THE OCCUPATION

Chloe Adams is the winner of the Penguin Literary Prize 2024. As a journalist and fiction writer, her work has been published by numerous Australian news mastheads and literary journals. She holds a master's degree in creative writing. Her love of literature was shaped by her mother, an actress and passionate second-hand bookstore owner. Chloe grew up in Melbourne/Naarm and has lived in the UK, Timor-Leste and Adelaide.

THE OCCUPATION

CHLOE ADAMS

PENGUIN BOOKS

UK | USA | Canada | Ireland | Australia
India | New Zealand | South Africa | China

Penguin Books is part of the Penguin Random House group of companies, whose addresses can be found at global.penguinrandomhouse.com.

Penguin Random House Australia

First published by Penguin Books, 2025

Cover design by Christa Moffitt, Christabella Designs
© Penguin Random House Australia Pty Ltd
Cover image courtesy piemags/GB24/Alamy Stock Photo
Typeset in Minion Pro by Midland Typesetters, Australia

Printed and bound in Australia by Griffin Press, an accredited ISO AS/NZS 14001 Environmental Management Systems printer

NATIONAL LIBRARY OF AUSTRALIA
A catalogue record for this book is available from the National Library of Australia

ISBN 978 1 76135 142 6

penguin.com.au

FSC www.fsc.org MIX Paper | Supporting responsible forestry FSC® C018684

We at Penguin Random House Australia acknowledge that Aboriginal and Torres Strait Islander peoples are the Traditional Custodians and the first storytellers of the lands on which we live and work. We honour Aboriginal and Torres Strait Islander peoples' continuous connection to Country, waters, skies and communities. We celebrate Aboriginal and Torres Strait Islander stories, traditions and living cultures; and we pay our respects to Elders past and present.

For Gillian

AUTHOR'S NOTE

Readers of *The Occupation* will note the inclusion of derogatory terms and slurs as well as troubling political and cultural views prevalent in 1940s Australia.

Some allowances have been made in the name of decency – for example, the worst slurs have been omitted, and those deemed unavoidable are used only sparingly.

Writing historical fiction is a game of balance – finding the measure of accuracy, sensitivity and plausibility. My intention was to confront the truth of that time while also carrying the weight of my words purposefully, acknowledging that the erasure of unpalatable histories also erases the experience of those who suffered through those histories.

'Into the same rivers we both step and do not step,
we are and are not.'

Heraclitus Homericus

1949

Almost at once the scene was drenched in motion-picture sentimentality. Cousin Tess, alone, in the doorway, pared back in effortless cream linen. She was clutching her crocodile-skin bag, the very one she'd carted about for years in an apparent show of Protestant austerity. And she'd come in from the hot squall of Collins Street drawn and harried – that much was clear to Mary, who was perched beneath a window, waiting.

But then Tess reached the fanned air of the lobby and her shoulders slackened, the pace of her heels against the parquetry floor slowed. At the verge of the parlour she took stock of the men and women in their finery, all the while tucking the bag under one wing, smoothing her frock, pulling the bag free, tucking it back again.

Finally a small man in a tailcoat approached and they exchanged a few words. Again, Tess's eyes flashed about the room, leaping from one pale frock to the next, one straw Panama to another. Mary imagined the man in the tailcoat was repeating the remarks he'd made to her only minutes earlier.

'Awfully warm out, madam.'

'Indeed.'

'At least ninety degrees they say, before the change.'

'Yes.'

'In March, madam. *March.*'

Tess pressed the back of a hand against her cheek. Perhaps she could feel the heat of the day under her skin. Or perhaps she was thinking what a fright she looked. Not that she did – she did not. But perhaps she was thinking that. Thinking of her mop of curls that no doubt objected to weather and haste.

There was a last, idle moment of anonymity before Tess turned a small degree further and practically cried across the room, 'Oh, I see her!' And sure enough, she was pointing at Mary, who was suddenly aware of her stiff jaw, her heels entwined, the frame of the enormous arched window beside her.

Inside her body, Mary felt that new sensation, a kaleidoscope of butterflies.

Tess made her way between the tables, amidst the high ring of cutlery on china and the lower clink of teacups meeting saucers. Behind it all, the constant hum of the revolving fans. The room was heavy with ladies' perfume and the smell of scones, and the temperature, Mary realised, was really only a few degrees cooler than outside.

Tess was nearly upon her, and Mary was on her feet. They were reaching for each other, pressing cheeks together, grasping arms with delicate fingers.

'Tess, darling.'

'Oh look at you. You haven't changed a bit in . . . in . . . how long has it —'

'Three years?' Mary offered.

'Gosh, has it been that long?'

'I suppose.'

'Yes.'

'After the boys came home.'

'Of course.' And then another thought passed over Tess, who was now gripping Mary's hand in earnest. 'I'm so sorry. The trams were a calamity, backed right down to the Shrine . . . And I, well, I should've cut my losses, of course, but you sit there, don't you, thinking, any minute now.'

'It's honestly fine,' Mary said.

Tess smiled, and there was a second flash of time, another lingering moment, as they stood face to face in their square-shouldered frocks, letting go of each other, their arms falling to their sides. They could have been sisters, Mary thought. Same height, same frame. Merely a year between them. Tess's chin was weaker, though, and the flawless skin across the cheeks – no Irish speckles. Still, there was an uncanny likeness.

Mary made a point to not look down, not inspect the slender shape of Tess, not think of the thickening at her own waistline.

Instead, she gestured to the table. 'Shall we?'

So, chairs were pulled, bodies seated.

At a nearby table, a little girl dressed in a summer frock that bunched over her chubby legs was gnawing on a scone with big, open-mouthed chomps, her jam-smeared cheeks working hard to manage the treat. Her mother was leaning in, vainly attempting to catch the crumbs as they fell from the girl's lips.

Mary forced herself to turn away, back to Tess. 'And how have you been?'

'Oh, please, let's not talk about me. Tell me about Japan – I'm dying to hear.'

Mary gathered a napkin between her fingers, laying the length of it onto her lap. 'Well, it was a wonderful adventure. Very difficult to explain, though.'

'Of course. It must have felt like another world.'

'Everyone's keen to know, and you try to conjure it . . . It's the strangest feeling, stepping onto another land after all those days at sea.'

'But knowing you were doing it in service, what a thing to be proud of.'

'Well . . . truthfully, we were spoilt rotten. We had our own girl to do all the chores around the place. One barely lifts a finger.' Mary let out a light chuckle, smoothed her napkin across her knees. This superior voice was not her own, not at all. It seemed to be following a script entitled What They Expect. 'And in the warmer months,' the voice continued, 'there's swimming and picnics and boating.'

'How wonderful.'

A second man in a tailcoat appeared then, spreading black-framed menus across the table and commenting again on the extraordinary weather. 'More than ninety degrees, can you imagine?'

Beyond the line of her menu, Mary watched as Tess flipped pages back and forth, eyes darting from item to item, making a sort of quiet huffing sound. Without any apparent thought, she suddenly swung one leg over the other, shifted a little in her seat, then swung the leg back again. In contrast, Mary noted how perfectly still her own body was – steady, even. Held in place, it seemed, by an invisible ballast.

And now the menu between Tess's fingers was shaking, and she was lurching for the water jug, misjudging, fumbling. The splintering of glass on timber rang out around the room and faces turned, brows arched.

'Oh my!' Slipping off the chair and onto her knees, Tess began to gather shards into her napkin.

'Dear. Tess, dear.' Mary reached out to touch her cousin's shoulder. 'The steward can manage.'

And true enough, one of the tailcoats arrived promptly, steering Tess back to her seat and busying himself with the clean-up. Presently, the tea was served in a gold-rimmed pot, and two china cups were placed down between the women. Mary poured for them both, and for a good few moments as they sipped their tea, they lapsed into silence. Out the vaulted window, a man on a bicycle sailed past at such speed it was as if he were being pulled on a string. He was followed by the shudder of a tram and next a lorry. On the footpath, the flow of pedestrians carried on ceaselessly.

When Mary looked back, she saw Tess take in a shaky breath. The ensuing exhale was conducted with such intent, Mary knew immediately, with a throat-tightening queasiness, that the time had come.

'When I rang, you surely wondered . . .' Tess began. 'It must have felt quite out of the blue.'

Mary placed her teacup down on its saucer and fixed Tess with a piercing stare.

'I . . . I . . .' Tess went on, 'was told something in great confidence. And I cannot know for sure if it's . . . well, whether I should be here, saying these words. Saying anything at all, really. Because Mary, dear, I would never want to upset you. That's the furthest thing from my mind.

'But I wanted to – knowing what I believe I know – I wanted to share something privately. That is . . . that Rodge and I, despite the years now, well, our doctor says it's unlikely we can . . . It would have happened by now, if indeed it was likely.'

Mary said only, 'I see.'

'Eight years of waiting. It's been very hard.'

'Of course.'

'I hope you understand . . . I ask you this with the greatest sincerity, the greatest respect for you and your situation. It's only that I feel I must ask, or I would never forgive myself.'

There was another hollow between them that lingered far too long.

Tess tried again. 'You know we would love it with all our hearts, don't you? Love it like it was our own.'

Tess, it seemed, could barely bring herself to look up in the face of Mary's silence. Her complexion had turned terribly pallid.

'I'm sorry,' the poor woman forged on. 'I'm not being clear, am I?' She took in a gulp of air, a lifeline. 'My question is this . . . If indeed you are with child, as I am led to believe, would you please – please would you give me your baby?'

Around them the chatter of ladies and the whoosh of the fans and the chaos of clinking seemed to intensify. Tess fell mute with the astonishing words she had just uttered. On the other side of the table, an ocean away, Mary turned and gazed out the window. Turned back. She knew she must speak, must find words, but language had abandoned her. The seconds ticked by with excruciating persistence.

'Say something, please,' Tess whispered.

Mary took a slow, even sip of her tea, placed the cup in its holder. She picked up the napkin, wrung it, folded and unfolded it, brought it to the corner of her mouth, blotted delicately, then reversed the whole action until the napkin was laid back on her lap, and finally, finally, she looked up, directly at Tess.

'There's a whole world out there,' she heard that peculiar voice say, 'that we didn't know existed. You wouldn't believe it if I told you.'

Tess stared at her, bereft.

'A world where men decide everything, on a whim, in the blink of an eye. Where the good perhaps aren't really good at all, not even a tiny bit. Or at least it's hard to say. One loses the belief that one might judge these things correctly.'

'I . . . I'm not sure I follow . . .'

'You may have the child.' Mary planted the napkin on the table and rose to standing. 'She'll be here before spring.'

Tess followed suit, urgently jamming her heels into the floor, the chair behind her all but tipping over. Mary was already tucking her own seat under the table, gathering up her handbag.

'Please,' Tess said. 'Please, Mary, won't you stay a little longer?'

'I'll miss my train. And it's done. The answer is yes. The child . . . the child is yours.'

'Oh, but won't you —'

'Please,' Mary said, insistent now. There was pain, of course. And some sense that she was apportioning blame crudely. But mostly she had a deep and burning need to be free of this place, before the tears came. 'You have your answer.'

The din around them endured and, in the background, the small child with the summer frock and sticky cheeks was laughing, and the mother was smiling back, an enormous grin that shattered any illusion of social decorum.

Tess again. 'May I ask just one more thing?'

'All right.'

Her face had transformed into something soft and hopeful, sickeningly so. 'You said *she*. You think it's a girl?'

'Oh, Tess.' Mary felt herself react with a wry smile. She shook her head. Felt that terrible conceit bubble up again. 'Not *think*. Somehow I just *know*.'

And she swept past Tess, a graze of fabric against her shoulder, a blur of cloth and hair.

1948

It was still early when land came into view. It emerged first as small particles of matter in the great cosmos of the dark horizon, distant and immaterial. Above, white wheeling gulls transmuted into stars.

Mary cradled the railing, let the cool morning mist fall to her face. She'd left Noreen asleep in the cabin, and she was glad for it. Glad to savour this moment with only strangers alongside her to murmur and bleat at the crags that sprung from the water, which were beginning to resemble solid earth. The sun winked on the skyline and, just like that, the land flashed green, and there was none of the wretchedness of humanity, nothing but the drift and rise of isles mapped out across the Inland Sea. A feeling swelled in her chest – certainly excitement, but perhaps also a long-awaited hint of peril. After all the years of war, cossetted in the snug confines of Melbourne, she was away, across an ocean, seeing what the men saw. Across a galaxy, as it were.

They inched closer over hours. She took breakfast in the dining room and returned to deck. Now the mist had cleared and the emerald land glowed ever more brilliant. There were signs of habitation. Terraces carved into the earth. Tiny dwellings dotted across the treeless hills and even tinier people moving about. This was a place of cultivation, a place for ploughing and planting, tillage and nurture. It was not as she'd expected, but with every minute that passed, the imagined shores of Japan sharpened into something far better.

With four months at least until the summer typhoons threatened, the air at Kure Harbour was still and bracing. Having swept down the gangplank in their fresh khaki and felt hats, breath issuing from their mouths in white veins, Mary and Noreen were made to stand under a shelter on the dock for an inordinate period of time while instructions were barked and kitbags inspected. They rubbed their hands together, huddled deeper into their greatcoats, stamped their polished lace-ups against the boards. Beside Mary, Noreen's cheeks were marbled pink, her lips colourless; in one hand she clutched her Kodak 35.

Finally, they were ushered out of the shadow of the ship, away from the water, and into the township. It was only now they saw the piles of dross still waiting to be dealt with, all these years later. Twisted steel girders, turbines, other large structures mangled beyond recognition. In the streets, streams of mud had washed in from the hills and dried solid, forming small dunes of crusted earth. And from a doorway, a local man, fluted by old age, surveyed the new arrivals. War had come, the scene seemed to say, and then, just as suddenly, it departed.

It was the weekend and the streets were almost empty, so they walked in messy bunches up a desolate promenade. Mary was struck by the size of the place; it was small, likely smaller than before, framed on three sides by a veil of hills that rolled back in graduating shades of haze like the layers of a theatre set. It was more village than city, and the bleak grey streets and unadorned facades did nothing to counter the provincial impression. And yet, she immediately liked the scantness of it, the soundless avenues, the absence of towering buildings, the modesty of the architecture.

The significance of their journey seemed to crystallise in this moment. It came to Mary as a sharpening of the senses; an absolute thrill at seeing objects wholly foreign to her, an inconceivable place made real. Even the touch of the chilled air was somehow different and unexpected.

Noreen turned back to the harbour and aimed her camera at the ghastly wreckage behind them. Against the dark scrim of the sea, a thin line of smoke rose from a pile of coal.

'Rather uninviting,' Noreen whispered.

'Well, let's see what the quarters are like.'

'I heard the Yanks have got it made, up north. Coca-Cola and fries and the most wonderful parties – the whole kit and caboodle. And we get . . . this . . .'

Mary held a flat hand across the brim of her hat and examined the glare-lit city to the west. More pale, squat buildings.

Noreen again: 'Oh gawd, I think I miss the boat.'

She had screwed her delicate features into a childish sort of pout, which made Mary snort a 'c'mon now' and bump her encouragingly at the hip.

They walked on.

'But it doesn't exactly scream fun, does it?'

'No, I suppose not.' And yet. And yet. 'At least it's not home.'

At least it wasn't going to the pictures and being made to sit through the newsreels of other young women with their proud chins marching in perfect formation, digging slit trenches, working on engines, wearing overalls paired with glamorous hairstyles, while she – Mary – was trapped with the little ones in her father's home, hopelessly unmarried, permitted at most to serve in a different way. Her father had only come around to the idea of her provisional emancipation late in the year prior, well after the war had ended – *now that the children are old enough,* he'd said.

The mist rolled in again, and they trudged on until they reached their destination, a wide boulevard lined with trees dappled in colour and a heavy concrete wall skirting a military base. Prouder, more commanding buildings rose up from behind the perimeter. Familiar flags languished on poles.

Mary nudged her new friend's arm – 'look, cherry blossom' – and in an instant Noreen was happily cooing, animated again. Mary had come to understand this was the special quality of her cabin mate, the country girl who hadn't laid eyes on a tram car until she was of age. Whose childhood sweetheart had skipped out on her without even an elementary missive – she'd only learned of her fate when word got around town that he was gone. Off to Brisbane to work the docks, or so it was said, leaving Noreen condemned to dreadful whispers. She was, it seemed, both immensely courageous and bewilderingly naive.

Noreen sighed and, trailing Mary towards the nearest pink-budding tree, said she'd been a spoilsport and she was sorry to have brought the tone down and she would not hear a word otherwise from Mary – 'no, really, I have'. Under the tree, she tugged at a thin bough and said the blossoms had reminded her to take the good with the bad.

With that, Mary reached for the Kodak in Noreen's hand. 'Well, how about a snap then?'

And so there by that spectacular tree, Noreen posed, one foot in front of the other, hat tucked behind her back. The mist had settled like flecks of snow on her face and across her shoulders, making her the very picture of a pretty English rose. She poured out a huge grin, uncanny given her mood moments earlier, and Mary captured the transformation with an emphatic click.

At twenty-nine years of age, Mary Ainsley Egan had been blessed in many ways, not least with the gift of a youthful face. A face that at fifteen had looked twelve, at twenty-five looked twenty, and so on. Now, as she squinted through the viewfinder of Noreen's camera, her new life before her, nothing but a high wall to pass beyond, she thought not of home – of her dead mother lost unspeakably young, her father silent and hardworking, her older brothers all thankfully returned from the war – no, what she thought was that she'd lived an alien life already, and so what difference could one more queer addition make? The sole girl amongst all those boys. A series of disinterested suitors and then a good one killed to round off the list.

Sometimes, after she'd decided on this trip to Japan, she was even happy she hadn't wed. If she'd married, her days would be spent sterilising bottles and rubbing nappies back to whiteness, each day passing with the next easily foretold. Certainly she wouldn't be here, in this remarkable place. And she liked this feeling of unknowing; she liked it very much.

Mary thought all this as she stood before the Australian army base on that dirty street, breathing in the fresh March air, ecstatic at the prospect of a real adventure. And even though she knew the big world lay all around her, in this moment she could not help but feel central to it.

They moved through the gates and caught sight of an altogether different terrain – sentry boxes, army trucks, men with rifles, swept paths and immaculate lines. In the courtyard behind the main building, they presented themselves to an older woman. When it was Mary's turn, perhaps because of that feeling of her own importance, it came as quite a shock to hear the woman say something or other about the 'Y'. It seemed only natural that Mary should ask her to please check again.

'Mary A Egan, is it?'

'Yes ma'am.'

'Pearson Street, Beaumaris?'

'Yes.'

'Private, you are most definitely listed here with the Y.'

The woman scribbled something illegible on a small scrap of paper and beckoned Mary to take it.

Mary began again with politeness. It was terribly important that the woman understood – there had been a mistake, she was with Dental, at HQ. And because those words did little to convert the old woman's demeanour, she added, 'with *Colonel Logan*.'

'Says right here, love: Dew Drop Inn, YWCA.'

'Dew Drop Inn . . .' Mary echoed dumbly.

'Yeah, make lovely cakes and biccies, they do.'

'But I'm quite sure I'm with Dental,' she said, as if repeating the phrase might effect some alchemy.

The woman sighed and flapped the piece of card in the air between them. 'Ask inside, then. Last I heard, dental hospital's closin'.'

She was directed through the caliginous bowels of the place to the office of a Major Marshall. There, at the doorway, a young man was waiting, scratching into a notepad, tie-less, daringly casual in a thin shirt and civilian trousers, more American jazz man than military forces. She hesitated, searching for a name on the door.

'Looking for the Major?' the young man said, head down, still scrawling.

'Yes.'

'That's him.' He motioned towards the office.

Inside, a small man perched behind a large desk was framed by neatly stacked towers of books and papers. She saluted, then explained the situation, and the Major listened almost sympathetically, she felt. He nodded, coughed. Finally, he spoke.

'Not sure what to tell you, sweetheart. Logan was discharged Tuesday. Halfway back to Oz by now, I'd say.'

'But . . . but I don't understand.'

'What's not to understand?'

'Why wasn't I . . . informed?'

It was then that his face changed. 'Informed?' He smiled, pressing back into his chair and broadening his chest. 'Well I don't know, darlin'. We've got twenty million Japs to think about and thirty thousand square miles of land to disarm, so I'd say it fell through the cracks.'

He looked at her plainly. He had seen war this man, real war, not the kind disseminated to the masses in grainy black and white. He had the insignia to prove it.

'But is there not another way?' she heard her own voice squeak. 'Something else I might do?'

His smile widened; a twinkle appeared in the eye. He was making no effort to hide his amusement.

Mary thought about the open door behind her, and how the young man in the hallway must surely be taking in this mortifying entreaty.

'Because, you see, I'm really only trained for one thing. As a nurse, not a . . . a mess girl.'

'All right,' the Major said, leaning two elbows on the desk, pulling his face into an imitation of bureaucracy. 'Think of it this way, sweetheart. Your country needs you.' And then he laughed outright. A great big guffaw. Evidently, she had really made his day.

In her rush out the door, of course luck would have her bump chest-first into the young man in civvies.

As if to steady her, he took her shoulders in his hands. 'You right there?' He said this smiling; he too was amused by her.

She muttered an apology and felt the heat of this encounter rising up her neck and into her cheeks. He was so close she could smell him, a fleeting draught of earthiness. When she looked down, she saw on his feet two indecently scuffed shoes.

Something about the ordinariness of these artefacts, or perhaps the carelessness with which they'd been handled – so antithetical to military principles – was enough to motivate her into action.

'Excuse me,' she announced with the firmest sense of dignity she could summon.

The young man stepped aside, albeit still grinning, and she bolted.

So her demotion to shop girl was not, as she'd hoped, the result of some erroneous scrawl of a pen, but instead a solid, immovable fact.

For half a moment, as she dashed back through those corridors of middling power into the sharp sunlight of a Japanese day, she was reminded of the many occasions over recent days and weeks in which she'd described her position – deputy to a Colonel – with short-sighted vanity. To family members, friends, neighbours, to Noreen and other women on the ship.

The thought came shrouded in ignominy, but also bewilderment. She had trained, quite especially, for this role. There'd been months of tutelage under the dominion of Matron Wester; the memorising of all the tiny metal tools, the excavators and scalers and probes that had, at the start, seemed identical or substitutable, but over time had each revealed themselves as uniquely necessary for precise circumstances. Not to mention the medicinal protocols, the hygiene practices, the etiquette with regards to addressing the assigned dentist and the VIP patients. It had not been unsubstantial.

But also, it occurred to her now, she had paused her life. This in itself was hardly a small thing. She had come across the ocean for one thing, not another. Instead, she was to prepare sponges and shortbread. A full five thousand, unfathomable miles away, and yet not so different to home.

The girls' quarters were not nearly so nice as their cabin on the ship. Located in a corner of the base, miles from the men's residence, the dorm had a certain utilitarian style that leaned towards despondent. A large, hand-written sign taped to the front door – *Out of bounds* – did the work of chaperone.

The room Mary and Noreen were assigned to was at least warm. The sweet smell of expanding timber fixed in the nose. There were three beds; iron camp stretchers mercifully topped with real mattresses, not straw palliasses as she'd heard women moan about during the war. The beds were made up in crisp white sheets, with a stack of army-issue blankets neatly folded at the base. There was a large plain wardrobe, and a dresser and mirror set against one wall. One bed, they saw, had already been taken, so Mary and Noreen made for the untouched cots under the windows, collapsing into them like children.

'Good god,' Noreen sighed. 'I'm pooped.'

Through the walls, Mary could hear the hubbub of other women coming and going from the dormitory, the banging of a door, laughter. Her thoughts lurched wildly back to home, to the boat, to the Major, who had so comprehensively humiliated her, and then the other man, the younger one, who had witnessed the whole exasperating affair.

On the ship, she and Noreen had talked around the issue of why – why come all this way? And especially now that the war was over and all the truly heroic work was done. Neither woman had offered up a particularly satisfying answer, instead grasping at sentimental truisms like 'to do my bit'. To speak of travel was quite beyond them, she supposed. To utter the truth, the very kernel of it all, the thing that pressed against her chest like a creature hoping to be set free. What was she to say? *I should like to know how it feels to cross an ocean.*

By and by, there was the rattle of a doorknob, and a woman appeared, naked but for a towel wrapped around her lean body. Noreen and Mary sat up like a shot.

'Well, well,' the woman said. 'If it isn't my new girlfriends.'

Her words, though, were uttered with equivocation – she hadn't yet decided if they would, in fact, be friends. But she'd deign to consider it.

'How do you like our digs?'

'Could be nicer,' Noreen started.

'Pitiful is what it is, especially after HQ. But you'll get used to it.'

'Oh, you've been – to HQ?'

The woman walked to the dresser and threw off the towel. Now completely bare – large breasts, flat stomach – she turned to them and made a show of dabbing at her arms. 'Course. I lived there.'

'What's it like?'

'The Hilton in comparison to this dump.' She turned back to the dresser and extracted undergarments, a blouse. 'Welcome to Japan's hillbilly backwater, ladies.'

'Oh geez.' Noreen flopped back onto the bed.

'But don't fret. We make our own fun here.'

Noreen let out a squeal and rolled onto her side. This new mien came as something of a surprise to Mary, who was realising that perhaps she'd met on the ship only the smallest fraction of possible Noreens. She had to admit this other, more excitable model did have an inevitability about it.

The naked woman – Ida was her name – turned to Mary then and said, 'You're very quiet over there.'

'Oh, I'm just . . .'

'Mary's had some bad news,' Noreen offered with pep.

'Oh?' Ida raised an eyebrow in a way that reduced sympathy to an easy arrangement of the face and waited for Mary to elaborate. There was a moment of silence while the two women appraised each other.

It was Noreen who could not bear the discomfort any longer and spoke next. 'Anyway, I heard we get some . . . help.'

'Ha.' Ida wagged a finger at her. 'I like a woman who thinks about her rights. Yes, we have a girl. When you shower, she'll take away your soiled clothes and leave the fresh ones here on the dresser. She's terribly shy – hid behind the door the first time I spoke to her – but you can't fault her, really.'

Ida pulled a skirt on and sat at the mirror, examining a perfectly symmetrical face.

'We have a nice rec room down the way. You can entertain there, in daylight hours. And we're each allowed two bottles of beer after work. It's a Jap brand, but still, it's all right. Oh, did anyone tell you? You're not allowed outside the grounds without a bloke – a local girl was murdered in broad daylight a couple of weeks back.'

'Oh my.'

'Yes, terrible stuff. They say it was one of our fellas, but the daft witness couldn't pick the perp out of a line-up. Said we all look the same . . . can you believe it?!' She laughed, and leaned in to apply her lipstick. 'I doubt it was one of ours, anyhow,' she muttered between dabs. 'The local men . . . well, we all know what they're capable of.'

Having completed her enhancements, Ida then stood and took another moment to straighten herself, fluff her curls, pout at the mirror. Finally, she turned to them. 'I'll catch you gals later. I'm off for a drive.'

Late in the day, when Mary was alone, the promised housegirl appeared like an umbra, weaving between hidden and shadowed places, gathering items left strewn about by Ida, pulling sheets. She wore black trousers and a simple dark blouse. Mary sat up on the bed, ready to utter her first attempts at the language, but the girl did not look up, did not say a word. Her long hair lay against her back, silken like it had been pressed, and she moved in a bowed way, seemingly shrinking from Mary's corrosive sight. Out the window, there were the muffled sounds of men speaking, a vehicle groaning in the distance, but inside there was merely the soft clack of the girl's sandals across the floor, the thwap and crack of sheets being fanned out over beds.

It was a strange thing, the two of them sharing this space in this moment, but Mary couldn't say what precisely made it strange or how indeed to fix it. Simply that a new feeling had arrested her, one that reminded her she was alien, or perhaps the girl was. She doubted that words could make them the same, or even similar.

Mary knew this girl was not responsible for the atrocities committed against their men, her brother Joe included. She was not culpable for the half-dead pack of bones that stepped off the train that spring day in '45; she would barely have been of age. On the other hand, the girl was one of them, irrefutably. Therefore, she was a villain of sorts. And yet, how did one reconcile that with the provision of manners? Civility was all that remained of Mary's mother's influence. The sit up pleases. The elbows off the table now. The say hello to the nice gentleman, dear. These were things that held up the world. So when the girl was finished with her work, when she was headed for the door, Mary was struck by the need to administer sounds to the wound of their silence. She sputtered out 'arigato gozaimasu' and the girl turned to face her, the look in her eye unreadable. She bowed, and took her leave.

The room fell silent again. Mary stood, stretched and hauled her kitbag and case onto the bed. She pulled out the contents one item at a time and laid them across the sheets. Her whole life now, she thought, reduced to so very little. Summer uniform. Two frocks, one for good, the other everyday. A pair of casual slacks. A pleated skirt. A blouse. A red woollen cardigan. Gloves. Stockings. Handbag. A bathing suit. The London Tan pair of heels her aunt gave her as a passing out gift. Sandshoes. A navy felt hat with feathers, a little worse for wear despite her packing it with care. Photographs from home. A silver hairbrush. Handheld mirror. Powder compact. Lipstick. Joe's bible. And her mother's Venetian glass rosary beads, which she held now in the palm of one hand and, after a moment's thought, slipped under her pillow.

There was also a tidy stack of novels, and a guidebook titled *Know Japan* that had been distributed on the ship. The opening passage laid out their mission – they must help the Japanese make themselves worthy to stand beside the peoples of the civilised world. And it was through this text that she knew fraternising with the enemy was expressly forbidden. The Japanese people were, in every way, different to the British; each man a mass-produced product shaped by obedience and enforced humility, each woman commanded to work devotedly, untouched by Western liberalism. The Aussies might learn the language and try the food, but really, the way to live in Japan was to have absolutely nothing to do with the people.

Noreen returned soon after, and together they made their way along the lovely swept paths, past a series of two- and three-storey buildings, a warehouse, a sports-yard, and on to the mess, a huge hall situated in the centre of the base. It was barely service time and already the place was discordant with occupation members, mostly men, sitting, standing, uniforms deconstructed at the neck and sleeves. Several long wooden tables were lined in smart order, and at the far wall, the meal lay hidden under a procession of silver lids.

Amidst the bedlam of this hungry crowd, Noreen found Mary's hand, squeezed it, and raised a nervous brow. 'Where shall we sit?'

Mary gazed from table to table. It was unclear if a system of etiquette existed here, and if so how to observe it. But she saw Ida, not far away, draped over the lap of a dark-haired man. The sort of chiselled, muscular bloke one would expect of this scene, cast from a universal mould. Despite Ida's earlier signs of hostility, there seemed no better solution, so Mary pulled at Noreen's hand and led her through the crowd. As they neared, Ida turned, saw them coming and raised her chin with haughty consideration. After a long beat, she sniffed, 'All right then, c'mon' – and she snapped two bony fingers at the men beside her, beckoning them to shift along the bench seat.

Introductions ensued. Jimmy was the dark-haired boyfriend. Two others, more dubiously, were known as Sicko and Turnip.

There was a Prescott and a Chipper and a small ginger fellow named Speck. All were swigging intermittently from bottles of Japanese beer.

Immediately, the men wanted to know of the newly arrived: when did they land, and did they bring booze, cigarettes, sugar or wool? A communal groan went around the gang when the answers were reluctantly confessed: that morning, no, no, no and no.

'Ah hell,' said one of the men, 'we need to get the word out back home.'

'Why on earth would we bring wool?' Noreen asked, happy to utter the silly question that Mary was repressing.

'Make you a mint at the marketo,' said the man named Speck.

'See, we bring it out for a pittance and sell it for gold bullion,' said another.

'All part of the service,' added Jimmy. 'Democratising the hell out of 'em.'

A cheer went up around the group, and Mary couldn't help but be pulled along by the force of the conversation.

'That's what we're all about,' said the one named Turnip. And in a staccato, staged voice, he began reciting the force objectives, 'Maintaining . . . and enhancing . . . Commonwealth . . . prestige.'

'Sure,' laughed Ida. 'You're all about prestige, T.'

'Aren't I just,' the man said, eyes bulging with heady glee.

Soon, supper was served – sausages and mash with a watery tomato sauce, which Mary practically inhaled despite the audience of all these men. Then there was the walk back to their quarters, down a dirt track under a brooding dusk sky.

There was that cloying smell again of the timber inside their room, and an introduction to the bathroom down the way. The showerheads that released either blazing hot water or slightly chilled. The decisions about what to wear in the communal areas and how to handle one's nakedness after a wash. Each choice, each determination, became more and more difficult as the night wore on, and it was only when Mary was easing back the firmly tucked sheets on her bed that she realised she was so bone-achingly tired, if a fire broke out she wasn't sure she'd even run.

At ten, they heard a distant cry down the corridor – 'lights out!' – and to Mary's enormous relief the light switch was flicked by Ida with surprising obedience.

In the dark, Mary conceded a long, slow breath and let her body unshackle itself from the day. A momentous day. One of the more memorable, perhaps, of a whole life. Begun somewhere in the Inland Sea, an utterly foreign locality, and ended here, a mere dot on the grand canvas of the world. And yet also a place, a real place, where she now resided.

A vision came to her of kneeling on her father's big chair in the study, many years ago, leaning her little elbows on the oak escritoire and spinning a pale globe anchored in a block of dark timber. It might have been the only evidence in their home of a world beyond Australia, and she would watch its continents and lines of longitude and masses of water whirl by at their odd angle and wonder how many people were scattered across this place called Earth. She'd once asked Joe if he knew – *might it be a thousand, or even more*? – and he'd laughed and laughed, his thin lips curling into his mouth, and then he'd ruffled her hair, and she hadn't minded so much that she was way off the mark.

There was plenty more to think of, but her body was so thoroughly depleted she began to lose the thread of ideas. It was now, just as she was drifting off, that she heard the strange, muffled cry of an animal in the distance. Mary's eyes snapped open. Again, that sound.

Ida whispered theatrically into the blackness. 'Ooh, hear that?'

It could be a bird, Mary told herself, or just as easily the howl of a woman in pain.

Noreen. 'What is it?'

'Well . . .' Ida paused, letting the cry endure for a moment longer until it vanished completely. 'Well . . . I don't wish to alarm you but . . .'

'Urgh, c'mon.'

'They say —'

'Don't, Ida.'

'They say on full moon nights you can hear the cries of the lost children come back to seek their revenge.'

Noreen responded with that same hysterical squeal and in the nearly pitch-dark Mary saw a pillow sail across the room, thudding against the metal frame of Ida's bed. A laugh erupted into the night and the pillow was lobbed back with even greater force.

Mary turned away from Ida and settled her body to face the window. 'What rubbish,' she muttered.

'You don't believe me?'

'No, of course I don't.'

'All right, suit yourself.'

Mary pressed her lips together, determined not to provoke Ida any further.

'Think what you like,' Ida went on, 'but it's a fact that the entire children's hospital was flattened by the Yanks in '45. The entire joint.'

'Oh my word,' Noreen murmured.

'You couldn't really blame the poor blighters for a little vengeance, could you?'

Nothing about Ida's voice conjured empathy, though. She might even have sounded pleased – with herself as much as the story.

Mary woke to a band of light, shockingly bright, painted across her face and pillow. So that's why the beds under the windows had been empty. She rolled towards the centre of the dimly kindled room and let her eyes adjust. Felt the cool air coming off the windowpane at her neck. Somewhere far away, a cockerel blasted out a provocative call.

The other women remained asleep. Their dissonant breathing worked an odd syncopation, and Mary inched deeper under her covers, trying to snuff them out. There was an enormous relief in having a moment to herself, to ruminate quietly without the frenzy of the past twenty-four hours to crowd her mind.

She thought of home, incongruously really, given the ship had set sail more than two weeks ago. But yes, there it was, in nostalgic clarity; the old place worn by time and sea air. In her room, the floral bedspread, the embossed wallpaper, the lovely brass lamp passed down through her mother's side. On the ground floor, her father and Penelope in the master bedroom, and the two little ones bunked in down the hall. Two empty rooms upstairs – forsaken by her brothers Michael and Bernard, both happily married.

And finally Joe, in the attic room, sleeping always until late, hopelessly unproductive. But, now that she thought of it, rather a comfort to have in the house, so it was not just her against the world.

Because of Joe, and because of his difficult turn in the war, it had seemed at times impossible that she would come to Japan, of all the far-flung destinations of the world. And yet when thinking of this oddity from a different angle, it occurred to her she might have been destined for this place after all.

Her thoughts shifted now to the day ahead, the uncharted quality of it. Some kind of job to attend to that she was utterly unprepared for. Meals in the mess. Making friends, if she could manage it. Another night's sleep in this bed, which was, truth be told, not entirely unpleasant.

She turned back to the window and, pressing up onto an elbow, nudged the blind aside. The view – white-washed wall, a patch of garden bed, spindly tree pushing up out of pine-needled soil – was bland, certainly nothing to write home about, and yet even this prosaic outlook filled her with the thrill of the new. That word, surreal as it was, bubbled up again – Japan. I'm on the other side of the world, she thought with a smile.

The Dew Drop Inn sat at the north-east corner of the YWCA building, a large structure given the paltry number of women on base. Its entrance was a wide, curved, multi-panelled aperture – Art Deco crossed with Japanese minimalism – and when Mary pushed the door open, she was comforted by the flood of warm air that coursed out. Inside, the café was small, basic, cosy. The counter, topped with all manner of glass jars and cloches, seemed to have been fashioned from salvaged hardwood, but the tables and chairs were quality numbers. Across the walls, someone had plastered cheap posters of bare-shouldered, misty-eyed starlets.

She gazed around the empty space. From an adjacent room, a sliver of light drew her attention, and as she stepped closer she heard the low rumble of human activity: a shuffling across the floor, the growl of a machine. She stepped closer still, had her hand on the precipice of the doorknob, when behind her a woman tore through the entrance and hooted, 'Goodness, girl! Not in there.'

Mary spun, felt the colour rush from her face. 'I'm sorry, I . . .'

The woman was a striking, narrow-shouldered dame in her fifties with a spine like a steel rod. She snatched off her gloves with precision and tucked them into a coat pocket. Her face was unusually small and round, almost infant-like beneath the veneer of cosmetics, with seraph cheeks and high-swept hair. Thoughtfully, she evaluated Mary, then spoke with an acutely cultivated accent courtesy of the ABC.

'You know numbers, dear?'

'Yes,' Mary said, 'well enough.'

'They said you were a nurse.'

'Dental nurse. That's right.'

'Good.'

Mary must have appeared confused, because the woman launched into an explanation. 'Well, there are volunteers, of course, plenty of them from the dependents group, but they're a fickle bunch. Come and go on a whim, constantly off touring the country, and I dare say half of them couldn't do a sum to save a life.'

Mary felt she should nod in agreement, so she did.

'I've been campaigning for you for some time,' the woman declared.

'For me?'

'Well, not *you*, precisely. Any of the uniformed girls would do.'

Mary nodded again.

'And you look like a reliable sort.'

'Yes, ma'am.'

There was something about the woman's imperious demeanour that triggered a juvenile response in Mary. She even felt her hands clasp behind her back.

At last the woman seemed to come to from her trance of appraisal and she explained in a softer tone that she was Mrs Richards, newly appointed Secretary of the Y and wife to Group Captain Harry Richards. Mary nodded and smiled, and Mrs Richards descended into a lengthy homily about the YWCA, its history and mission of supporting women in service.

As she spoke, an elderly Japanese man dressed in chef's whites emerged from the kitchen, balancing a large tray of cakes and tarts. He moved behind the counter and, one by one, transferred items onto platters. Without giving the vaguest indication that she'd seen him, Mrs Richards gazed out the window and carried on a story about her terribly devoted housegirls – three girls because . . . well, rank. Finally, after several minutes of this, the old man disappeared back through the crack in the wall from which he'd come and Mrs Richards' performance seemed almost pointless without the additional audience member.

'So,' she said presently, moving along the length of the counter, pointing at various objects. 'Price list. Serving utensils. Apron. Instructions for the register. Tea break's at ten, and luncheon's served at midday. Oh and now you know, don't go in . . .' she screwed up her small baby face and prodded a finger towards the kitchen, 'there.'

'Yes, all right.'

'Tremendous.'

Now, in a frightening display of finality, Mrs Richards flipped up the collar of her coat and moved towards the door. Surely she didn't intend to desert Mary already, with so little training to speak of.

'Sorry —' Mary spluttered, her hand springing up.

The woman turned to her, eyebrows raised.

'Won't you stay? It's just . . . I don't . . . I'm not sure I know what to do.'

The woman released a half grunt from the nose and checked her wristwatch. 'No, dear. At this very moment, I'm expected upstairs in the language school. The little Jap darlings will be waiting for me.' As a final consolation, she sighed and gazed at Mary, gentler now. 'Look, you just take the money and clear the plates. It's not so very difficult.'

'All right.'

Mrs Richards departed in one swift motion, and a gust of wintery air rushed into the café to fill the void of her not insignificant presence. Mary stood a moment in the centre of the room, paralysed almost. She took in the expectant scene around her, the faint din in the kitchen. Morning sunlight poured in around the large painted letters on the window – D, E, W – and cast sharp-angled shadows at Mary's feet.

By ten, it seemed the entire occupation had adjourned to the Dew Drop for their morning break. Mary was run off her feet, pouring tea from the urn, serving little cakes, calculating sums. After the initial terror, she found there was a pleasure in it. Not a scholarly satisfaction, but a cerebral pleasure nonetheless. The constant problem solving. The streamlining of orders to maximise time. The building of number patterns in her head. As the hours passed, she learned to move less, think faster, breathe more.

At lunch, it was soup and sandwiches and more of the same baked goods. The elderly Japanese man came and went from the kitchen, soundlessly taking the piles of dirty plates and magically turning out clean ones, never once making eye contact with her. Once or twice, she stole a glance through the kitchen door and saw half a dozen men of varying ages, all dressed identically, labouring away.

In the quieter moments, a smattering of army dependents made their way into the café. Small children wrapped in winter garb. Wives in lovely thick coats, hair spun into fine creations under felt hats. They left small tricycles on the path outside and, once sated, the children streaked off out the door, leaving their mothers to chat. Mary observed these groups with interest. It seemed an odd life. To travel such an awfully long way, but with no real prospects. Still the children and a house to maintain, only one cloistered away in the corner of a military compound.

In the afternoon, Mrs Richards appeared through the front door, followed by a bevy of Japanese schoolgirls – at least ten in total – all impeccably dressed in stiff dark uniforms. Mrs Richards had embraced the role of governess with great solemnity, ushering the girls over to the counter with brisk flaps of the hand.

'Chop chop, girls,' she was saying. 'Chop chop.' When they were crowded around the counter, she gestured to Mary. 'Say good afternoon to Mary-san.'

'Good afternoon, Mary-san,' the group recited.

'How do you do?' Mrs Richards prompted.

'How do you doooo,' the girls repeated.

'Remember what we say. Courtesy demands courtesy.'

Mary smiled at the gathering of little faces. She was just about to say something when Mrs Richards' high register cleaved the air once more.

'Now, see here, this one.' She pointed to a passionfruit-topped cake under a glass cloche. 'Spoooonnnge.'

'Spoooooonge,' the chorus replied.

'And here, saaand-wiches,' Mrs Richards said, wrapping her lips around the word with a determined rigor.

'Saaand-wiches.'

'Neeeeenish tart.'

'Neeeeenish taaaart.'

'Scone.'

It went on like this for several minutes. An amusing production, and already Mary was thinking how she would convey the humour of it to Noreen at the end of the day, perhaps even to Joe back home. There was something about this Mrs Richards that delighted the senses. One might have dismissed her as caricature, if not for the fact she was standing right there, real flesh and blood. And perhaps it was not so much Mrs Richards but Mrs Richards in Japan that heightened the comic effect. Back home, she'd be swallowed up, barely discernible in a room of her peers.

At four, the elderly man emerged again from the kitchen. He was dressed now in a threadbare woven jacket and loose pants, and he bowed at Mary with a quick tug of the body. 'Madam-san. We go now.'

He stood there a moment longer staring at the ground until Mary realised with a snag of understanding that his words were not so much a comment but a directive. *She* goes now, was what he meant.

She sprang into action, gathering up her coat and scarf. He ushered her to the cash register with a meek beckoning motion, and one step at a time mimed how she must empty the contents of the register into a safety box and carry the safety box outside.

'Offisu,' he said, pointing emphatically around the side of the building. 'Offisu,' he said again.

It was clear from the pressing tone and the jabbing motion of his gnarled fingers that it was of the utmost importance *she* take the money, and that *he* at no time be made to touch it.

At the door, she nodded and thanked him. It was only when the door had clicked behind her and she was breathing ribbons of white into the cool air, she realised she did not bow at the man as she should have, nor did she ask his name.

The days, and then weeks, passed. The cherry blossoms burst into full splendour, then almost immediately waned. Brief patches of sunshine became inordinately exciting, hinting at happy times to come. And for Mary, Noreen and the other fresh arrivals, these days passed with a rare haste. There was something about the newness of Japan that was most preoccupying. It was the challenge, perhaps. The learning of tricks to make life less arduous. For example, showering in the mornings to avoid competition. Doubling up your stockings on the coldest days. If you could sneak two hard-boiled eggs into your pockets at breakfast, they'd keep your hands warm for at least the time it took to walk to work.

For one full week, they became fixated on perfecting their salutes. That then led to impersonations of other members – the lazy and the overly earnest being of particular significance – which inevitably left them in fits of laughter.

In the Dew Drop, Mary stumbled awkwardly towards greeting the old man in the kitchen whites, and finally, after days, learned his name was Nakajima. He was the most diligent, self-possessed man she'd ever come across. It was as if he was still a boy in a classroom with the weight of his teacher casting a long shadow over him. Only it seemed she was the teacher. Or perhaps the shadow. In any event, she understood she played a role, unwittingly, in this graceless dance they were in.

Every so often, Mary would think of the job she had trained for and wish for it a little; for the title and status perhaps most of all. But she could not say she disliked the Dew Drop. The constant bustle allowed her to feel in the thick of things, and she quickly came to know many of the Australians by face if not name. Through snippets of conversation, she began to piece together an impression of the world beyond the walls of the base – a provost raid on a local tea house, a rat infestation at Customs, the boys in Disposal finding another cache of explosives in the tunnels west of Hiroshima, months after they thought the last had been discovered.

And she came to understand this role in the Dew Drop was, in a sense, a privilege; one that could not be replicated in the Colonel's clinic or by sitting at a desk in a hushed room, tap, tap, tapping away, as Noreen and Ida were required to do, or by ordering the Japs about at the railroads or the warehouses, as the men seemed chiefly engaged with.

Letters from home arrived in the girls' rec on Wednesday evenings, tied with string into sizable bundles. They were distributed by the House Sergeant after supper, setting off little eruptions of shrieks and wails. On the third Wednesday, there was a pleasing stack of three letters for Mary; a lengthy state of the union from Joe, who confirmed, as always, that the world was indeed going to hell in a handcart, another of gentler tone from Aunt Mildred, and a brief dispatch from her father that said almost nothing but felt utterly precious nonetheless. In the same envelope, another sheet of paper – it'd been folded by amateur hands and creases dashed the page at unusual angles. Sallyann, she saw, had sketched in crayon a large figure in a triangle dress standing between two smaller ones, a little red house in the background, a bright spiky sun in the sky. In the bottom corner of the page, dear little Robert had marked a small patch with artless scribble, and Mary smiled to herself, thinking what it would have taken of Sallyann to surrender that fraction of the parchment.

She sat down at once to compose her responses, but found the task less straightforward than she'd hoped. What to tell them of Japan? How to convey the unparalleled newness of it. How the place, the work, the people, had filled up her mind and now little else could take root. She settled for entertainment – *everything is upside down in Japan, even the light switches* – and deposited the envelopes into the little postbox in the rec without further thought.

The first time she was allowed out, into the streets of Kure, it was after work with a gang of Y girls and an Aussie guard. Wrapped in their greatcoats and scarves and hats, they made their way past the last vestiges of European familiarity – a huddled bunch of card-playing, gum-chewing occupation fellows who looked up and studied them as they passed – out through the main gates and into a grey blustery afternoon.

The streets were far busier than the day she arrived, and as they approached the commercial precinct, the spectacle became thrillingly abundant. Gleaming new vehicles. Old men with carts. A battered lorry rattling by. Cases of apples stacked high beside a fruit stall. Street cobblers and paperboys. Japanese characters plastered on walls and signs.

A boy on a bicycle churned round-nub knees in swift rotations as he skimmed past on the pavement, then dropped back into the traffic with ease. Outside the cinema, a woman and child sat perched on two old tea chests and scanned the windy streetscape with slack faces and lashed hair. Every so often, Mary caught a glimpse of the sea far off in the distance, a matte sheet of pressed metal studded by fishing vessels moored well offshore.

There were other surprises too. Many of the men and women were dressed in European clothes. Yes, there were kimono and monpe and geta, but Mary's eye was constantly drawn back to the lovely arch of a woman's heel, or the pleasing cut of a businessman's suit. All of this – the briefcases and satchels and modern hairstyles – painted an image of a different kind of Japan. Not a country of death and extinction, but alive with movement and colour; certainly something far richer than upside-down light switches.

They made a turn into a market street where stalls stretched out under the eaves of large buildings. Mary wandered close to inspect the curious wares: dried persimmon piled in wicker baskets and mountains of fresh octopus, slick speckled suckers turned to the light. The stallholders were noticeably poorer in this neighbourhood, thinner too, and between the tabletops she spied several young children playing in the dirt. An unpleasant smell of life, or death, perhaps both, advanced on her and she swept on, eager to be free of it.

She came to a stall where two Aussie officers were remonstrating with a vendor over tins of condensed milk. Their voices cut awkwardly between English and Japanese, between affable and flinty. One was saying, 'No tricks, Mister Honda-san. Good stuff. Totemo yoi.' A third, their friend presumably, a sandy-haired teen, was down on his haunches beside the shop display, luring a child from the shadows with the offer of a Hershey bar. He was humming a tune, a familiar tune, and it took Mary just a moment to recognise it. 'You Are My Sunshine'. By now she understood these Aussie men could make enough in this marketplace to live quite comfortably. It was a lucrative business, if ethically questionable – frowned upon, but rarely policed.

She walked on, thinking about the peculiar ways a culture could reveal itself in another land. Those little hints of the West that had made it across the shores and into the minds of the Japanese, seemingly at random. Jimmie Davis songs. Gold-wrapped chocolate bars. Nice ladies' shoes. Pushy young men with freckled faces and sticky-out ears.

At the final stall, a young woman with a baby strapped to her back scooped up a handful of loquats and wrapped the package in cloth, tying the ends with a firm knot. Her fingers were strong, muscular things clenched around the fabric as she tied and tied again. One of the Y girls called out from a few yards away that it was time to head back. But Mary hesitated, admiring the stallholder's deft movements, the precise handling of the fruit, the way each parcel was slipped along the countertop and another was reached for. The woman's dark hair had fallen across her face, and although there was a veil there, Mary felt that she knew this woman. She could not, but she *felt* that she did.

The woman seemed to sense Mary's presence, and as she raised her face to the light, as the dull afternoon sun fell onto the woman's features, Mary jolted back in shock. She had seen men without legs before, others without arms. Several in wheelchairs making their way into the training hospital with grim, tense jerks of the shoulders. But never had she seen a face like this. Waxy, with gullies and rifts like sand after the tide had washed out. One eyelid seemed to have melted onto the thick of the woman's brow, pulling the eye into a most unusual form.

Mary made a point of clamping her lips shut and pressing them into a smile. The woman returned the expression, and Mary felt again her own body, treacherous in its transparency, step back by instinct, turn, and walk away.

When she'd caught up to the other girls, she let out a long exhalation. Someone thought aloud, 'I wonder what's for tea,' and they walked on, into the capricious gale, back towards the corrugation of hills that rimmed the city, and closer yet, the thick cement wall that signalled home.

Mary woke that night to the sound of muffled sobs in the darkness. Noreen, of course. Certainly not Ida. She thought she should whisper something reassuring, perhaps get up and sit by her friend's bed, stroke her lovely downy hair. But it was so cold in the night here – too cold to release even a finger from under the bedcovers. She would have to find her greatcoat on the other side of the room, and that would wake Ida.

Mary lay deathly still trying to make up her mind what to do, and all the while the weeping continued from the next bed. Noreen was so young – too young, perhaps, for this posting. And yet a little seed in Mary felt affronted. They'd all suffered, had they not? The woman in the market with the melted face. All the mothers, millions of them, who'd lost their sons. Every single person who'd lived through the past few years. Indeed, even Mary, who'd lost her own love to the great disturbance of their time. She had flapped a hanky just as enthusiastically as the next girl as the train had swept out of Spencer Street Station and into the distant beyond.

Admittedly, the boy – Thomas – was by now a perfect stranger. She could hardly picture his face. But still, there had been a time when she thought she would marry him, spend an entire life with him, gazing at each other over the breakfast table and the dinner table, the bookends to a day worn down by children and housework and scrubbing and mending. He'd been kind; that's why she'd agreed. Even as a girl, she'd thought better of kindness than any of the other, more exciting qualities young women tended towards.

Yes, Thomas was kind and quiet. In fact, he barely spoke a word. Perhaps that's why the memories of him had faded so profoundly. And it was such a brief affair, all in all – six outings, a proposal, her lips never once brushing his, and then they were at the station, him clunking up the metal train steps to his fate, looking rather skinny in his khaki and slouch hat, proudly thinking he was off to make some kind of difference. Yet, he never even made it to the front.

Two years before that, when the slow ringing timbre of Menzies' voice had cut across the wireless, she'd been inside, washing up. *No harder task can fall to the lot of a democratic leader,* he had warned. Joe and Bernard had been out in the street playing after-supper cricket, and naturally word got around quick. Theirs being one of the nicer and larger houses in the street, the neighbourhood boys had pressed into the living room and crowded around the radio, all in filthy sports clothes and trying varying disguises of manhood on their sweaty faces. Little Phillip Thiele was still knobby-kneed and thin across the chest, the bulge at his neck protruding conspicuously.

How utterly abstract that time remained in her memory, with at least three of those local boys dead and gone and never to be returned, Phillip among them, and her brothers magically saved. Her father had said once that they could thank their mother; that the very act of losing her was in some way protective, because she was up there making sure of their safety. The idiocy of that position hadn't occurred to Mary at the time. To think one terrible event made anyone immune from another was quite preposterous. And yet she'd grasped on to the notion with little persuasion. They would be all right and, by some stroke of grace, they were.

But not Thomas, of course. Dear old elusive Thomas, who lacked a dead mother to keep watch and who had died at the hands of a terrible banality – too much drink and a hardwood door swinging shut at precisely the wrong moment. The senselessness of the whole fiasco had given new texture to Mary's conception of destiny, and left her more accepting of his death than she might otherwise have been. She realised now, she could not evoke the sadness she felt his memory deserved; being so indistinct, it was a memory that seemed to have taken shelter in a different life.

And, if she was honest, perhaps her discontent might have simply been impatience at Noreen for having woken her. In the end, terrible as it was, she did not a thing; did not slip out of bed to comfort Noreen, did not say a word. To do so, she decided, would be false. It would demand that she feigned kinship or sisterly love; sisterly love being something she in truth knew little about. So instead she waited, and in time Noreen's weeping turned to whimpering, and the whimpering in turn fell silent. The last thought to consume Mary before she descended back into slumber was a vague, wondering notion. Were Thomas's eyes brown or green?

'Quick, get dressed – you can thank me later.'

Brimming with self-satisfaction, Ida had torn into the room like a perfumed twister.

'C'mon,' she was saying, 'up and at 'em.' Bailing up a grubby towel from the floor, she proceeded to snap the end of it sharply against the lump in Noreen's bed. From under the covers, Noreen flinched and mustered an aggressive moan.

Mary now, from the other side of the room, 'Leave her, Ida. She's —'

'I'm well aware.'

'Perhaps she needs —'

'What she *needs* is a good spanking. Now Noreen, dear, get up. Not only is it your day off, it's also Sunday, and one has an obligation to make the most of a holy day without a whiff of holiness.'

Indeed, Sundays had been the hardest day by far to acclimatise to. Without Mass, or an elder in sight to insist upon their piety, the day had become a strange void in the week. Mary could not bring herself to attend service willingly, nor did she wish to tempt the heavens by finding something fruitful to do. Lying about and waiting out the time had seemed, up to this point, strictly the right approach.

A good few moments passed while Ida towered over Noreen's huddled frame. 'Fine. I'll just tell Jimmy not to bother then, shall I?'

A pause descended and Mary thought she might have almost counted down the seconds to Noreen's reply . . . three, two, one – and yes, here was Noreen emerging from under the covers, blinking into the light.

'Bother with what?' she asked, almost but not quite smiling.

'Ferry us to HQ.'

'Oh my word, really?' Noreen was upright on the bed almost immediately.

'Yes, now get up. No more moping.'

'He's really going to do that?'

'I told him I had a sourpuss on my hands here and, well, he solved it for you. But you have to promise to be cheerful. No sourpusses.'

'Oh, I absolutely promise.'

Noreen swung her legs to the ground, hands clasped in a confused prayer. Her face was as bright as Mary had ever seen it.

'You coming, Mare?'

'Yes. All right.'

Of course she was coming. She was as excited as anyone to see the much talked about headquarters on the small island of Etajima, where all the important men resided, along with their wives and children.

'Bring your togs then,' Ida was saying as she rifled through her belongings. 'They have the most wonderful natural baths there. Three pools, three different temperatures.'

Not a few minutes later, Jimmy appeared at the window, a cologne-infused bluster of casual wear and ropy muscle. His hair was set into dark, gelled rills. At home, he was an engineer, but here his work involved running patrols out to the countryside and looking for trouble – a job, Ida enthused, that came with a great deal of power.

With one great charge of her tiny shoulders, Ida drove the sash window up, then greeted him with a kiss and a rough hand through his freshly arranged hair. He allowed this, of course – her impudence was perhaps even welcome – and Mary saw that it was all part of the courtship. Yet another example of the game the clever women played, shifting between devoted attention and abject neglect, thereby keeping their man on his toes.

The Jeeps had already been snapped up by other weekenders, so the group donned their greatcoats and traipsed to the ruined docks on foot, down the quiet Sunday streets, so different without the tenacity of human endeavour. For Mary, there was a sense of déjà vu about this journey; it took her back to a time, mere weeks earlier, when she knew almost nothing about this place, only what she had seen on that first day, and in black and white pictures in the newspaper, a few carefully curated shots in the army medical women's brochure. She was hardly a seasoned veteran, and yet this replay through Kure was a reminder of how familiar this town and the base and her life in Japan already felt. What might another week, or month, or year do to her senses?

The sight of the docks welcomed them from a good distance; the wretched, twisted objects along the shoreline were still hard to fathom, bearing no sign they were once useful machines. At the water's edge, a mound of casting nets lay piled on the jetty like sea-drift, and beside them a handful of local fishermen were launching a small craft into the shallows. The men's faces could not be properly seen under the rims of their hats, nor did they glance up at the foreign intrusion.

'This way.' Gripping Ida's hand, Jimmy led them past the local men to the far end of the docks. There, a small barge, skippered by a young Australian officer, was picked out of the clutter, and the women were helped over the gunwale and told to sit on a bare bench. Jimmy stood at the wheel with the officer and the two of them spoke in lost murmurs as the barge putted into the bay, out past a floating chain of oyster farms and a rocky isle crowned by tufts of green, towards a near cluster of silhouetted hills. Beyond the ripples made by the boat, the sea appeared almost crystallised in the chilled air.

As they neared the island, the outline of a waiting man and a vehicle could be discerned beside a small quay. Jimmy's friend from home, it turned out – Chet Walker, a medical officer with a dark, low brow and outrageously large mouth. The kind of bloke you felt had an infinite number of grins in his armoury, none of them genuinely kind.

'Gee, what a set of crows you've got yourself here!' Chet cried as they climbed out of the boat. 'Practically a harem.'

Jimmy threw his head back and barked a laugh. 'Just my god-given charm, that's all.'

'No local sightseeing for you then, mate.'

Jimmy strode ahead and the two men shook hands vigorously, thumped their chests into each other, and embraced with more laughter. The women followed mutely, but when Mary turned to Ida, she saw that she was smiling along, quietly amused by the men's banter.

After the introductions, the women squeezed into the back of Chet's army vehicle while Jimmy sat up front. They followed a gravel path along the water's edge, hemmed in by a dense forest of pine trees. They passed a group of men and women unloading hessian sacks from a wooden vessel along the shoreline. Nearby, a small child turned to their oncoming vehicle and flung a tiny, futile pebble into its path.

In time, the forest disbanded, giving way to man-made structures; traditional homes with rock gardens, rectangular living quarters, a school, a brand-new building marked 'Corporals Club'. Behind the village, the hills had been carved into giant green steps upon which the locals might plough and harvest. A woman with a wide grass hat led an ox and cart up a steep path. Water trickled from raised bamboo pipes. The last of the blossoms lingered determinedly on branches here and there, waiting for a gust of wind to whip them away, but there were other tremendous flowering trees preparing to take their place in bloom.

The landscape was far prettier, more mythic and charming, than the weary confines of Kure, but it was not until they rounded a corner and saw the grand, white-washed walls of the hospital laid out over greenery that Mary really understood what had been forsaken in her secondment to the Y.

Noreen gave her a nudge. 'Almost like a fairytale, this place, isn't it?'

'Yes,' agreed Mary.

'Imagine what we'd say about Japan if this is all we knew.'

'Well, perhaps it's better not to be sheltered.'

Noreen laughed half-heartedly. 'S'pose so.' Then, half a moment later, 'Still, wouldn't complain for a week or two.'

Chet turned into a driveway that ran down to the former naval academy, past another impressively large building, to a series of sporting fields marked out over a vast lea. He stopped the truck next to a small construction site where two local men were laying mesh across a hut wall. A third was hauling gravel in baskets suspended from a yoke, his face grim under the weight of his load. Beyond them, a group of Aussie men in rugby jerseys stood about chatting. One was tossing a ball high into the air, catching it again with a thud against his chest.

Chet and Jimmy clambered from the vehicle and Mary turned to Ida, asking the question with her face. Ida shrugged and said only, 'Twenty-minute halves. Won't take long.'

So it became apparent that before the eating and the promised bathing and the merrymaking could begin, the women would be required to stand around in the fierce cold, watching the men smash their bodies into the mud.

They did what was necessary, of course, and in time they were joined by a handful of other women, neatly clad in nursing uniforms, who wandered down to the oval and stood on the opposing boundary, nestled into each other for warmth. One of them was quite beautiful, a real Rita Hayworth type, and when the ball bounced their way, they spooled out squealing, great smiles on their faces. Mary eyed them from across the field, thinking how silly they looked shrieking like piglets, determined not to fall into the trap herself of being so shrill and eager.

Mary could be prideful at times – this she knew already. But also, there was some sense to it. Why should she pander to the men over a game she had played countless times herself, right up until adulthood in fact. On a family picnic or after church, she would join her brothers in games of union or cricket, or she'd follow them out into the ocean for a dip, right out to the depths where only the brave souls went. They would not insist she join them, nor did she have to ask; it was a given that she would participate, because she was one of them and had forged by accident or otherwise a shared history.

On the field, the men wrangled each other to the earth until one broke free to race and duck and weave, the muscles across his thighs swollen with comic power, only to be caught by another and towed into a new mess of arms and legs. They played without an umpire, so at times the game was paused and a friendly altercation ensued. Someone would cry, 'C'mon!' Someone else, 'Don't be a dumb mug, Finnegan!'

Although she could not pretend to be interested, she saw Ida and Noreen beside her were performing their roles with aplomb. Cheeks flushed from the chill, they whooped and cheered at all the right moments. Ida even flaunted a miraculous capacity to whistle with her fingers, like a man, but prettier.

Mary gazed out to the tree line, a spiky pine canopy, then back to the men, impatient for the game to be done. Over at the construction site, the local men were now slopping wet muck onto the mesh-lined walls of the hut. They bore their labour in silence, tacking between one another like noble vessels far out to sea. It occurred to her then that had she been alone, she might have felt quite frightened of these local men. She thought of the terrible words her brothers had used to describe them. At least two were quite young – young enough to have worn a uniform. Yet they didn't look cruel or sadistic. In fact, in their straw hats and loose trousers, they looked nothing more than quotidian.

After the game, the whole rugby crew headed up to the 'club house', a conventional Japanese dwelling with sliding doors and grass mats, that had been repurposed for European tastes. An ochre couch, a handsome standing lamp – these were the cultural markers that took possession of the place. As it turned out, the club house was simply one of the men's homes. His wife and children were away, sightseeing in Tokyo, and being the oldest and most accomplished of the lot, he had nominated his home as base.

It was barely midday, and there was not a morsel of food to speak of, but someone pulled out a bottle of liquor and a great cheer went up around the room.

'To the atomic age!' a deep voice hollered.

'Make your own fun!' several others chanted back.

Minutes passed. The women, nurses included, were offered mugs of the sharp-scented spirit, and with the benefit of time and an accepted universality, they began to introduce themselves. There was a Dulcie and Barbara and the great beauty, Vera, who was going with Chet and who – it was made crystal clear – expected a proposal any day now. They crammed into the lounge, four bottoms to a two-seater, and sprawled out on the mat, watching the men watching them.

Another unmarked bottle materialised, and the men became looser and louder with each hour. Lunch was forgotten. Someone glanced out the window and mentioned casually that rain was falling. Another had the idea to turn the electric heater up to the top setting, and the room quickly became sultry. The women were forced to disrobe to their blouses. Beads of sweat formed on the men's brows.

It didn't take long for Ida and Jimmy to disappear, and in the miasma of the drink and the sweltering room, Mary saw that other couples were forming too, sliding into each other with some sense of inevitability. Noreen went to the bathroom only to return fluttering her eyelids at a tall man named Macalister.

Through all this, Mary remained an observer to their game of courtship. Perched on the floor, her legs tucked under her dress, she held up her mug dutifully when the owner of the house, the patriarch, wandered by with the liquor, and she was reminded of that out-of-place feeling she so often had. The never quite knowing what to say and what to do, how to hold her body, wear her face. Being young was so peculiar, and she knew with absolute certainty that it had been largely wasted on her.

After two o'clock, Chet announced with a resonant clap that it was time for a dip. So the women crammed into a bedroom, pulled the blinds and slipped into their bathing costumes. One of the men made a show of banging theatrically on the door, so they took turns standing guard, holding the door shut with mock outrage.

When they were ready, the women covered themselves with their greatcoats and appeared in the doorway giggling at the waiting band of bare-chested men. From the house, they trudged a good distance towards the mountains, down and then up a ridge, until they saw white wisps of steam rising from the flat summit of the next hill. The men, frozen stiff by now, raced in a barrel-bodied, deep-phonic contest towards the first pool, jabbing and shoving each other until one cracked the surface and a spray of water was sent into the cold air.

Although the hill was steep and there was effort required, Mary experienced this pilgrimage as if she was wafting high above it all. As some celestial being. Her head felt wrapped in gossamer, her free-floating fingertips discrete from the whole. This feeling, she knew, was a consequence of the liquor, which had been much sharper, and frankly more plentiful, than any nip of sherry her father had offered her over the years. But it was not an unpleasant sensation; it simply allowed her to feel beyond herself, borderless.

She waited until the group's attention had shifted to the far end of the pool before slipping out of her coat and into the water as quickly as her slow limbs would allow. Once inside, she released a trapped breath. There was the niggling thought that at some stage she would have to ascend out of the pool, wet and dripping, practically naked, for these men to gaze at her, but for now she could relax. For now there was the warm water like a bath, and the fog drifting around their bodies.

Someone had suggested a game of tag, but Mary was satisfied to sit on a step and rest the back of her spinning head against the cold stone. She stayed like this for some time, eyes closed, water lapping at her collarbones, assigning the hollers and squeals from the crew to some distant enterprise, until a voice penetrated her trance.

'You holding up okay?'

She opened her eyes. It was the patriarch, the owner of the club house.

She sat up straight and smiled at the man before her. 'Yes, I'm all right.'

He leaned an elbow on the side of the pool. He was perhaps forty years old, with distinguished grey streaks above the ears, a broad, hair-covered chest.

'How long you been here?' he asked, and she had some work to do thinking of the answer.

'Oh, well, let's see. Five weeks, I think.' She dabbed a wet hand against her sweaty forehead. The man stood close, and she could smell his stale, sharp breath caught in the heat radiating off the surface of the pool.

'It's a riot, isn't it?'

'Yes, I s'pose it is.'

'Bet you didn't think you'd be lounging around in a hot pool like a medieval queen, did ya?'

'No,' she laughed. 'I certainly didn't.'

'Bit of a change of pace for us all.' He was serious now, gazing around at his company of red-faced, hooting men. 'Head north and make some dough. Meet some nice crows. Go home and start your life afresh.'

She nodded, unsure how to respond.

'Some of these fellas did it pretty hard in New Guinea. They deserve a little comfort, don't you reckon?'

'Yes,' she said, 'they do.'

'You been over to the bombsite yet?'

'Not yet.'

This brought on a change of voice in the man, a growl across the pool. 'Hey, Jimmy!'

'Yeah, boss?'

'You haven't taken these girls to Hiroshima yet?'

'No, boss.'

'Why the devil not? Every Aussie's gotta get there. So we can tell the folks back home what an absolute mess we made of 'em.'

Jimmy laughed at this, and splashed a little water playfully across the pool.

It was when the man turned back to her that he really saw Mary, or at least that's how it seemed. He narrowed his bloodshot eyes. Grinned.

'You're a pretty girl. Why don't you have a bloke?'

She smiled at him, felt a rush of heat across her already hot face.

'I'm not sure,' she whispered.

'You could find a fella here, no problem. Just gotta loosen up a bit, hey?'

And with those words, his hand under the steam and water slid across her lower belly. She reacted without thought. Flinched. Groped at the foreign object, which only made him laugh.

'Not like that, girl. C'mon on, you can do it.'

His hand, detached in a way from his body, returned to her belly, then slid down to nuzzle into the place between her legs. It was a challenge as well as an act of possession. This time she froze.

'There's a girl,' he cooed. 'No one's looking.'

The fog in her head had suddenly lifted, and she could feel her heartbeat like an alarm in her temples, in her chest, worst of all in that private place down below.

She saw the scene anew. The patriarch, whose name she still didn't know, standing beside her, completely motionless above the waterline, amicably chatting, while the others frolicked and bellowed and carried on, utterly unaware. His face was inscribed with a strange indifference, and she understood that this was the face of hubris. He was a man so sure of himself he would pursue a trophy he didn't even desire.

She clamped her legs shut. Roughly thrust the man's hand away and, with one great burst of unthinking courage, duck-dived into the centre of the pool. Kicked furiously, bubbles rising around her. Under there, the world was even more surreal than above, with its long watery shadowed legs, but it was also quiet, protective. She came up for air. Didn't look back. Duck-dived again, kicking until she reached the far end of the pool. She bobbed up and took in a desperate lungful of air.

'Oh, there you are, Mare.' Noreen turned her fine shoulders to greet Mary. 'I'd almost forgotten you!'

'Here I am,' Mary said, running a hand over her wet hair.

'Come here then, lovely. Have you met Macalister?'

Noreen pulled Mary into a sideways hug. She was beaming a luminous red-cheeked smile. Somehow the heat of the pool had softened not ruined her features, and she was even more pixie-like, enchanting.

Macalister was clearly taken by her. He was standing very upright, a performance of the reliable man.

'Pleased to meet you,' he said, dipping his head. He had a proper English accent and Mary wondered how on earth he'd got mixed up with this horde of Aussie savages.

The conversation continued around her. When she was brave enough, she glanced back across the pool. Half their group had relocated to the next lagoon, a little tarn set into a depression on the side of the hill. The club house owner had been commandeered by Jimmy, who had Ida under one wing and was laughing, practically spitting out a story with wild, wide gestures of the other arm. The father character was listening intently, his face fixed, contorted even, into an absorbed rictus. From thirty feet away, he had the look of a real elder, the patient benefactor, and already the episode from moments earlier was beginning to feel like a figment of Mary's heat-doped mind.

By May, the weather was erratic. One moment it was clear and lovely – a balmy heat that smelled like earth, clouds like spun sugar – the next, a downpour had them racing across the yard in their brown lace-ups, a swish of wool against rayon, as fat drops of rain dashed the ground. It came down the sides of the hills, rushing and trundling with gathered speed. In no time, the paths were transformed into streams of mud, and they were compelled to slow their pace, creep even, to avoid ending up on their backsides.

Nonetheless, in the evenings the women were grateful for the tiled roof over their heads. The galvanised iron of the men's quarters, it was widely reported, amplified the sound of rain to the point of utter bedlam. Mary would watch the sleepless men stumble into the mess hall at breakfast bleary-eyed, soft-limbed. Even the officers seemed to have lost their strength, and when they came wandering in, they drew gentle smiles in a most unusual way.

Then one morning Mary overheard one of the girls confide to another that those nights – the stormy ones – were the best for the men of a certain persuasion to sneak in their girls. And the men who refrained – from dogged idealism or perhaps misfortune – were forced to lie awake listening not just to the music of the sky but also the clap of clogs on bare floorboards, squealing bedframes, the urgent low groans of release.

The act of settling in happened in covert ways. One day, Mary failed to straighten her back when Mrs Richards appeared in the Dew Drop with yet another task to attend to – knitting for the orphans, charity drive for the housegirls. Likewise, Ida's bragging and preening became the backdrop, not the foreground, to Mary's evenings. She learned to live alongside it, she supposed – stopped expecting anything different.

She was forming habits, too, if she cared to consider them. Habits that mimicked home. Instead of reading under the elm in Beaumaris, she sought out a large camphor on the base, the largest tree by far – no giant, but large enough to comfortably sit under. Its pale, rough roots nudged up out of the ground, forming natural chambers. So now, most afternoons after work, she went to the tree with a book, dragging a chair from the mess to perch on. On wet days the awning of glossy leaves made for an effective shelter, and on clearer days she could watch the people move around the base. Sometimes they'd nod or exchange a few words. But mostly Mary felt the relief of solitude, the freedom to say nothing at all.

Empire Day arrived and there was a merciful reprieve from the rain. A Yankee brig had been deployed from the capital to observe their big parade, and it was tacitly understood by all that an event of this magnitude, especially with their American superiors in attendance, must be executed with absolute fastidiousness. This was no time for laissez-faire larrikinism, lest they substantiate the Yanks' enduring prejudices.

At three, Mary and Noreen made their way to the yard. The women were not required to march, but of course they were dressed in their uniforms, freshly pressed, with their hair pinned under their hats. The promise of all the men spick and span in their parade attire, their spotless white belts and gaiters, slouch hats and rifles, had Noreen practically skipping.

'Oh, do you think he'll be there?'

Mary smiled. 'I would imagine so, yes.'

'But do you think he'll be able to see me, in the crowd?'

Mary caught Noreen's hand and pulled her into a more relaxed pace. 'My word. What's got into you?'

Noreen looked to Mary and took in a gulp of air. 'Love.'

'It can't be love! You barely know him.'

'All right, desire then.' Noreen delivered this word like some second-rate starlet, throwing an open palm across her forehead.

'Oh dear.' Mary laughed. 'Even more dangerous.'

They approached from the southern end of the yard, and already many people had arrived; the buzz was not Noreen's alone. Indeed, there was a palpable feeling in the air, something that could be gleaned from people's faces and the shapes of their bodies. A small man was racing up and down the threshold of a roped-off area, yammering instructions to various others. In the distance, the VIPs were being guided towards a raised platform. Beyond them, as if placed there for dramatic effect, a half-bald hill lay creased and scrappy, a great sunken animal.

Almost immediately Mary lost Noreen in the mix of other women, civilians, even some permitted locals dressed in their Sunday finest; the men in sharp black suits, the women in colourful silks, hair rolled and pulled into extravagant whorls. The sight of all these people thrown together – Aussies, Kiwis and the

Japanese – still struck her as pure anomaly, and she wondered if she would ever grow accustomed to it. Could she un-know what she had always known?

Finally, a horn rang out and the proceedings began. Like some masterpiece, the men rose above their antipodean deficiencies and, led by the regimental band, streamed into the yard in meticulous lines, khaki arms swinging like pendulums, feet chawing sandy earth. They surged in, one contingent after the next, battalion by battalion, the armoured car squadron, artillery unit. One quota appeared in round helmets. Another in slouch hats. A smattering of garrison caps and dark berets. There were badges and medals, of course, that meant things. And there were variations in size and shape and complexion. But, for the most part, the men flinched and halted, swerved and spun like starlings in the sky, as if a singular organism.

The sight of all this pageantry was captivating, and for a moment Mary did not register the body beside her. Taller than her, but only by a little. The certain air of amused distance, pleasantly occupied by the spectacle and yet never one with it. She had not laid eyes on him since that first day outside the Major's office and yet the young man was immediately known to her. His mere presence was a reminder of the humiliation she had endured.

Evidently, the memory was fresh for him too, because he turned to her, raised an eyebrow and grinned. 'Oh, it's the nurse.'

The word hung between them, and she felt a glare blow across her face.

'Oh,' she replied, matching his tone. 'It's the jazz man with the ratty shoes.'

He threw his head back, letting out a real shock of laughter. 'Very nice. I mean, really, that was swell.' He pulled his trousers up an inch, bent at the middle and gazed down at his feet. 'You're absolutely right. I'm desperately in need of a polish.'

She breathed in deeper, raised her chin a small degree.

The men in lines paraded past, brittle bodies, their faces flat planes of duty.

'Tell me,' he whispered, leaning a little closer, 'how is the job going?'

'Shh . . .' she said sharply.

She would not move, not an inch. She would not soften for him.

'Cripes, don't take it too seriously. It's just a working holiday for most of them.'

She remained silent, eyes fixed ahead.

'I mean, look at them . . . so serious —'

'Because it is serious,' she snapped.

'What, all that buffoonery with not an adversary in sight? Sure, it meant something in '46, but now? Now, well . . . it's occupation for occupation's sake.'

'Don't be absurd.'

'Meanwhile, we've got India and Pakistan at loggerheads. Palestine in all sorts. A coup d'etat in Czechoslovakia.'

She turned to him. She could not help herself. 'What on earth does that have to do with us?'

'The point is . . . the point is that peace was and always has been a relative term. Conflict abounds! And this, this —' He threw a hand up, capturing the full breadth of the parade before them. 'This is just a parody.'

She inspected his face – the broad cheekbones, the pale smudge of lips, the hair longer than permitted. The eyes, pale brown, flashed with some insight that evaded her.

'*You* should know,' she said with a strength that surprised even her.

'I should know what?'

'About parody.'

He laughed again, lightly. Bobbed his head up and down. 'That's fair.'

'You're a reporter, yes?'

'Yes.'

'So shouldn't you be taking notes or something?'

'Nah, could write this tripe in my sleep. Same as all the other times.'

She huffed. 'You are . . .'

'Roguish? Beguiling?'

'Impertinent,' she said firmly.

A whistle blew out across the yard and there was a loud, crushing stomp. It commanded their attention. The line of men swivelled, and another blast pierced the air. There was a long heavy silence, and just like that the parade was over.

The crowd relaxed in on itself, and she thought she would turn to him and say something civil. Perhaps she would ask his name. But instead he was tipping his hat, smiling and saying, 'Well, nurse, always a pleasure.'

And in a shot, he had broken away and disappeared into the mass of people.

The figures of them, three women and a man climbing into a Jeep outside the Kure base, might well have been observed with interest by the locals who happened upon them that day. Then again, perhaps there was nothing substantial or novel about the moment at all. Perhaps a handful of occupation members dressed in civvies had become so commonplace as to barely warrant a second glance. The dark-haired man standing by the side door holding out a hand for one then another woman to press up into the high vehicle. The most striking of the women being helped into the front passenger seat. Finally, the man himself immured in the driver's position and the engine announcing itself to the street: *look at us, we're off to Hiroshima to see your destruction for ourselves.*

These were the peculiar thoughts that flooded Mary's mind from time to time. She wondered about the locals, but did they wonder about her? There was something faintly shameful about what the Aussies were doing, she decided – making a point of witnessing the suffering, not by happenstance, but by establishing it as the central event of their day. Still, she was here; she had not refused the invitation from Ida and for that reason she was as complicit as the rest.

It was a pleasant day, and they'd dispensed of their cardigans and pullovers. Jimmy in the front wore trousers and a shirt that clung to his robust shoulders. Behind, Noreen sat primly in a blouse with a scalloped collar. The drive was surprisingly brief, and it felt to Mary as if they'd barely escaped Kure before they came around the headland and the outskirts of Hiroshima appeared on the horizon: small dwellings scattered across pasture; plots of land cultivated with rice and other crops Mary could not name; in turn, a tightly knitted cluster of homes, remarkably still standing or perhaps rebuilt.

Finally, just as one expected the city to reveal itself, great empty spaces emerged. Some stretched out unspeakably, cleaved by streets and avenues, broken up only by the odd tree, a bowed pole or a mound of rubble. The whole arena was carpeted in a startling green and, as Jimmy slowed, the movie-reel flicker slackened and Mary could make out thistles surfacing from the earth.

Still, there were homes about too, plenty of them, and many more coming up. One was moated by the most exquisite garden – daffodils, jonquils, a madly blooming azalea bush. And there were patches of surprising industry; construction sites where men worked in teams, and along the roadside, a constant flow of workers on foot.

The Jeep pushed on, passing over a bridge and then another. More homes appeared. And more still. A shuddering, screeching streetcar crammed with locals loomed into view, then receded behind them. They saw now, ahead, the emergence of a civic centre – modest shops, lean-tos and food stalls, a large gathering of local people come to sell and buy wares. Reams of fish had been strung up to dry across the shop fronts, and along the footpath – a tattered, uneven affair – men and women mingled, some in nice clothing, many others in workwear. Hunched over in the dirt, a solitary bootmaker laboured. An ox lumbered by.

All of this had a baffling effect on the eye. Mary had imagined nothing. A wasteland, they'd said. A hell on earth. But this was . . . well, not the prettiest of towns, but it was a town all right. The beginnings of one, in any case, materialising out of the ashes, running in a canvas of light and motion towards the horizon and the shimmering, impervious sea beyond.

They drove on until they reached the largest of all the old structures. Square block below, a dome on top. The remains were barely articulated, more bones than flesh, certainly not habitable, and yet one saw enough to understand the former grandeur of the place.

Jimmy pulled up at its base and they climbed out of the vehicle.

'So, this is it. Centre of impact.' He put his hands on his hips, stretched his back one way, then the other. The hoods of his eyes were low as he surveyed the landscape, a casual imitation of a tyrant's gaze. He was at pains to impress them with his total lack of discomfort.

'Shocking,' Noreen muttered.

'But remember what the emperor said,' Ida offered with a smile. 'We bear the unbearable. And they sure as hell did.'

Jimmy moved to embrace her as if sightseers on honeymoon, arms wrapped around one another, almost nose to nose.

Mary caught Noreen's eye and they shared a secret understanding, before breaking away and returning their attention to the ruins set out before them. So, this was what they had come to Japan for. Not the parties or bathing or courting. This. The most colossal of all humanity's deeds laid bare in one tract of indescribable landscape.

They spread out to explore. Mary wandered away from the grand building with its bony-fingered dome and into the flat earth behind. She walked slowly, head bowed, watching the ground for clues of human existence. A little melted crockery, or a cooking utensil perhaps. But there was nothing. It seemed the place had been raked clean over the years. Eventually, she found a collection of block-shaped tombstones, marked with characters, sprouting innocently from the earth along with the weeds and the grasses.

The four of them orbited one another for several minutes until they gathered back at their starting point and, without uttering a word, instinctively climbed back into the sanctuary of the vehicle. Jimmy lit a smoke and passed it to Ida. For a moment they were silent as they gazed out to that field of naught. Already, Mary knew it would never be sufficiently described to her loved ones at home. It was too bewildering. The nearly city and the terrible ruins and the empty spaces.

It was Jimmy who spoke next. 'All that fuss about a decisive weapon, hey? The joint's practically rebuilt anyway.'

And strangely it was Mary who replied. 'Oh, would you say that? I mean . . .'

'Yeah, well, not this patch. They're keeping it this way, to lord it over us. But the rest of it, over there' – he threw a finger towards the horizon – 'practically back to normal.'

'But wouldn't you need to know what it looked like . . . before?'

'Same as all their other VD-infested hovels, I should think.'

Ida snorted out a laugh. 'You know they made their houses out of paper, right? Paper!'

'I suppose it is rather a weak material,' said Noreen.

'An entirely predictable outcome, I'm afraid.'

Through the rear-view mirror, Jimmy fixed his eyes on Mary. 'Not convinced, I see.'

Somehow the cigarette had made its way to her, so she drew in a lungful of heat before responding. 'No, I'm . . . I'm, well, I'm not sure.'

'All right.' Jimmy fired up the engine and Ida's hand found the back of his neck. 'But let me just say, it doesn't pay to get soft about the Japs.'

They drove back to Kure under a brilliant mid-afternoon sun, and Mary found she was able to enjoy the drive in a way she couldn't earlier. She was comforted by the lovely undulating sweep of the hills as they whooshed by. Homes clung to their sides like barnacles, and they seemed so thoroughly unaffected by the devastation, busy in their naivete, she thought if she could just keep her head turned this way, if she didn't glance back, she could pretend away the city that lay behind them.

That afternoon, the housegirl appeared in their room. Nancy was her name, or so Mary had been reliably informed by Noreen, who heard through a friend's girl. She was hauling a large bucket, and the slosh of water against the metal sides marked her intent at once.

When the girl saw Mary sitting on the bed, book hung open between her hands, she briefly dropped her head in a gesture of respect. Mary bowed too, and taking in a deep breath, blurted out, 'Konnichiwa, Nancy.'

A tremor of surprise passed over the girl. 'Good afternoon, Madam-san.'

'Oh, you do . . . speak English, that is.'

The woman's face peeled open. 'Ah, yes. A little.'

'Would you like me . . . to . . .' Mary leapt from the bed and started gathering Ida's clothes from the floor.

'No, Madam-san. Please, no.'

'It's honestly fine,' Mary said as she continued to bluster around the room. 'I don't mind. It feels so strange to not —'

'Please, Madam-san.' Nancy's voice was insistent, almost but not quite brusque. Her hand was out, reaching for the clothes in Mary's grasp.

'All right,' Mary said finally. She returned to her bed and drew up the open book while Nancy began to move again around the room, shifting items, then setting to work with the mop, driving it across the floor with graceful, whole-body arcs.

Mary passed her eye over the shapes on the page, but they failed to convert into ideas. Instead, images of Hiroshima came into her mind. Those expanses of nothingness, that strange arcane city. She wondered what the last few years must have been like for this girl, Nancy. She was young, but not so young to have been sheltered from the horrors.

The objects of our profound solicitude. That's what Hirohito had said in his surrender speech, and she tried now to impose those words on Nancy. To somehow make Nancy the object of her own profound solicitude.

She heard her voice break the silence before she had the urge to speak. 'Nancy?'

Again, a surprised look on the girl's face. She straightened up.

'Yes, Madam-san?'

'I'm . . . not much of a madam, I'm afraid. Maybe . . .' She placed a hand across her chest. 'Would you call me Mary? Watashi wa Mary desu.'

There was a long pause while Nancy considered her words. Finally she said, 'Hai . . . Mary-san,' and smiled, and moved on with her work.

'Do you wonder about them?'

Mary was still waking up to the day so she didn't quite comprehend Noreen's question as they walked to breakfast.

'Who?'

'You know . . . them.'

Ahead, a local man in worker's attire approached. He was a young man, walking hurriedly, expressionless save for a vague awareness that he was passing two European women and should avert his eyes.

After he'd gone, Mary said, 'Yes, yes, of course.'

'What do you think they make of us?'

Mary considered this for a moment. The bite of their feet on the gravel path allowed for this sort of interruption, as did the familiarity that Mary felt existed now between Noreen and her.

'I'm not sure,' she said finally. 'They don't seem to hate us, but —'

'Exactly,' Noreen said with a snap of her fingers. 'You can never tell, can you? It's such a terrible mystery, but I'm . . . I'm just dying to know.'

They walked on a little more before Mary felt Noreen's arm graze against hers. 'This one,' she heard Noreen say quietly.

Mary looked up. Another man – older, middle-aged perhaps. Again, he passed without incident.

'I think he does,' Noreen said matter-of-factly.

'What?'

'Hate us,' she said, which produced a laugh from Mary.

'We can't know, not for sure.'

'Ooh, perhaps he was one of those . . . what do you call them . . . kamikaze pilots.'

'No, he's far too old. No, no, I think during the war he . . . worked in the ear-plug factory.'

'Well, that's a bit dull,' complained Noreen.

But a little spark had awakened inside Mary and was running ahead. 'It was near here,' she said. 'I read about it. They made ear plugs for the air force and the navy men.'

'If you say so.'

'What's more, I think he has . . . three children. A son and two daughters. And after the war ended, he made ends meet by collecting nightsoil, you know, with one of those iron-wheeled handcarts, and even though we think it's a nasty job it wasn't such a bad way to pass the time, because it was so lovely and peaceful in the city at night after all the years of air raids.'

'My word, Mare.'

Mary laughed again. She was on a roll now and could hardly stop herself.

'Life was hard in other ways though,' she went on. 'Food was in short supply, and having only a small quota of land they could not grow enough to stave off the hunger.'

The women rounded the corner of the mess hall and fell into

line behind a group of other men and women who had congregated near the door.

'Finally,' Mary said, 'his neighbour Denichi —'

'Denichi?!'

'Yes, Denichi,' Mary said, deadpan.

'Is that a real name?'

'I think so. And in any case, it is now. So Denichi was a gregarious fellow and knew some words in English, and told our friend back there, Toshio —'

'Toshio?!'

'He told Toshio there was work going with our lot for honest good men. So Denichi brought him here one morning and introduced him to one of our boys who said he could come back the following day and there would be work for him. So now he sweeps paths. It's not his favourite thing to do, but he would never complain, not ever. Because in every house as far as the eye can see, someone died . . . but in his house . . . by some miracle, no one did.'

Noreen was silent, gazing at her. 'Mary . . . I can hardly believe it.'

Mary smiled, emptier and lighter now.

'Did you just invent all that? On the spot?'

'Yes, I suppose I did.'

It seemed Noreen was still a little baffled by her, but the line was moving. And although Mary felt she should be sheepish about this outburst, secretly she was rather proud of herself. For that moment, at least, she entertained the notion that the man who had passed them on the path was in fact Toshio and that she, by some extrasensory detection, had hit upon an essential truth.

The following week, a dance was held at the camp theatre. The organising committee had constructed a sorry-looking torii from slabs of pine, and it stood at the entrance for all to parade under. Their construction might have had the feel of a school art project, but still there was an undeniable thrill as the three women passed under it and descended into the depths of the cacophonous hall.

In a navy frock with her breasts spilling out like two alabaster pillows, Ida was one step ahead, almost but not quite disowning them. Mary and Noreen followed behind in their roomier, higher-necked dresses.

Inside, the low-lit room unfurled before them. Ribbons of crepe paper had been suspended between the windows and the central light fitting. The band was a cobbled-together, United Nations kind of affair: a Japanese man on double bass, the Kiwis on brass, Aussies on the piano and drums. The sound they were making had an unusual quality – swing, yes, but ever so slightly asynchronous – and yet couples were dancing, adding fat to the din with an ensemble of feet on trembling boards.

Some of the men were paired with Japanese women – the aberration allowed out of simple necessity. Even so, it was clear the girls were outnumbered. Mary had been warned that, as an unattached European woman, she would be required to do the right thing and make herself available, lest some poor bloke be left high and dry for the entire evening. The nurses had travelled from the island too. Even the married women, Ida had confirmed, would do their bit for the cause.

A local girl handed them each a bottle of beer, and Mary followed Ida's mince across the room, submerging into the sea of people who bounced out and into pairs with a thrust or a tug of the arm, sweeping between one another with magnificent ease. Mary was keenly aware of the unpartnered men on the fringes who turned and noticed as they passed.

At a small table, they sat and deposited their handbags, and Ida gathered her fine features into a pucker to yell, 'Didn't I tell you the band would be a disaster?'

'Oh, but it hardly matters,' Noreen cried back. 'This is just exquisite.' Face lit up like a Ferris wheel, eyes bright as jewels, she gazed around the room.

Ida took a swig of her beer and looked to Mary. The raised eyebrow insisted upon solidarity.

'Are they a little out of time – is that it?' Mary offered at last.

'It'll be the Jap fella. Jimmy says they're terribly slow. Lucky we have the Aussies to liven things up.'

Ida leaned back in her chair and scanned the room. They were late by a whole half hour only because Ida had insisted she never arrived anywhere on time if she could help it and that it was always better to arrive after the bloke you're going with had been waiting a good deal of time. But Jimmy was nowhere to be seen, and it was Noreen who was asked to dance first, by a new recruit with rubbery cheeks and freshly shorn hair. He was not Macalister but he'd do.

When they were alone, Mary noted the change in Ida: a rigidity in the neck, a shameless streak of contempt upon the face. Mary thought she should say something to ease Ida's pain, to distract her at the very least, but the right words wouldn't come, and she knew the wrong words were better left unsaid. So they sat like that, pretty shags, sipping their beers, watching the men and women shift and tack to the clamorous rhythm. The trumpet player let out a run of wobbly proclamations and the crowd erupted in delight.

Soon, two men appeared beside them. The more handsome of the two – fair hair, dimples – approached Ida. The other – small, scrawny, barely eighteen – shuffled awkwardly behind him, and now it was Mary's turn to acquire a steel gaze. She did this by instinct; it was that pride again. She could not say she understood herself in this moment, but she was sure she did not want to dance with this boy, and she knew that by turning a shoulder ever so slightly, taking on a harsher expression, pretending she did not see him, he would – indeed he did – dissolve back into the crowd.

The song ended and a slower one began. The couples moved into each other, swaying now rather than spinning, and if she squinted, she felt almost underwater at the sight of them in the half-dark, as surreal as marine life. She could feel the bounds of her own body: an edge, hard up against the world. One knee stacked upon the other. The length of her wrist against the table. Fingers wrapped around the cool glass of the bottle. Breezily unbothered. And so it was, then. Even when she invited the solitude, she was unhappy with it. She saw there was something irredeemably defective about her, something that could not be overcome.

This moment of self-indulgence was penetrated by the fact of his voice over her shoulder.

'Nurse.'

She turned to him, scarcely tried to hide the look on her face. He saw her expression and laughed.

'Oh cripes, it's like that, is it?'

'It's like . . . nothing,' she said loudly over the swelling music.

'And here I was thinking we could put our differences behind us.'

He was still standing, she sitting, and the disparity between them and the intensity of the music served to make her feel even more watched, more exposed.

'I doubt that's possible,' she found herself saying.

She thought for the first time that he was probably younger than her, although maybe it was just that baby face, the open steady smile that seemed to both ask a question and answer it all in the same venture. She knew she should turn her body to him, thaw her face, make things easier for them both. But for some reason, mysterious even to her, she did not do this. Instead, she turned back to the dance floor and took a swig from her bottle. The way to solve this problem was to commit fully to the mythology that she did not – absolutely did not – want to dance, and she certainly did not want to dance with him.

In her peripheral vision, she saw him fold his hands into his pockets.

'I'm Sully, by the way.'

'Hello,' she cried back, the volume of her voice utterly at odds with the casual indifference she was trying to foster.

'And you are?'

'Mary,' she said. 'Mary Egan.'

The music had brightened again, and she spotted Noreen in

the crowd of revellers, smiling joyfully. She had found Macalister, or perhaps it was he who had found her.

'All right, Miss Mary. So, shall we just pretend that you're not sitting there alone, waiting for a partner, and that I myself have no one to dance with?'

'Perhaps that's best.'

'Because you're waiting for a real bloke. One with a gun, not a pen?'

She snapped her face towards him, firmed her lips into protest. There was something very unusual about this man. The strange all-in-one smile. The crinkled, unblinking eyes. The shoes that remained in need of attention. But she had to admit he was not unattractive. He might even have been handsome.

'Are you a Red?' she blurted out.

He laughed then – at this, at her. A baffled guffaw that released something between them.

'Well, are you? Before I agree to a dance I should know.'

He looked utterly perplexed. Courageously, she let the moment stretch out, the uncertainty very much a part of the thrill. Finally, he narrowed his eyes and pointed a finger at her. 'Cripes, you really had me going there.'

She turned away from him so he couldn't see the proud grin that had spread across her face. When she turned back, he was still there, smiling, watching her intently.

'C'mon, then. How about one spin around the room? Then I'll hand you over to the real men.'

He offered a palm, and she sighed in jest as she took it, stood, crossed the threshold of the dance floor and suddenly was in his arms, being held by this strange specimen who was stronger than she'd imagined.

They were silent as they moved, but the bedlam of the not-quite-right band did the job of conversation. He pulled and shifted her with ease; he was, she discovered, a rather proficient dancer. There was an elegance there that made the process comfortable for them both, and she let him sway and twirl her across the rough timber.

The music slowed and he drew her closer, still facing her, but not touching body to body, not that close. He smiled, almost apologetically, at the intimacy, and she tried her best not to stiffen.

Finally, he spoke.

'It's not the first time I've been asked.'

'What?'

'The Red comment. I hear it a bit.'

'Oh.'

'It's the darn shoes that give me away.'

She smiled. 'I didn't mean anything by it. I say things sometimes . . . queer things.'

'Nah, it was funny. You got me.'

There was another moment of silence.

'I catch myself sometimes,' she went on, 'saying these silly things, not at all appropriate, and then carry on all the same. I can't imagine why I do that.'

'Well, while we're at it, I'm sorry I ragged you about the job. It was an attempt at . . . humour.'

'Yes. I suppose I knew that.'

Mary felt something inside her body loosen. It was the smell of him, perhaps, or the heat of his hand at her waist. These tiny wonders.

'Why don't I see you around the base?' she asked.

'Ah, well, I cover the whole country. If I'm not coming, I'm going.'

'I see. So you must have many adventures.'

'Suppose you could say that.' After a beat, he added, 'It's not all rosy, but it is truly an adventure.'

The song petered out, and she wondered if there was an opportunity for more. She could not bear the thought of returning to the table alone, to wear the proud gaze, to be preyed upon by pimply teenagers. But then another man was moving towards them, gesturing to Sully.

'May I?' the man asked.

And Sully was tucking his head in, a bow of sorts. Not another word was spoken, but somehow she'd been shifted into the hands of this other man, and he was firmer, pulling and jerking her this way and that. She relinquished Sully to the press of people, didn't even try to keep track of him – this other man was a distraction. Big and broad, his upper arm was practically geologic under her small hand.

'Having a fine evening, miss?'

'Yes,' she smiled.

'Committee's put on a cracking show, huh?'

'Yes. Quite something.'

He smiled a big toothy smile, and she thought, yes, I can be that girl if I try. I can be that fun and frivolous girl.

The night continued like that. A multitude of men spinning and twirling her. Small breaks to powder her nose. To sip at another beer. To gossip about the men with Noreen. Then back to the dance floor to be swept around and around in aimless cycles. She could not deny there was something heady about it all, being so sought after. And she could not help thinking of her school friends at home, with their babies and endless chores, who would never in a million years have an opportunity like this. Of course there were dances in Melbourne too, but not this kind, steeped in this strange, wonderful foreignness.

After the final song, Noreen found her and they ambled out into the still, cool night arm in arm, heavy with exhaustion and yet light as feathers.

'My friends back home will never believe me,' Noreen said.

Mary laughed. 'No, perhaps not.'

'So many fellas.'

A sharp shriek of laughter caught the air, and for a moment Mary assumed the sound, so perfectly timed, had come from her own body. But no, it was separate. It had come from the dark edges of the night, from another body altogether.

'C'mon.' Mary pulled at Noreen's arm, and they followed the sound across the yard, towards a group of people amassing beside the kitchen block. There were other sounds too. Whooping. More laughter.

The only light flared from the windows of the hall, a good fifty feet away, but it was enough to see them now beyond the bystanders, in the blackness – a man and a woman entangled. They were grappling with each other in the most unutterable way, and Mary's face ran hot in the night air. Why on earth was she here, walking towards an act of intimacy? Why were others watching too? And what kind of woman would . . . would . . . The thought could not be finished.

None of it made any sense, and yet they stepped closer, somehow compelled, permitted even, by the presence of other people, men and women.

Finally they were close enough and the scene was fully realised. The woman, a local girl, was clothed. Pale fabric against the black night, a trick of the light. So it was not what she thought, after all. It was something quite different. It was . . . Jimmy clutching the girl's hair, a thick plait held in one solid fist, and with the other he was lashing her side with a sprig of birch.

He was roaring, 'Giddy up, horsey, giddy up!'

The men nearby were hollering, laughing, but the girl was silent, almost expressionless in the dark. Her pale face caught the light as it jerked back and back and back. Enduring the unendurable.

Beside Mary, Noreen was mute. The darkness seemed to contract in on them. There was just this pantomime, grotesque as it was, and a sickening abstraction of sound. Snap went the hair. Crack went the whip. Snap. Crack. Snap.

Now Jimmy was clicking his tongue as if he was coaxing his unfaithful filly to budge, and this brought on another round of laughter. More snorts and snickers. Another crack at her side and the girl's knees buckled under her. Her hair went taut in Jimmy's fist but she did not cry out, and still he went on.

Mary understood Sully was next to her before she even saw him. In the darkness, watching this man ride a feeble girl, it seemed that everything was possible in this world, good and bad. She turned to Sully, his face sequestered in the shadowy light.

'What the devil . . .'

She barely recognised this serious man, suddenly devoid of all levity. She thought he would say more, but he was moving forward, deep into the crowd, pushing larger bodies aside.

'Oi!' His voice sliced the night, and the crowd hushed. 'Not in front of the women.'

Jimmy froze, took in Sully, then turned his attention to the bystanders as if they might provide a response on his behalf.

There was a deathly, inordinately long beat of quiet.

'Our women are watching,' Sully said.

With a wounded wrench, Jimmy released the girl, and she scurried into the night, bent at the middle.

Jimmy stepped closer to Sully, almost nose to nose. Inhaled. Exhaled. The smile was gone, his face misshapen.

'Whose side are you on, mate?'

He spat at Sully's feet and then he too was gone.

There was a sigh and the crowd shifted in the moonlight. One by one, men and women moved away either dazed or energised, who could say. Sully remained in place, his back to her. She wanted to step forward, to put a hand on his shoulder, but Ida was suddenly there, saying, 'What on earth was that?'

'Ah . . .' Mary and Noreen exchanged a look.

'Something rather ghastly.'

'But what?'

'A fella . . . he was . . . gosh, I don't know.'

Noreen's face was blanched.

'C'mon,' Mary said. 'Let's go home.'

So they walked in a trio, barefoot, carrying their shoes, back to the dorm. Mary did her best to explain the bizarre episode to Ida, who asked insistently, 'But which bloke was it? But couldn't you see his face?'

'It was no one,' they said. 'No one we know.'

Mary climbed into bed in her underclothes, hair and make-up untouched. She rolled towards the window and watched slivers of light stir and weave through the blinds. The dancing was far away now, almost make-believe.

Not in front of the women, she said to herself. As if that was the issue. As if bad things could be made good if only one adopted the right company.

Early on Monday, Mrs Richards appeared through the café door, a stack of printed brochures pressed against her chest. Immediately, it was clear to Mary there was something peculiar about the woman today.

'Mary, dear,' she started, then stopped.

'Is everything all right, ma'am?'

'Would you be so kind as to . . . help me?'

'Of course.'

Mrs Richards stepped a little closer, hesitated again.

'What is it?' Mary asked.

'You see, it's come to my attention that all these little girls don't have the faintest notion of what their countrymen were really up to during the war. So I . . . I had the idea to . . . teach them.'

'I see.' Mary nodded, still confused but realising with every passing moment that she would need to be patient with Mrs Richards today, that the woman was not herself at all.

'My bigger half had these brochures made . . .' She fanned the pile out across the countertop. Each copy bore an image of Pearl Harbor, a jetty and palm fronds framing a ghastly explosion in the distance. Plastered over the picture, someone had cut and pasted a handful of words and a clumsily positioned Japanese airplane.

'Lovely idea.' Mary smiled encouragingly.

'But I'm afraid . . .' Mrs Richards' face wavered. 'There's been a small error.'

Mary took up a brochure from the counter and whipped her eyes over the printed copy. 'What kind of . . . Oh!' She couldn't help but let out a small laugh. 'Pearl Harder! Oh dear.' She laughed again, stopped herself.

'I had a hundred done,' Mrs Richards said by way of confession. 'I thought, well, I thought the girls could take them home, share them amongst their family members.'

'Right, good idea.'

'But that silly, silly girl in Harry's office . . .' Mrs Richards' voice trailed off, and Mary thought surely the old dame could see the error was no accident. But no, Mrs Richards would not entertain the idea of a conspiracy, or at least not today. 'It won't do, will it?' she said in review, her voice firmer, almost back to its usual self-assured register.

'No,' Mary agreed, 'perhaps not.'

'I have these . . .' The woman rifled through her handbag and pulled out a ream of sticky labels and a black pen. 'I thought we could do it over.'

'All right.'

Mary glanced at the door, then to the small clock suspended behind the counter. In half an hour, the troops would arrive demanding their teas and coffees and cakes and scones. But she could not deny Mrs Richards this indulgence. And so that's how she found herself sitting with the Y secretary in an assembly line of sorts.

Now that the confession had been dealt with, Mrs Richards had rediscovered her equilibrium and was quick to instruct Mary on each and every step of the process. 'Not like that, dear. We need to snip the ends of the sticker a little to make it fit.'

'Of course, I see.'

The two women toiled at the fiddly job, Mary sticking, Mrs Richards as scribe. Outside, a couple of uniformed members wandered past, boots crunching, trailing smoke from their mouths.

'How do you like Japan, dear?'

'Oh, I'm . . . I suppose I'm becoming accustomed to it.'

'Yes, well, we're a long way from home, aren't we?'

'Certainly.' Mary passed the next sheet over. 'How do you like it, ma'am?'

Mrs Richards' face brightened. 'Oh, very much. The life of a group captain's wife is first-class here.'

'Better than home?'

'Well, I'll give the Japanese women this: they certainly know how to care for our boys. I barely lift a finger most days.'

Mary smiled and continued her sticking.

'You know the little darlings are raised from the cradle to think of a man's every whim, every desire.' Mary nodded and Mrs Richards continued. 'Of course, that can present . . . challenges from time to time.'

'What sort of challenges?' said Mary, feigning innocence.

'Well.' The woman seemed on the precipice of launching into a scandalous story – only to catch herself mid-thought. 'Oh, I don't think I should say.'

Mary smiled and returned to her sticking. 'All right.'

'Then again. Perhaps I'll just say, some of our men – not mine, of course, certainly not mine – but some . . .'

'Yes,' Mary gently nudged.

'Some have been known to indulge in rather unusual bedfellows.'

'No, surely not.'

'Yes, my dear. *Yes.*'

Mary carried on the shocked pretence but she was already thinking how to retell this story, committing each detail – Mrs Richards' voice, words, posture – to memory.

'And, as a result, there are some rather shaky marriages around these parts,' the woman said finally.

'Oh that's a pity, isn't it?'

'Indeed.'

There was a silence now while they both mulled over this revelation. Perhaps Mrs Richards was castigating herself for saying too much, but there was also the prospect that no such thought existed.

'Mrs Richards?'

'Yes, dear?'

'Do you think the girls . . . the local girls, I mean . . . do you think they're willing participants?'

Mrs Richards reeled a little, her eyes white orbs of conviction. 'Of course, dear. Our men may be simple-minded, but they're not brutes.'

'No, no, of course.' Mary smiled an apology. 'You're absolutely right. Silly me.'

In July, Mary came down with a mystery ailment and was forced into quarantine in a small house at the edge of the base. She spent ten days in the little hut, delirious with fever. Each day snaked into the next, marked only by the medic's visits, Noreen bringing meals and the promulgation of camp gossip uttered through a small, cracked window. Ida and Jimmy had officially parted ways. Her new bloke had a tattoo. The housegirls had been made to line up for venereal checks much to their distress. And a group of Aussie girls who'd been up to Tokyo came back raving about the gardens and the shrines. They'd even spotted the emperor's cavalcade in the city: 'Reckoned the Japs were practically throwing themselves at the wheels of his shiny automobile!'

When she returned to normal life, or at least the Kure life that no longer felt foreign, she was shocked to find the weather had turned tropical. Even without a fever, she was drenched in sweat just as soon as she was out the door. The air was so thick it seemed to cascade in hot breaths down the hills behind the city, settling into the basin of the township like treacle in a lacquer bowl.

There was a determined quality to the heat that endured into the evenings, that did not bow to the moon and the stars, so after work they returned to the dorm, showered, changed, and flopped onto their beds, staring at the ceiling and bemoaning the absence of a mechanical fan. A cotton frock was a better prospect than their stiff summer uniforms, but even so, they lay there practically able to watch the perspiration surface from their skin.

When there was truly nothing else to occupy their time, Noreen would say, 'Oh, do that thing, Mare, that game you play.' And she would not let up until Mary complied.

The way it went was this: Noreen or Ida flipped through the occupation newspaper or the *Know Japan* book and pointed at random to some page or other. And then Mary was obliged to examine the face or faces on that page and, on a whim, tell a peppy tale of imagined lives.

Truth be told, Mary did not mind this game, despite her protestations. She liked the fact she could spin a yarn from almost nothing. One day it was Ren, the navy man who buried his uniform in the garden after the war ended – she'd read about this phenomenon, so knew it to be true. Another time it was the watermelon seller who gazed flat and questioning at the camera. This, Mary said, was Fujie, who had learned the art of growing melons from her parents, who had learned from their parents, and so on. Because Fujie covered her crop well and tended meticulously to the job of pest control, she was renowned across the region for offering the first and last melons of the season, and for being a reliable source of quality produce.

August was no less humid, but somehow their bodies had adjusted to the savage weather. Their energy returned. The nights became less intolerable. Now they could go out after work, wandering quietly around the base, with their make-up staying put on their faces.

On the first Friday of the month they were given leave to attend the third anniversary of the bomb blast, so in frocks and sunhats, the three women caught a train to the outskirts of Hiroshima and then a streetcar into town. The transportation had been marked for occupation use, and there was a whole string of streetcars in action today, thus it was a pleasant journey, and they were able to stretch out with ease. An early morning downpour could still be seen in the muddy fields that flashed by, and as the car rattled on, the hills vanished behind them and dazzling views of the sea loomed ahead.

They emerged onto the busy streets of Hiroshima after ten. In the distance, the decimated skeleton dome stood witness. As before, the centre was more shantytown than anything; it seemed rather little had been accomplished since she last laid eyes on it. But it also felt different now that she was in amongst the crowds, people weaving between makeshift shops and street stalls, many Australians among them. There was an atmosphere of festivity and cheer against the backdrop of destruction.

The local men were dressed in suits, some very nice, others rather forlorn. Many of the women were in colourful frocks and blouses and simple summer hats. Small boys in spotless white uniforms appeared in the gutter, sticks aloft, screaming gleefully at one another before racing on.

Out of all this commotion, an old man as bent and buckled as the town itself stepped forward and grabbed Mary's arm.

'Souvenirs?' he bellowed.

He gestured behind him. A shop, to some extent. Laid out on a table was an array of objects drawn from the ashes – a melted bottle, a twisted tile, a broken cup. In poorly rendered English, a sign announced 'Atomic remnants'.

'Here, madam-san, here.' He beckoned urgently.

'Thank you, but I'm not —'

He snatched up an item and placed it firmly in the palm of Mary's hand. It was a mysterious, beautiful thing. Small and curved, with an intricate pattern interrupted on one side. Made from bone perhaps, or porcelain. She ran a finger along it's smooth edge.

'Very special,' the man whispered.

'What is it?'

'For lady's hair.'

He broke into an elephant sound, trumpeting with one wild hand flapping up and down.

'Oh for god's sake.' Ida was beside her now. 'It won't be the real deal.' She seized the object and handed it back to the man. 'Kyoumi arimasen.'

'But it was sort of lovely,' Mary protested as they stepped away.

'All the genuine stuff went years ago. He's a shyster. Now c'mon, this way.'

They fell into line behind a large group of military folk, wandering past more stalls and eateries and a constant barrage of commerce, until finally they reached the banks of the Ōta river. Before them, the Aioi bridge stood like a fierce recalcitrant child, a little untidy at the edges but refusing total collapse.

They followed the trail of people over the bridge towards the skeleton dome, onto a wide expanse of sodden dirt. Many hundreds of onlookers were already gathered, local folk as well as occupation forces. A lucky few were seated; the rest stood behind. There were men with bicycles, women clutching babies. A couple of uniformed fellows had climbed onto the hood of a vehicle to secure a better view.

Above it all, a billboard screamed in enormous black lettering: 'NO MORE HIROSHIMAS'.

The formalities took place on a wooden stage, nicely decorated with ribbon and white fabric. There were speeches from local and Australian politicians that carried on for more than an hour, but strangely there was no mention of the plane, Enola Gay, nor the pilot, Paul Warfield Tibbets Jr, who had named that plane after his own loving mother, nor the weapon that was so gaily referred to as 'Little Boy'. And certainly no one mentioned the fact of tens of thousands of people losing their lives in an instant.

Even the Japanese speakers were uneasy in their handling of the event, skirting the details delicately. The particulars had been obliterated by politics, and Mary had the absurd idea spring into her mind that perhaps the tragedy that befell the people of this city was caused by some kind of accident, a stroke of fate, not a real piece of machinery, delivered by a real plane, named after a real mother.

Ida beside her was shifting impatiently on the wet ground, glancing at her nails, then her feet, making a clucking sound at the sight of her muddy heels. And it was then, to their right and several rows of people away, that Mary discovered Sully. He was standing next to a local boy, scribbling into a tiny notepad, shoulders hunched with the effort of gathering words at speed on the page.

Mayor Hamai, in a lovely suit and softly spoken English, was saying, 'Let us join to sweep away from this earth the horror of war, and to build a true peace.' He repeated the words in Japanese, and the crowd applauded.

Then there were dancers and singing. Doves were released. A camphor tree materialised and was planted in the soil below the platform.

The final speaker was Lieutenant General Horace Robertson, the highest-ranking Australian in all the land. He strode to the stage, and Mary strained to catch a glimpse of his moustachioed face. He wasn't an overly large man, no bigger than the mayor, and his thick uniform seemed to envelop him. Yet his face carried the weight of his title. His pale cheeks sloped away from his eyes solemnly. Unsmiling, he opened his mouth to speak, then paused. He gazed out across the masses, found a cluster of local people and appraised them with a master's scowl. Finally, as the great empire man that he was, he spoke in a barking, plummy tone, apparently unaware of the microphone not three inches from his face.

'I commend you,' he blared, 'for your sentiments for peace.'

He paused again. The crowd waited.

'But at the same time, I must remind you that you caused this disaster yourselves. *You* brought this disaster upon your city.'

There was a moment of deep and confounding silence, like that which follows the firing of a gun. The mood had shifted so suddenly, so unexpectedly, that the citizens of Hiroshima seemed not to know how to respond.

The great man spoke on, but what came next was made obsolete by the outrageous words he'd already lobbed into the throng. A spell had been cast over the collective, or a curse perhaps. It was only broken when a squadron of Mustang fighters roared overhead with earth-shattering noise. People recoiled, shrouding their ears, catching their hats before they were blown from their heads.

'My god that's low,' Noreen screamed into the blast.

One small child threw himself to the ground, burying his head in his arms. His mother stooped low after him and drew him into her body.

The Mustangs looped around, flew over a second time, then

disappeared into the horizon. When they were gone, it was intuited that the proceedings were over, and people began to move away, returning to their lives.

As the crowd dispersed, Sully appeared again, not twenty feet away. He was deep in conversation with the local boy Mary had seen him with earlier, his notepad now tucked into his shirt pocket. She watched on, captivated by the familial easiness that seemed to exist between them. The boy was tall, lean, with a serious face framed by horn-rimmed glasses. He had that studious look that traverses all nations and all races.

'Mare, you coming?' Noreen asked, and Mary realised she'd entirely tuned out the conversation taking place around her.

'Oh.' She looked to her friends and back to Sully.

'What are you looking at?' Noreen asked.

'Nothing, nothing.'

Ida also was peering in the direction of the men, raising her eyebrows, smiling. 'Well, well. Quite the dark horse, aren't we?'

'No, no, it's not that kind of thing.'

'Which one is he?' The women continued to strain their necks to make sense of Mary's eyeline.

'It's no one,' Mary said firmly.

'Oh my word, it better not be the Jap boy!' Ida howled.

'It's no one,' Mary protested again.

Despite herself, she looked over one final time, and then Sully saw her. He raised a hand and began to move towards her group. She had just a brief measure of time to collect herself, to arrange her face into something resembling poise.

'Miss Mary,' he said, removing his hat and hugging it to his body. 'How are you?'

'I'm fine, thank you.'

Mary could feel her friends' lips pressed into strangled smiles. Noreen had even locked her hands behind her back, a child caught in the act. There was nothing else to do but introduce them and let them laugh.

'This is . . . Miss Harris . . . and Miss Creighton,' Mary said dutifully.

Sully smiled at the women. 'Hello.'

And now, the inevitable release. 'Hello!' they spluttered in unison.

Sully turned to Mary, smiled again, knowingly. 'Do you feel like a wander?'

'All right.' She looked to her friends. 'I'll see you back at the —'

But Noreen was already guiding Ida away by the elbow. 'Of course, of course,' she was crying out with a big grin.

'Have fun!' Ida squealed, followed by muffled laughter.

Mary could not be happier to see the back of them, and yet their juvenile display seemed to linger between Sully and her, the echo of Mary's incurable singledom. Perhaps also the unorthodox man she had ostensibly selected. Not a military man. Smallish. Mop-haired. Non-conforming.

'Shall we try this way?' Sully asked.

'Yes,' was all she could muster.

They wandered back over the bridge. Took the quietest street they could find. It was spotted with vacant marshy blocks, places where homes presumably once stood. Behind them, the clamour of the city could still be heard, but the sound was distant, abstract. She waited for Sully to speak and, in time, he obliged.

'What d'ya think of Robbie's little performance back there with the aircrew?'

'Felt a little . . . hostile, didn't it?'

'You know they're all scared witless of airplanes, don't you?'

'No,' she said. 'I didn't.'

'Understandably.'

'Oh yes, yes, of course.'

They walked on. Eventually the ground below their feet softened and the fenced-off properties eased into muddy pastures. The sun was high now, a great white-hot sphere above them, and Mary could feel the sweat pooling between her breasts.

'What I'm confused by,' she said, 'is the way it had the feel of a carnival. The singing and dancing and souvenir stalls.'

'Ah, well.' He tucked his hands into his trouser pockets. 'Chamber of commerce thought it might revive the economy. Or that was the idea, anyway.'

'I see. But it didn't feel quite right to me.'

'Nor me,' he said.

What Sully was thinking in this next moment was his alone to know, and yet Mary found herself longing to ask. There was only the mundane to return to.

'Was that your boy back there?'

'Yes, yes, my interpreter. Haruki.'

'How do you find him?'

'Very pleasant, actually.'

'And was he assigned to you, or could you choose?'

'Funny story, really.' He smiled and turned his body a few degrees towards her. 'Stumbled upon him in a field.'

She laughed, baffled. 'Really?'

'Yup, my first week here. I got lost traipsing around the countryside out that way.' He indicated a spot over a hill to the east of the city. 'Stopped a bloke in a field, thinking he could set me right. And lo and behold, in flawless King's English, he pipes up with, "Sir, do you need help to find your way?"'

'But how?'

'His father was an English teacher, before the war upended everything.'

'How astonishing.'

'He's not alone. There are others like him.'

To their right, a woman in loose trousers lumbered heavy-footed across a plot of land, sinking then rising as she navigated the soft patches. It was only when she turned and headed towards a ramshackle house in the distance that they saw the sleeping child strapped to her back.

'I admire the Japanese,' Sully said. 'Or I've come to, anyway. It's the honour, you know? The quiet, stoic pride. You can't help but be moved by it.'

Mary was silent. After a beat, he turned to face her, perhaps aware of some subtle shift in mood.

'Did I say the wrong thing?'

'No, no,' she said, shaking her head.

'I think I must have.'

'Well, it's only . . . they did do terrible things. In the Pacific, in China.'

'Yes, they did,' he nodded. 'But to state the bleeding obvious, they . . .' and he pointed towards the woman and child in the field, 'they didn't do anything.'

'Yes.' She smiled a small smile. 'It's just . . . well . . .'

He looked up and waited for her to continue.

'My brother was in the camps, at Changi.'

'Oh cripes.'

'And on the railway. Came home half dead. Just a bag of bones, really. And eyes like . . .'

'Stone?'

'Yes.'

'I see.'

'He was the happiest of us all. Before, I mean.'

'I'm sorry, I shouldn't have . . .'

'It's all right.' And for some indescribable reason, it was. It may even have been a relief to have it out in the open.

'Does he speak of it?'

'No, never.'

He nodded thoughtfully. 'It's often the way.'

'But he has a lot to say about the Japs. In general, that is.' She laughed to hide the truth of this fact.

'Like what?'

'Like . . . like we should've dropped a bomb on every one of them. Like, they're an evil race, better wiped off the face of the earth.'

Sully sighed. 'Ah well, plenty of our blokes would agree with him.'

They fell quiet again, walking, listening to the sounds of the city in the distance. Underfoot, the mud was thicker, squelching under the soles of their shoes.

Eventually, Sully spoke. 'I was a war corro for a time.'

'Oh, you served.'

'In the Middle East, mostly. And a brief stint in New Guinea with the Ninth.'

'I didn't realise.'

He smiled at her. 'Well, can't blame you. I never did fit in right with those blokes.' He laughed, and they walked on. 'But if there's one thing I learned in all that time, it's that there's no such thing as the enemy. There's only the powerful and the desperate, that's it.'

She nodded.

'And you can be either, or both, at any time.'

'I see,' she murmured, feeling a tingle in her limbs despite this treasonous statement.

Soon they agreed to turn back, and they ambled towards town, using the cadaverous dome in the distance as compass. Above, beams of sun sloped down through the clouds like a divine offering. As they neared the train terminal, a row of newly planted trees, slender and elegant, guided them the final stretch.

There was not much they could find to say on the journey back to Kure, caught between the ground they'd covered and the company of others who were still upbeat from the day's events.

The two of them farewelled outside the mess hall. A quick nod. A smile. Nothing more. As soon as his body was turned away from her, those hands eternally tucked into the pockets of his trousers, his silhouette assumed an archetypal quality. Like a long-held memory.

What was it to know someone, Mary wondered. To really, truly know them. Did it take a lifetime? Or could it all be distilled into one moment of genuine connection?

Back at the dorm, Noreen and Ida were lounging on their beds in the darkened room, cooling themselves with the flutter of handheld fans.

It was Ida who made their thoughts known. 'Have a nice time, did we?'

The tone was teasing, jovial, but all the same, Mary was irritated by it. If only she had responded in such a way every time Ida spent a moment alone with a man.

'Yes,' Mary said. 'Thank you.'

'*That* bloke, of all of them? That's the one that tickles your fancy?'

'There is no *fancy tickling*.'

Ida rolled onto her side. Stopped the fan. 'Be careful, dear.'

Mary looked at her. She didn't hope to hide her disdain.

A moment passed between them before Ida flopped back and started up the fan again. 'Well, I'm just saying. Did you girls hear about Edna?'

Noreen responded immediately to her tone, sitting up with a flush across the cheeks. 'No. What?'

'Honestly, you must live under a rock. Everyone's been talking about it.'

'Well, c'mon,' Mary said, intrigued now despite herself. 'Tell us.'

'It's been obvious for weeks. Have you not noticed?

'Noticed what?!' they said together.

'Dorothea says Edna had to ask for a new skirt – a bigger one! And she didn't even have the smarts to pick up her sanitary rations,' Ida squealed. 'Silly fool!'

'Oh my.' Noreen's eyebrows were arched in amazement.

'Finally, the matron had to ask her outright. "Are you up the duff, dear? Kindly do let us know so we can ship you back to Melbourne in time for someone else to take charge of the problem!"'

Ida broke into hysterical laughter, and Noreen joined in, hiding a big open grin behind her fan.

'Poor girl,' Mary muttered.

'Oh, don't be such a bore, Mare.'

'Well, I'm sorry, it sounds awful.'

Ida rolled off the bed. Paced across the room. 'Still, it's better than the girl they found dead in a gutter.'

'What?'

'Yep, back in Melbourne – she was one of ours. Tried to have her little problem sorted. Day before her nineteenth birthday, apparently.' She wrenched the blinds open and gazed out to the spindly pine tree and bare wall beyond. 'Younger than all of us.'

Mary was silenced by this news, old as it was, but fresh to her. It was too shocking to contemplate, and yet immediately an image surfaced in her mind. A girl like them, peach-skinned, supposedly protected by the mysterious forces of the Commonwealth, dead in a gutter.

What followed was an even stranger thought, one she could not really begin to explain. But it started with the realisation that she could picture *this* dead girl in her mind's eye far more readily than the aftermath of the atom bomb. One situation felt instantly real, the other impossible. One came to her in colour and with detail. The other flashed and flickered in a confused, uncertain flux, turning to liquid before she could fully grasp it.

'Anyway,' Ida said from the window, 'the point is we all need to be careful and look out for each other.'

'Yes,' they agreed solemnly.

'Yes.'

The weather was as unbearable as ever, but in the shade of the camphor, Mary saw that she was beginning to embrace its luxurious weight. She might have said she was even happy to be seated there with a book between her fingers, the modest canopy over her head, lost in words with no sense of where her warm skin began and ended. From time to time, people wandered by and nodded an acknowledgment, but mostly she was left to her quiet seclusion in a manner that would've been unthinkable in the rec or the dorm.

By and by, a shadow passed over the pages of the book. She glanced up to find Mrs Richards standing before her. The old dame was carrying an umbrella for shade – not an ornate parasol but an ordinary umbrella. Still, she held it delicately, with her chin high and her breastbone stuck out like a well-fed bird.

'Reading,' she said. The word was uttered as a statement of disapproval, not a question, but nonetheless Mary felt an answer was required.

'Yes, ma'am.'

'Aren't you a little lonely, my dear?'

'No.'

'At your age, solitude is unnatural.'

Mary gave a polite smile and dropped the book onto her lap.

'No, no, this won't do,' Mrs Richards continued. 'Fun is the order of the day. More fun.' She made it sound almost as if one could buy this thing – fun – at the marketo, and how on earth had Mary managed to miss that fact?

'I'm fine, honestly.'

But Mrs Richards did not seem to hear her and was already one step ahead. 'I'm organising a little furlough,' she said, 'for some of my dear friends. A little lay-off. A little R and R, as they say.'

'A little . . . fun?'

'Exactly, my dear! Now you have it.' Mrs Richards released the umbrella and rapped the tip of it twice on the ground. 'Up in the highlands, where the upper classes escape to during the warmer months. Even the emperor himself, I'm told.'

Mary dog-eared her spot in the book and shut it. 'Oh,' she said, 'I didn't know that.'

'Well it makes sense, doesn't it? This weather is impenetrable.'

'Yes, it is.'

Mrs Richards gazed off towards the docks, grimacing a little at the disobedient weather. Suddenly, her eyes shot back to Mary.

'Would you like to join us, this weekend?'

'Oh.' Mary sat up a little straighter. 'All right.'

'Tremendous. We'll meet Saturday outside the main building at precisely six o'clock.'

'All right.'

'Six in the morning,' Mrs Richards clarified.

'Yes, I see.'

'Very well. And it shan't cost you a thing. It's all seen to.'

It took Mary a good few seconds to process the invitation, and Mrs Richards was already halfway down the path when she remembered to yell out a hearty thank you. It was unclear what had possessed the woman to bestow her kindness on Mary, and yet Mary was grateful for it. To escape the heat was one thing, but more pressing was an escape from the suffocating social scene of Ida and the rest of them, and the opportunity to go someplace new, to experience that thrill again.

At dawn on Saturday, they gathered on the footpath beside a convoy of Jeeps. It was already warm and the air breathless. Above them, the British and US flags hung limp on their posts.

Mrs Richards handed her a clipboard and pen. 'Mary dearest, will you manage the roll?' The woman was shrouded in a brilliant mauve frock and matching sunhat. Her chest had been veiled with layers of sheer fabric, and from her hat sprouted feathers and tulle. She looked set for a visit from the Queen, not a drive through the mountains on a rutted road to a far-flung place.

Mary in her plain cream frock and sensible lace-ups proceeded to wander from group to group ticking off names on the list. There were familiar faces among them – the telegraphists Joan and Betty from HQ, two contemporaries of Mrs Richards whose children were all grown up, an older gentleman, Mr Hanrahan, and a handful of younger men she knew from the mess by face, not name. The eclectic party, she saw, had been handpicked by Mrs Richards, but by what criteria it was unclear. It was only when the last of the bags were being loaded into the vehicles that Mary noticed a name scrawled in light pencil at the bottom of the page:

Sullivan Darling. She looked up and, like an apparition, Sully was there, out of breath, grinning.

He dropped his kit to the ground. 'Made it.'

'Well done.'

She had this sudden urge to say something else, something playful to counter the flush that had swept across her cheeks, but Mrs Richards was clapping her hands together and bellowing, 'All eyes this way, please!'

She went on to reel off facts about the cars, the location of the property, the distance they would drive and the dangers they would face on the journey. There were men with rifles, she said, who prowled the mountains at dusk and dawn, but 'they shan't worry us because we have our own handy men with rifles, don't we now'. This was answered by a roar of agreement followed by sycophantic tittering.

It was becoming clear that their little vacation would be curated inch by inch by their benevolent benefactor, whether they wished for the generosity or not.

In the back row, Sully leaned towards Mary and whispered ever so quietly, 'What is she wearing?'

Mary hiccupped a shocked laugh and nudged him in the side. She had the clipboard pressed to her body, and she suddenly felt more childlike than she could ever remember, flushed not just by shyness but also anticipation.

'Of course, you're right,' he whispered then. 'The thing is . . .'

'Don't,' she warned, giving him a sideways look.

'Can't you just see her skipping jauntily through a forest, two little wings peeping out the back.'

A laugh shot out of Mary and she disguised it quickly with a cough.

'Are you two listening up the back there?' Mrs Richards blared.

'Yes, ma'am,' they countered in unison.

They climbed into the vehicles, four or five apiece, and by design or fate Sully and Mary were cleaved off into different cars. They headed in convoy away from the harbour, directly inland, straight into the heart of those barnacled hills. The windows were down, and the warm air rushed through, making conversation untenable.

They drove for some time, an hour or more, as the inhabited land gave way to larger swathes of pine and maple forest. The road grew serpentine, and they wound up and up, down and down, their stomachs turning somersaults with each dip and jerk. At one point the lead vehicle came to an abrupt halt, and they saw the lilac shape of Mrs Richards race into the bushes to dispense of her dignity. She returned several minutes later ashen faced. They carried on.

They felt the air outside becoming cooler and, in the roadside mist, the forest trees seemed strung together with gossamer. When they reached a small village, the little homes were almost like toys packed with cotton wool.

Eventually they arrived at the inn, an unpainted building perched snug in the saddle of two peaks. The simple timber lines and elongated roof said so little in the landscape, posed so little threat, one could almost hear the hushed meditation of the man who had designed it.

They disembarked onto the gravel drive, and Mary was immediately grateful for the unyielding ground beneath her feet. Three young women in matching kimono ushered them into the building with smiling nods and served them green tea in handle-less cups.

This was the first truly traditional building Mary had set foot in and the feel of it – the effect it had on her senses – was extraordinary. It was incomparable to the Japanese home she'd seen on Etajima, which of course she understood now had been modified for European customs. This place was so spare, so preternaturally quiet and clean and uncluttered, the only thing to do was to gaze out beyond the interior, out to the vegetation that hung aloft, deep and moody like a Rembrandt in a gilded frame. It was as much an homage to mother earth as to the power of man, and she was spellbound by its restrained dignity.

She stepped towards a window, and soon Sully was there, touching the small of her back, then recoiling playfully.

'Are you . . .?' He looked at her closely, wrinkled his brow.

'No, I . . .' She realised her eyes were indeed wet. 'It's just so . . .'

'I know.'

'Breathtaking.'

'Yes.'

They stood at the window for another moment, side by side, looking out at the exquisite broadleaf jungle. Then the severe tones of Mrs Richards' voice could be heard over the chatter in the room.

'Righto, ladies and gents! We have a full schedule ahead, so we'd best prepare ourselves.'

The group gathered around dutifully.

'Our hosts will show you to your rooms, but don't faint if you find it empty. No one is supposing you will sleep on the floor. They have a quaint little notion here that one should put away one's bed in the morning and lay it out at night.'

There were faces made amongst the guests and a kind of awkward teeheeing.

'We shall all do our best to assimilate, shan't we? We shall summon the adaptive qualities of our colonial forefathers!' She let out a shriek of laughter. 'What a jolly enterprise,' she finished with, rubbing her hands together with a great smile.

Then the arrangements began. Mary would be bunking in with the two telegraphists. Once they'd been shown to their small empty room, the young women all agreed the roll-out beds were just as good as any cheap military mattress but, of course, Mrs Richards wouldn't have a clue about that.

They dumped their cases and returned to the living area, where a breakfast buffet of fish, rice and some unknown vegetables had been spread out over a table. Those that could manage it sat on cushions on the floor to nibble politely at the strange food, while the elder members of the group were accommodated on the lounge.

Next it was time for a walk in the forest, which Mrs Richards declared would be guided by the village headman, a Mr Ogawa. The old man who appeared was a tiny thing with a boyish face, a little flash of suppressed humour in the eye. He spoke very quietly, entirely in Japanese, and it was at this point that Mary realised with amazement that Mr Hanrahan, the older gentleman among them, spoke the language, conversing with Mr Ogawa in a spool of fitful, lurching sounds. Together, the two men would be their tour guides.

They set off on a track through a tunnel of knitted trees, passing two great boulders blanketed in green velvet. The forest seemed to have warmed ten degrees at least while they were eating breakfast and the bracing air had succumbed to a more familiar, sticky aspect. The smell of it was deep and rich and somehow could not be teased apart from the feel of it.

Mary broke off a small branch and used it to fan herself as they continued on. She stayed close to Sully, and she felt, or hoped perhaps, that he stayed intentionally close to her.

'Warm now,' he said.

'Yes,' she smiled.

Behind them, they could hear the huff and pant of Mrs Richards and another older woman.

They reached a large fallen log, and Sully asked only, 'Can you manage?' He seemed to resist the temptation to touch her, to presume she needed the help.

'Of course,' she said. She hitched up her skirt and with some pride navigated the tree alone. When she turned back, Sully was grinning at her.

Ahead, Mr Ogawa did not wait for the stragglers, forging on with the athleticism of a much younger man. Those who wished to keep up did, while others fell behind into a tail that stretched back into the forest. Every so often the front of the pack reached a fork in the path and the headman slowed, turned back and muttered, 'Kochiradesu.' This was followed immediately by Mr Hanrahan's eager translation – 'This way, this way.'

They arrived at an open glade. The trickle of a brook could be discerned from behind a wall of trees. The laggards were allowed to catch up, and Mr Ogawa waited with unnerving patience until the group was silent. Then he began moving from tree to tree, touching leaves, uttering words alongside fine gestures of the fingers.

'This one – an oak, I think,' Mr Hanrahan stammered. 'This one, evergreen conifer. Japanese cypress. Maple tree. Native cherry.' It was clear the Australian gentleman was not comprehending every word, perhaps not even every sentence, as the headman's words carried on and on for several minutes. 'He says there are many kinds of birds in this forest . . . And flowering plants. He named a few but I'm sorry, I'm not sure . . . Oh and now he says there are deer that live amongst these trees too, and a weasel that stays close to running water.'

Abruptly, the old man turned and headed towards the river. They followed suit. The creek was shallow; the kind of burbling, lichen-edged, glass-clear stream one associates with a children's story. On the near bank, Mr Ogawa stopped beside a small stone statue.

'O-Jizo-sama,' he said, slowly, clearly. He patted it twice on its bald head. 'Ji-zo,' he said again. It seemed important that his foreign acquaintances understood the weight of this word.

After a long pause, he launched into a rhythmic, softly spoken speech and Mr Hanrahan did his best to keep up.

'Jizo is . . . an ancient protector,' he said. 'He has rejected . . . jeepers, I'm not sure. Nirvana, perhaps. And he's stayed here on earth to watch over the souls of dead babies and children.'

The old man continued to speak on in low, exacting tones. There was wisdom to be garnered; this was understood from the lowering of his eyelids, the way he clasped his hands together, the rocking into and out of a quarter bow.

'He says when children die they cannot cross the river to the afterlife. They are stuck here, besieged by demons. What they must do, over and over, in perpetuity, forever, is build stacks of small stones.'

'Oh, like Sisyphus?' someone asked.

'Yes, it seems so.'

'How ghastly,' Mrs Richards said.

'But Jizo has renounced his right to move on and has stayed with the children, to comfort them in place of their lost parents, and to drive away the demons.'

Mr Hanrahan became subdued, and the group waited for Mr Ogawa to speak again. The old man's eyes were practically closed, and Mary had a sense the mannerisms were by design. Far off in the distance, a bird released a high-pitched cry, mysteriously complicit. Finally, Mr Ogawa opened his eyes, and spoke again in a low grave tone.

'These past few years, he says. These past few years, many, many Japanese children have been trapped at the edge of the river.'

The group were silenced. This was more than a folk tale; this was admonishment.

'Jizo is very, very busy, he says.'

The heaviness of the moment was soon forgotten in the clamber back up the hill, and lunch was dominated by minor gripes and whines. Someone was unhappy about the state of the meal. Another yearned for English tea, not this inferior oriental brew. Amidst it all, the shrill intonations of Mrs Richards: 'Now, now, friends. Assimilation is the task. We are but a lump of clay, eager to be moulded.'

The housegirls shifted in and out of the room, attending to tasks wordlessly. The sliding doors had been flung open but still the dining room was stiff with heat.

Sully found Mary alone at the buffet table, her plate aloft.

'I have an excursion in mind,' he announced. When she looked up at him, he grinned, forced his hands deep into his pockets and rocked back on the heels of his shoes. 'Would you join me?'

She flashed a look at Mrs Richards, who was chastising one of the young men for his poor handling of chopsticks. She looked back to Sully. 'Would Mrs Richards approve?'

'Does Mrs Richards ever approve?'

She laughed.

'I'm kidding, of course. I'll speak with her.'

She studied his face a moment longer. 'All right, then.'

'Excellent. We'll leave at seven. Once it's dark.' He saw the sudden look of alarm on her face and smiled. 'It's all above board, I assure you.'

'All right.'

'I'll ask the girls to prepare us an early meal,' he said. 'Oh, and do you have sandshoes?'

She let out a quizzical yelp and he grinned again as he stepped away.

'It won't be nearly as much fun if I break the surprise.'

'Very well,' she laughed, waving him off.

By seven, the night was ink black. A girl from the inn guided them down the side of the building and along a stony path. At the first signs of hesitation, she seized Mary's arm at the elbow, steadying her. Sully found his way ahead of them, pointing out depressions in the ground, calling out when the track became unstable. There was a sick excitement in Mary's belly, navigating the rough ground in the dark, but the girl was deceptively strong, like a wiry wood sprite, and in time they managed a kind of synchronicity. They walked like this for some distance until the ground flattened out and the forest ran full-tilt into darkened walls.

'Are we in the village?' Mary asked.

'Seems so.' Sully uttered a few words in Japanese to the girl and spoke again to Mary. 'Only a little further, she says.'

They passed several dark homes capped with steeply pitched roofs until they reached a stretch of ground lit by lanterns. The girl released Mary's arm and pointed them to the start of a small timber deck.

It took a few seconds for Mary's brain to grasp the change in terrain and orient itself. 'Oh, it's a jetty!'

Sully laughed, as if that part of his plan, at least, was evident.

Now, slowly, her eyes adjusted. She edged carefully along the wooden planks. The river below them – hemming and hawing – was a dark stain, just the peaks of its bluffs catching the light. Above, the blot of night was moonless and colossal. When Mary turned back to the village she saw the girl had disappeared, and although there was no doubt life in amongst the trees, the whole scene was disturbingly quiet.

A charge of fright bolted through her. Perhaps, perhaps, had she walked into a trap? She took a deep breath. This time, she did the work of steadying herself.

'Will you tell me now?'

'No, c'mon, you'll see.' He leaned out over the edge of the jetty, carelessly cheerful, looking into the blackness for god knows what.

'Sully, I'm . . .'

'Here we go.' He turned back to her proudly. And indeed, there in the distance, a boat appeared; a tiny, brilliant speck winding its way towards them. As it neared, the source of the light revealed itself. A large fire basket had been suspended in front of the narrow vessel. A small flaming pyre as figurehead.

On the near side of the boat, several birds ducked in and out of the water, frenetic like wind-up toys. They were fastened to a fisherman on lengths of fine string, and the man, dressed in a grass skirt and curious turban, reached for them as they popped and sprang from the river.

'My word,' she said.

'It's quite something, isn't it?' Sully whispered.

'Yes.'

The fisherman drew the birds, bright-eyed and obedient, onto the deck, and another man, almost invisible in dark clothing, steered the boat towards the jetty. She understood now that they would board the vessel.

'Konbanwa,' a voice offered into the night.

'C'mon,' Sully said, touching her arm. The man in dark clothing reached out a hand and she took it, straddling the running water below. He signalled to sit on a narrow panel that ran port to starboard, and Sully soon joined her, their bodies pressed against one another. The summer air was still warm. It smelled like fire and fish.

They pushed off into the night in silence, moving into the current of the river. Mary and Sully watched as the men returned to their work, the one in the bow steering the barge onwards, the other – the usho, she learned – releasing the birds back into the water. The animals' wet coats sparkled in the firelight as they dipped and bobbed and plunged. Every so often one surfaced wrestling a fish in its long beak, at which point it paddled back to its master. The usho's pale hands on the string moved in surprisingly tender ways, but also swiftly, confidently, governed by a skill acquired over years, maybe even generations. There was something solemn about the process, she thought. Almost ceremonial.

In time, Sully whispered, 'Cormorants. Expert fishers.'

'But how do they . . . why do they give up their catch?'

'The string around their necks,' he said. 'The fish won't pass.'

Her eyes sharpened in the half-light . . . oh, yes, now it was clear. The birds were not so much obsequious as enslaved. More apparatus than tamed beast.

'Oh.' She inhaled. 'How terrible.'

'No, this is their way. The birds seem to enjoy it, don't you think?'

'I'm . . . I'm not sure.'

Her mind remodelled the scene before her, taking in these small adjustments. It must take a certain conviction to tie a length of twine around an animal's neck and pull it tight – to be so sure of your place in the world.

Sully turned to her and saw the expression on her face.

'You old softie.' He nudged her gently, and she smiled. 'I believe they're fed well afterwards, if it's any consolation.'

'So everyone wins.'

'Precisely.'

Another bird had snagged a fish. It sculled back to the boat with urgent thrusts, and the usho gathered up the catch, muttered something approvingly at the bird and tossed the fish into a large woven basket. He looked up at the two trespassers and said, 'Sweet fish. Very good.'

Mary smiled back at him, and Sully uttered an endorsement in Japanese.

They drifted on, then eventually turned and headed back upstream. She kept her hands tucked tightly in her lap and thought about the warmth of Sully's body, electric next to hers, the boundless sky and the sharp smell of the river, the hungry animals who nonetheless stalked on, knowing all the while their hunt was futile.

Beside her, Sully was bright, jolly even. He was heedless to her perspective, that much was clear. But could she blame him? Could any sane woman expect a man to fathom the relentless suffering of servitude?

———

The girl was waiting for them when they returned to the jetty, so they traipsed back uphill unspeaking, their shoes damp, chests heaving with the exertion.

The inn was dark upon their return, and the girl explained that Mrs Richards and the gang were still at dinner in town. They peeled their shoes from their feet and the girl lined them up neatly at the door.

Inside, the blinds had been drawn and a standing lamp cast a soft, yellow patina over the otherwise commonplace: the lounge, the low table, the mostly bare walls.

As they entered, the fug of parched timber and exotic food caught Mary off-guard.

'Oh,' she said. 'It's still quite warm.'

'We'll get used to it,' Sully said.

They sat on the lounge, miles from each other. She could not have reached out to him even if she'd had the urge to do so. The smell, pervasive as it was, diverted her thoughts and she could only think of what not to say.

'Did you like the birds?' he said finally.

'Of course – yes.' She smiled. 'Very much. Thank you.'

'But something's troubling you?'

'Oh.' She could barely hide her surprise. So he did see. More than she imagined. 'It's difficult to explain.'

He nodded. 'Is it me?'

'No!' she cried. 'No, not at all. Hand on my heart, it's not you.'

He smiled and another long pause descended.

In the end he saved them by springing to his feet and pacing, one naked step after the other, to a small photograph hanging on the wall. Stuffing one hand into his trouser pocket, he extracted a hanky and slid it against the dusty glass, revealing the intricate scarps and troughs of the Inland Sea, those islands like listless bodies in the dark water.

'What did you think when you first saw it?' he asked.

'It was just beautiful, wasn't it? Thrilling.'

'Yes.'

'But we couldn't see the destruction.'

'No, that's right.'

They were silent again.

'So many strange things,' she muttered.

He looked at her and grimaced. Paced back to the lounge, sitting closer to her this time, and leaned his elbows against his knees, fists falling open.

'I spoke to a bloke who was on the first Aussie ship,' he said. 'It was winter, and he reckons the men stood on the deck, frost-bitten, cold as hell. Just packed up their camp in the jungle a few days earlier, and then they were here sailing into a frigid wind. Cripes, must have felt like the Arctic. Didn't have a darned clue where they'd sleep that night, and they gazed out at the islands, at the sides of the hills, and you know what he said? Apart from saying how bloody beautiful it was, obviously. We all did that. But no, he said they couldn't believe it was agricultural land. On terrain like that. All lumpy and dense. Another world away from the golden earth we grow on. Ours feels almost infinite in comparison, doesn't it?'

She nodded. 'No wonder the Japs were desperate for more land.'

'It's little wonder at all.' He touched the tips of his fingers together, forming a bridge with his hands. 'You know how they managed to get into the port that first day? Through that labyrinth of islands?'

'No, how?'

'A Jap,' he said. 'A local sea pilot pulled his tiny boat up next to theirs, jumped aboard, and directed them in.'

He shifted back in the shadowy space next to her, reaching an arm over the spine of the lounge.

'Don't you think that's absurd? That we, the occupying force, needed them – the conquered – to help us find our way to shore?'

She laughed lightly, relieved to have reason to.

'What kind of lousy, two-bit occupying force needs to ask for directions?' he said.

His face broke into a grin and they both laughed this time. It was one of the most profoundly idiosyncratic things she had ever witnessed in another human being, this capacity of his to shift so swiftly from light to dark and back again. The way his eyes cleared, then dimmed, then cleared again.

And it was in this strange moment of release that his hand reached out and touched her face, his fingertips like sandpaper. She looked at him, astonished. He tucked a strand of hair behind her ear. Traced the curve of her face, down the neck into the pit of her collarbone. Found her hand on her lap. Pressed into the fissures between her fingers.

All these moments happened like a mirage. She could not, would not move, for fear of disrupting the mood. The expression on her face surely betrayed her; it must have said everything he needed to know about her naivete, her inexperience, her complete and utter haplessness when it came to matters of the other sex. She opened her hand for him, let his fingers slip between hers.

'May I come closer,' he said.

'Yes,' she whispered.

He slid towards her. 'May I kiss you?'

'I —'

But he didn't wait for the answer, leaning in and blocking out the light of the world in one nimble action. Their lips touched, and she submitted to him. No longer could she smell the vinegary scent of the local cuisine. Now there was his smell, rich and loamy after the long day, indescribable, singularly his.

The kiss lasted barely a moment, she supposed, but already she knew it would exist in her memory for a lifetime, fully formed and perfect.

By and by, they heard voices outside, the movement of people approaching the inn. Mrs Richards was remonstrating in some fashion about the quality of the meal, saying, 'Lumps of clay, my dear, lumps of clay.' Sully smiled, touched her face a final time, and pulled away from the lounge. When the gang appeared on the back porch, he and Mary were just two people, quite a distance from each other, one sitting, one standing, barefoot but in every other way perfectly decent.

Mrs Richards came through the door, stopped, and eyed them carefully. 'My dears, I did not expect you home so soon.'

It was unclear whether she was appraising them for signs of impurity or taking in the scene with some nostalgic pleasure. Mary opened her mouth to speak, but words didn't come. And then the rest of the party came bundling through the door, chatting noisily, and the need to defend herself had passed.

So the friendship between Mary and Sully, so carefully crafted over the past weeks, had been replaced by something unnameable. The next morning at breakfast, it took a great deal of courage for her to look up at him, to say simple things like 'good morning' and 'shall I pass you the rice?' For his part, Sully seemed even more attentive. Each time she turned towards him, she was met with a direct gaze, a small smile.

After the meal, they packed up and headed back to Kure. And to transport herself back in time, why this – she found – was just as easy. The night before replayed and replayed on her, the birds, the boat, the fish, the kiss, and she could not, simply could not, resist the temptation to think of what might have come next had the others not appeared on the porch.

Her mind was a mess of obfuscating thoughts; notions of fact and fiction reeled on, jumbled and entangled. She'd been corralled into a vehicle with Mrs Richards and they sat in the back seat, fanning themselves with broad-leaf branches. In the front seat, Mr Hanrahan and their driver, a young army man by the name of Reynolds, were discussing the new Japanese constitution, penned by the Americans and radically democratic.

For a long while, Mrs Richards did not speak. She was wearing a garish green number, and a tuft of feathers in her hair. The return trip was just as winding, just as taxing as the first leg, but the woman made a point of touching her stomach and declaring to the car that she'd had only a light breakfast and didn't feel at all out of sorts.

In the course of time, she addressed Mary.

'Do you enjoy political talk, my dear?'

'A little,' Mary said. 'When I can keep up.'

Mrs Richards made a thinking sound and continued to fan herself.

'And you, ma'am?'

'Not so much.'

'But you're so involved in . . . all the charity drives and whatnot.'

'Civic duty is not politics, my dear. They're hardly one and the same.'

'Yes, of course.'

'And it's men's business, isn't it? All that very serious talk about very serious things.'

'Oh, well . . . I don't know.'

Mrs Richards snapped her head towards Mary, and Mary was silenced by her direct gaze, the thin-pressed lips.

'Do I offend you?' the woman asked with a sudden curiosity.

'No, no, not at all.'

'But you think of yourself as serious, I suppose. All that reading, and the serious expressions.'

Mary could not think what to say. It had been so many years since she was chastised by a mother figure, her own mother gone so long ago.

'No, I was just . . .'

'Perhaps your lot —'

'My lot, ma'am?'

'You know, younger women. Perhaps you think I'm silly. The costumes. The chitchat. The holidays. All my talk of fun.'

There was a wounded aspect to the woman's voice, and Mary had a sudden thought that quite possibly this conversation had nothing at all to do with her. Perhaps age was the culprit, or an uncaring husband, or a lost son. Or perhaps this was just Mrs Richards grappling with her own place in the world.

Mary realised she hardly knew a thing about the woman; not moving in the same circles, she knew only what Mrs Richards chose to tell her, with the particulars few and far between.

'I would never say such a thing, ma'am.' Mary turned away, but still, there was an instinct to respond further. 'On the other hand,' she began, turning back. 'On the other hand, I do think there's something rather honourable about serious matters.'

'But there's a place for fun, too.'

'Well, yes . . .'

'You had fun last evening, did you not?'

'Yes, yes, I did.'

'Mr Darling was pleasant company?'

'Yes.'

There seemed, to Mary, to be some implication that she ought to now spill the beans. The look in Mrs Richards' eye was a challenge. To indulge in some gossip as an act of gratitude. But then the moment passed, and Mrs Richards spun back to the window, to the blur of trees as they raced past.

'At my age,' the woman said, 'you've seen a few things. You know a little about life.'

Mary was vaguely aware of the men in the front seat still droning on about sovereignty and the bill of rights.

'When you look back on your life, my dear,' Mrs Richards went on. 'When you consider all the chores you have done, all the hours cooking and scrubbing and the caring for children and for men, the endless dreariness of it all, not to mention the heart-ache, the fact any number of people can be taken from you at any moment . . .' Her voice trailed off and Mary had a sudden terrifying notion that something truly awful must have occurred in Mrs Richards' life, that she would break down and weep right here in the car. But then her face hardened again, and she turned back to Mary with those brows. 'Well,' she said in summary, 'you might find, that really one ought to have fun when one can.'

Mary woke with the memory of Sully's lips on hers. More than an image, he'd become a taste, one that quickened her heart and sent sparks of heat down her body. She opened her eyes and gazed at the strips of pre-dawn light laid bare between the blinds. In the half-dark, she could hear the slow sleeping respiration of Ida and Noreen. Far off in the distance, a cockerel exalted.

It seemed uncanny that she'd slept at all, given her mind's absolute devotion to this titanic life event, aka the kiss. The flashbacks were so real, so embodied, if she just closed her eyes she could almost feel his breath in her mouth, smell the scent of him mingled with that strange aroma of the inn and the forest beyond, see the birds slick in the dark water.

How would she get through a day? And another? The feeling was total and incapacitating. There was only him now. And the deep urge to be near him, both painful and delicious.

She rolled towards the light and hugged herself, wrapping her palms across her ribcage. Through her nightdress, her fingers found the pitches and slopes of each rib, the bony ladder of them. Again, she closed her eyes and imagined they were his hands, edging ever so slowly, one depression at a time, towards the soft pillow of her breasts. This act of touching, and of imagining, felt like the most natural thing in the world and she thought only of being caught in the act by the girls, not god, who of course could see her, could see every incremental movement and, yes, could read her intentions. And yet she could not care less about damnation, because the warm feeling and the touch of the imagined him was total and incapacitating.

She held her breath and dared his (her) hands to cradle her breasts. In the very same instant, Noreen turned abruptly in bed and the rustle of sheets was so ear-splitting it might as well have been a party of nuns charging into the room to train a flashlight on Mary's wicked ways.

Mary exhaled sharply and lifted her hands from her body. An unholy few seconds passed as she waited, suspended in her shame. Finally, Noreen released a long, somnolent wheeze, and the room fell mute again.

The day that followed was long and hot and dreary. An excursion to the local orphanage had been lined up and a good number of members had joined in the party, heading off that morning with bags of boiled sweets and hand-stitched sunhats in tow. Sully too had been sent on assignment further afield, so there was no prospect of seeing him. There was just the thinking of him to run out the hours. Mercifully, Mary discovered that memories made for a ready substitute; they were almost like kindling, she thought, ready for ignition at any time, awaiting the tiniest spark. And the most satisfying part was that this fire was all hers. Mrs Richards need not know. Nor the girls. It would remain her own wonderful secret.

When she returned to the women's quarters in the late afternoon, Noreen was already there, and Ida not long behind.

'This blasted weather,' Ida complained by way of greeting. She stumbled into the room and collapsed onto her bed.

There was nothing much to say, because they were all living through it. The blasted weather. Not just hot, not just sticky, but grievously so on both counts.

For some time, they remained in companionable silence, each woman on her island of a bed: Ida spread-eagled, Mary reading, Noreen thumbing through old letters from home. This was the kind of silence that made living with other adults bearable. Indeed, the being alone while being together might have been the only thing that made it possible at all.

Eventually, Ida pulled herself up to sitting, kicked off her shoes and began to massage her stockinged toes.

'My feet are swollen beyond belief.'

Noreen murmured an agreement. 'It's my hair I worry about.'

'What on earth are you saying?' Mary smiled. 'Your hair is perfect.'

'Oh, but it gets so terribly fluffy.'

'It's fine.'

Noreen smiled a thank you.

'So . . .' Ida turned her attention to Mary. 'Tell us about the weekend? What happened?'

'Oh, well.' Mary was careful to arrange her face just so. It was not that she hoped to deceive the girls, more that the secret of Sully felt precarious and sacred. Beyond words, in fact. 'It was all right, I suppose. The place was rather lovely, and we went for a long walk in the mountains. The air was incredibly fresh, almost headache inducing.'

Ida raised an eyebrow. 'And was that it? Fresh air and old ladies?'

'In essence, yes.'

'How tedious.'

'Well, you know Mrs Richards. Always desperate for a party but —'

'Well past her prime.'

'Indeed.'

Nancy appeared in the doorway then, shuffling in her sandals, whispering 'konnichiwa', the courteous but distant bow.

Ida clucked. 'Rather late in the day for tidying.'

'Ida,' Mary hissed.

'Well, I'm just saying . . . it is.'

Nancy dropped her head an inch lower and moved past them to the far end of the room, where the washing basket stood. She bent at the middle and began gathering up the soiled items. There was something particularly defeated about the girl today, the long face, almost pained, and Mary was hit by a bolt of sadness.

'We should . . .' Mary cut a hand through the air, indicating some abstract idea of censorship.

But Ida was undeterred; perhaps she was even buoyed by Mary's attempts to suppress her. 'Not talk about the elephant in the room?'

'She speaks English.'

'Oh sure, a little.'

'More than a little . . .' Mary looked across the room for an ally, but Noreen had become enthralled in her letter-reading and was staunchly resisting the inducement. Mary turned back to Ida, determined now. 'And her name is Nancy,' she whispered.

'So she claims.'

'Oh Ida.'

'I mean, what do you want me to say? Her name is clearly not Nancy.' She released a haughty outburst and flung a hand in the direction of the girl. 'Look at her, Mare. She's a Jap. And the Japs don't call their children *Nan-cy*.'

Mary was struck dumb. What she understood about the occupation in this moment came to her in one blinding flash of knowledge: everything forbidden was now allowed, even wholesale cruelty.

In the corner of the room, Nancy remained head down, bundling the dirty washing up into her arms. Her pace seemed to have hurried, and in her rush to be free of them, a frock tumbled from her hands.

'Let's face it,' Ida went on, finally lowering her voice to a whisper. 'She has access to our most precious belongings, and we don't know the first thing about her.'

With arms stretched wide around the parcel of washing, Nancy straightened and walked past them, chin unusually proud, out the door. They listened to the footfalls of her sandals disappearing down the corridor.

Mary was about to say something diplomatic but firm when Ida blurted out, 'Oh, I just remembered!' Her eyes glinted with some new delight. 'I didn't tell you.'

Noreen gave herself away with one abrupt jerk of the head. 'What?'

'The signal twins heard from their girl, or maybe it was from Clarice's girl, I forget, but the gist of it was that Nancy had a child.'

'What do you mean "had"?'

'Well apparently, if you believe it, the child was . . . well, killed in the war.'

'Oh my word.'

'Yes, terrible stuff.'

'How?'

'No idea.'

'She looks too young, doesn't she?' Noreen added.

Mary gazed at the open door. 'But they all look rather young, don't they? The lovely complexion . . .'

The women pondered this fact for a moment. And Mary thought too of Nancy. Not a girl after all. A young woman. And perhaps even a mother – a grief-stricken mother at that.

'Could there be anything worse?' Mary asked the room. 'Than to lose a child.'

'I dare say no,' Noreen muttered.

Ida sighed and pursed her lips together. 'I suppose you're going to say I should be nicer to her.'

'Well . . .'

'After all, it's not her fault she's a Jap, is it?'

'No,' Noreen said, 'it isn't.'

'All right.' Ida sighed again. 'I suppose I can try.'

Sully and Mary. Mary and Sully. Here were two words that belonged together. There were other words, too, that dovetailed in rather a satisfying way. Like, Mary and Darling. Mrs Sullivan Darling. Why not? It could be.

Over the days that passed, in the cracks between work and reading and the arrival of letters from home and a sudden tropical storm that passed through one night with an inharmonious clatter, as well as all the blather about the Summer Olympics in London which had thankfully begun and ended without any major disturbance – in between all that, Mary dwelled on these pleasing thoughts of Sully more than a little.

The two of them had developed a kind of rhythm, within the limits of what could be managed. It was too early to declare anything official, and yet she could not help but feel a sort of accord had been reached between them, albeit unspoken. His careful attention was indisputable. A smile as they passed each other in a crowd. A look of wry humour across the café, the mess, the yard. He seemed permanently in the company of Haruki, the interpreter, which made launching into conversation that much more difficult.

But then, one afternoon, Sully came past the camphor tree cradling two metal cups steaming with tea, miraculously alone. The sight of him, this sudden emergence, felt to her almost religious, and her heart buffeted violently in her chest.

'Conrad,' he said with surprise, nodding to the book in her hands. 'Heavy stuff for such a beautiful day.'

Immediately she became self-conscious, realising she had selected from the rec library the most pretentious title imaginable. She dropped the book to the ground to distance herself from it and took up the tea with two hands.

'I've just begun.'

'And?'

She laughed. 'It's heavy.'

He was wearing his shirt the usual way, open-necked, sleeves rolled up. His hair was wilder than normal.

'You seem to like this spot,' he said.

'Well, yes. Strangely, it reminds me of home.'

He gave one side of his trousers a yank and perched on a large root that had broken free of the earth. She blew at her tea and took a tentative sip. The next question burst out of him as some pent-up, long-wrestled-with quandary. 'Mary. Do you think there's such a thing as a soulful person?'

She looked at him with curiosity.

'I suppose I mean . . . Well, do you think some people feel more deeply than others?'

'It's hard to know, isn't it? We have only our own experience.'

'But it must be the case, surely. Just as we come in different shapes and sizes and colours.'

'You've spent some time thinking about this, I see.'

'Far too many hours.'

She laughed and sipped again at her tea. She assumed the topic was exhausted, but Sully was speaking again.

'But seriously, that day in the mountains, in the inn, when you were crying at the window, at the forest. The look on your face was . . .'

'Was what?'

'Just as I felt,' he said.

Their eyes met for a brief time. It was Sully who broke the union, who began instead a sudden, one-handed search for his Chesterfields, patting himself down, discovering them finally in his breast pocket. 'Ah,' he said, producing the pack as evidence, then proceeding to search in the same vein for his lighter. All the while, his tea slapped committedly against the sides of the metal cup.

When he was done, he let the smoke waft out from between his lips, passed the cigarette to Mary and lit another.

At last, he was ready to continue. 'So maybe there are just some of us who cry at trees, or at the sound of a particularly exquisite violin, or the sight of a lovely painting. And there are other people who . . . don't. And those other people are wandering around among us, never even dreaming of doing such a thing.'

'Maybe they feel just as deeply but don't cry?' she said.

'Perhaps.'

'Or maybe they've been taught they're not permitted to cry. Or they have a fussy baby to feed, or bills to pay, or a country to save.'

'That's a generous perspective.'

'I don't know. It's a bit miserable to think I'm destined to a life of weeping, even if it's at lovely things. Maybe we're that person for a while, and then we're not. And meanwhile the other kind – the person who's gone their whole life unmoved – walks past an autumnal tree lit up like a flame one average Sunday morning and their whole sense of the world unravels.'

He smiled and took another drag on his smoke. 'So, it catches us all eventually?'

'Maybe,' she said.

'What a wonderful thought.'

The following afternoon, he again joined her under the tree. And the day after that. On the third afternoon, she brought out a second chair in anticipation of his arrival. So they sat, tea cupped in one hand, cigarette in the other, and they watched the passers-by, chatted a little, sipped at their drinks. Now and again, they lapsed into a glorious, utterly comfortable silence. Her book was soon relegated to spectator status, and she didn't care a penny. Who needed stories when you had life?

At one point, Noreen happened upon them, grinning a deliberate grin that Mary knew was bound to spread rapidly, but this time Mary didn't feel shy, and she wasn't a bit ashamed. Still, she would not say too much when asked about the liaison; she would not deny it, but instead assume a position of grace and humility and undecided discretion.

It appeared their little routine would carry on in perpetuity, or rather, she hoped it would. But on the fifth day he declared almost before his bottom had hit the seat: 'Haruki and I are off to Tokyo in the morning.'

A low panic struck Mary straight in the solar plexus. So, this was how he would finish with her.

She felt her lips tighten like a displeased headmistress. 'I see.'

He examined her face closely. 'Oh, don't be like that.'

'Like what?' she said. 'I'm fine.'

'I was about to say, it's just a week.'

She smiled another tight smile that she wished but failed to relax.

'I'm sorry,' she said. She looked down into her tea. 'I know I don't have a claim to . . . anything. Or anyone. It's just that, the last time a man went away, he . . . he died.'

'Ah,' Sully said, nodding. 'Well, that'll do it.'

She made a silly face.

'I'm not going to die,' he said then.

'Well, you can't promise that . . .'

'No, no, I absolutely promise you. I will not die between now and next Tuesday.'

She laughed. 'All right. But I'm holding you to that.'

'Please do. If I betray you, you're welcome to write to my mother and berate her for raising a perjurer.'

She laughed more heartily, felt the release of something trapped in her chest fly up and away and into the cloud-riven sky.

'So, I'll be seeing you next week, all right?'

'All right,' she said.

On Sunday, she tagged along on a boat trip with Ida and Noreen. Ida repeatedly referred to the event in a high, contrived voice as 'the launch picnic', which Noreen remarked was something surely the Hollywood starlets would be envious of, not to mention her friends back home. Indeed, Mary too would never have imagined picnicking on a boat in her old life, although the occasion was tempered by the absence of Sully, and the presence of Jimmy, who had appeared back on the scene after a short stint of Ida-enforced exile.

It was when they were gathered on the docks that Mary made sense of the numbers and why Ida had been so insistent on her coming along. They were a party of six – Jimmy and Ida, Macalister and Noreen, Mary and a sea captain named Fred. She smiled charitably at the bear-shaped man, balding under his nautical cap. To his credit, he appeared sufficiently embarrassed by the set-up too.

They swept out into the Inland Sea on his small craft. The sun was blazing above them, but the deceptive rush of sea air made it possible to imagine a spring day, or at the very least a pleasant

Melbourne summer day. Nonetheless, the women wrapped themselves in light scarves to cover their pale arms, and they clutched at their sunhats as the boat bumped at speed over white-tipped water.

After some time, Fred guided the vessel into the shelter of a bay and dropped the anchor in the shallows. The water was glass clear and when Mary leaned out she could see the seabed had been pummelled into perfect dunes. Not far from the boat, a stretch of white sand led to sparse forest, and beyond that a hill rose up into a jagged peak. It was undeniably spectacular, and Mary's immediate thought was, oh, Sully would love this. But then Ida was sharply nudging her in the ribs and demanding she shift to the other side of the vessel – next to Fred – to even out the weight. Fred smiled hopefully at her, and she succumbed out of sheer obligation.

'The tide'll be out soon,' he said as she came around beside him.

'Oh, lovely.'

'You'll be able to walk in, like the parting of the Red Sea.'

She laughed and said, 'Oh, I'm not sure I'm worthy.'

But the joke was lost on him. He was pointing out to the east, to the strip of land that hemmed the water's edge. 'See, they call it Horseshoe Bay, but I reckon it's more of a boot shape.'

'Yes.' She smiled. 'Yes, I see what you mean.'

He was silent for a moment, nodding at her with a wild look in his eye, and she had an urge to save him from the agony of the moment.

'I guess *they* don't call it Horseshoe Bay, anyway.'

He looked at her. 'Say what?'

'I mean, the locals would have another name for it, surely.'

Now he caught her meaning and was jerking his head up and down profusely. 'Oh sure, yeah, yeah – too right.'

She smiled again at him and looked back out to the east, to land's end and the hazy rise of another island beyond. A pair of cormorants skimmed past them, low over the surface of the sea. Long necks, mighty beating wings.

The purported 'launch picnic' was in reality a tin of slightly soggy tomato sandwiches supplied by Ida and a bottle of unlabelled booze, procured by Jimmy and served sans cups. They passed the bottle around and chatted about the next dance, scheduled for the following week, and other ideas for fun-making.

Soon, as promised, the tide had edged out far enough that they were able to slip off the craft and wade through ankle-deep water up to the island. She left the others in the shallows, splashing one another and squealing, and pushed on into the first tract of scrub beneath the forested rise.

There she was astonished to find a hidden lea of flowers growing wild beneath the trees. Clematis and azalea and lilies. Other species that she could not name. A spray of white. A tiny tubular yellow thing. She almost gasped at the beauty of it.

She turned to call out to the others, to alert them, then thought again. No, this one moment could remain hers. If Sully were here, she would share it. But not with them. Certainly not with Ida and Jimmy, who would more than likely race around roaring with their ugly self-regard, ripping the crowns from their stems with unthinking greed. Perhaps Sully was right; there are some special few who see the beauty, and there are others who do not.

In the glint of sunlight, she caught sight of Fred breaking away from the group and moving in her direction. His trousers had been rolled up to his knees and his muscular calves punched at the sand with each stride. She stepped down onto the beach and made her way towards him.

'Going for a wander?' he called when he was within earshot.

'I thought I might.'

'Mind if I . . .'

'No, of course, please.'

They set off towards the tip of the island, which felt unreachably distant and remained so no matter how far they went. He insisted she walk on the water side, with the cool tide lapping every so often over her feet. It was hot now and she was grateful for this small act of thoughtfulness.

'You've been here a while,' he said, not as a question but a statement of fact.

'No, not really. A few months.'

'Oh, you seem . . .' He searched for the word. 'Seasoned.'

She laughed. 'Oh dear, I think maybe that means embittered.'

'Nah, sorry. Not at all.'

She nodded, smiled. 'How long for you?'

'Just shy of a month.'

'Oh, I see. You're probably still thinking of home.'

'Some days.'

'And the war – were you . . .'

'Nah,' he said, 'got stuck in Townsville for the most of it.'

'Ah.' She looked across to him and saw in his eyes that this story had been – over the years – noted down as another disappointment. 'Defence of home and country is rather important,' she offered.

'Yeah, yeah, something like that.'

They agreed to turn back and watched as the tiny figures of Ida and Noreen and the men grew nearer.

'If it's any consolation, you stop thinking about home after a while. I don't know why. Maybe it's self-preservation.'

The conversation turned to his work ferrying Aussies over to Etajima and Iwakuni, the constant difficulties of finding the right parts for the vessels. All the while they edged closer to the party on the shoreline. Ida had stripped down to her bathers and was standing in the shallows, regaling the group while excitedly waving her slender arms about, the high, piercing shards of her voice carried away on the breeze. The others were stretched out on the sand before her, their features flashing with laughter, and Mary was struck by the notion that she herself – or Fred, or both – were the source of their entertainment. She chastised herself for such paranoia just as Noreen saw them and shifted ever so slightly. In that instant, their laughter dissolved.

Fred next to her fell silent – she thought perhaps he shared the same thought. But then he cleared his throat with a telling formality, and he was speaking again.

'I hope you'll understand if I ask . . .'

Her response was an immediate tightening of the shoulders.

'Do you have a bloke?'

She looked down to her bare toes as they pushed across the wet sand. 'There is someone,' she said. 'It's just, well, it's not exactly a fully formed thing. But I . . .'

He was quick to interject. 'No worries.'

'I'm sorry,' she said, looking up now.

'Nah, nah, please.' He straightened his broad chest a little. 'Seems like everyone has a someone around here. That's why I asked.'

'Well, I appreciate your frankness.'

'Sure, no problem.'

By the time they set off on their return journey, the sun had dropped in the sky and the breeze was cold against their damp skin. A flask of whiskey was shared around the group, but Jimmy hardly needed it. He was inebriated to the point of stumbling, every objectionable facet of his personality magnified. Over the wind and the buzz of the engine, he was screaming a story about a beggar child hounding him before a rugby game. How they had paid the boy to join in, called him Dusty and made him run drills just for the laughs.

Mary watched the sun-kissed faces of her friends as they listened to Jimmy. So beautiful, each of them. So full of careless youth. Ida, one arm draped over the side of the boat, open-mouthed, deep sounds erupting out of her. Opposite, there was Noreen, quiet but smiling, snuggled up in the crook of Macalister, his eyes shimmering with private thoughts impossible to read.

There was something grotesque about the lot of them, the whole ghastly scene, herself included. A strange image came to her: these people, many years in the future, dead in the ground; corpses stripped to bones by bugs and worms. Nothing lasts forever, she thought with an odd detachment, not even good fortune.

The engine gave an abrupt shudder, and in the blink of an eye her friends had transmuted back into living form. Jimmy was still, even now, droning on about Dusty the boy beggar and his inept left-foot kick.

That night, after dinner, there was a picture showing at the camp theatre. She let herself be swept along, although she was not obliged. She could just as easily have stayed in the rec. Claimed a little sunstroke, or an urgent need for sleep. She could have distanced herself from the only friends she had, grotesque as they were. But something made her go. Something made her take another swig on Jimmy's flask, too. Something about the whole day – the picnic and the island and Fred and the rugby-playing beggar boy – made her want to drink that horrible-tasting whiskey. If she couldn't beat them, she might as well join them. How hard could it be to disown oneself?

The theatre was already darkened when they arrived. A man's plummy voice was prattling on about the expulsion of the Soviet consul general from New York, rising tensions between Delhi and Hyderabad, Bradman's triumphant score at Lord's. The room was awash with the flickering light of the newsreel, silhouetting the crowd of heads. They stood in the doorway a moment, letting their eyes adjust.

Jimmy leaned into Ida and said far too loudly, 'Where the devil is Joan Crawford?' His complaint was followed by an echo of shushing and someone saying, 'Shut your face, mate.'

Amidst the din and in the dark, Mary didn't see Sully until he was right beside her, pushing his hand into hers and whispering, 'Surprise.'

The shock of him sent a shiver of euphoria down her. 'You're here,' was all she could manage.

'Pulled up early in the end.'

She smiled at him, and his face became discernible in the dark. The soft plane of his forehead, the elegant line of his nose, the white gems of his eyes.

'I'm so pleased,' she said.

'Me too.'

He guided her to two chairs in the back row and they sat. The newsman drew to a close and they waited in silence for the film to start. She was still too surprised to breathe naturally; she could feel the air caught in her chest coming out in excited little exhalations.

His hand remained in hers, a firm grip, and when the film began, he leaned into her and whispered, 'Have you seen this one?'

She shook her head. All she could think of was his breath hot on her neck, the mark of his fingers, his shoulder pressed against hers, all the places where their bodies met. She understood now why the Church reduced these deeds to sin. Each touch – each promise of a touch – was animated by impurity, a dangerous thrill. It elicited new meaning in this word, *want*. She had wanted before. That much she could be sure of. She had wanted ice-cream, sunshine, a day of rest. But these, these were desires of middling significance. They were curable. She had never wanted as she wanted now, in this moment, with the heat and smell and goodness of Sully radiating off him like light.

He squeezed her hand. 'Glad I found you,' he said. 'In the dark, I mean.'

She looked at the side of his face, stripped of colour, thinking of the right words. The right words being the bare, unholy truth. Unrestrained. Ungovernable. An invitation to anarchy.

With a surge of courage, she whispered, 'Sully, let's go somewhere.'

He looked at her and raised one brow in bewilderment. Read her face. A smile spread over his own. 'All right.'

If there was any rationalising to be done tonight, it was that her life in Japan had been, from the beginning, one transgression after another. The words they had spoken. A stroll. A touch. A boat ride in the dark. Birds. Fire. A kiss. She could chart them: a constellation of misdemeanours that rolled across the sky in glimmering clarity, a labyrinth of stars that had led her, with unqualified certainty, back to him.

And now, another thrilling walk in another black night to Sully's lodging, more house than room, set apart from the men's dorms. Somehow, beyond any thought or resolution, they were kissing – frantically this time, no room for civility – and he was removing items of clothing from her body, and she didn't say no because there was a trembling pleasure in every fingertip, in the wet belly of her mouth.

Astonishing thoughts were being produced amidst it all. Mrs Richards saying one ought to have fun when one can. Her childhood priest saying salvation comes through god's grace alone.

There was the easiness of it all. It was not nearly as confounding as she had imagined it might be. There was amazement at the sheer measure of naked flesh on display, almost glowing in the darkness as they found each other, lost each other, found each other again. And the bewildering sounds he made; unlike anything she'd ever heard. The way his breath came loose, through the nostrils, like a discontented horse. Only he wasn't unhappy. Somehow the pleasure, she realised, hurt in a way – and the hurt pleased.

Most peculiar of all, there were dead bodies, many of them, piled up along shores and in jungle landscapes, humans who were not so lucky as her. But here she was, life, ascending from the ashes. She should take this happiness, clutch it, embrace it, possess it. She should acquiesce, wide-eyed and giddy, to the wonders of this mortal cage. Let him press his fingers into the soft animal of her body until she released a skittish little gasp. Let him enter her. Make them a union. Indivisible. Consecrated under the great yawning canopy of the Japanese sky.

It took only minutes. That alone came as a surprise to Mary, who was of course discovering many new things on this night. But really, she thought, it was all over so extraordinarily quickly. What she was left with was the fact of the body; how adaptable it was, making astonishingly hasty adjustments in such a brief window of time. One moment you could think of nothing else and in the next you could hear some creature rustling on the roof. You could be amazed by how much the eye sees in the dark. And you could feel rather exposed lying naked next to a real-life man, wondering where your clothes had landed and how you might shimmy off the bed to retrieve them without being watched. Could one ask the gentleman to close his eyes? Then the thought came that she should have asked about a prophylactic, but not really having a precise idea how it all worked, and not knowing if it was the sort of thing a man had on him or could easily acquire in Japan, the thought was soon banished.

In fact, there were so many thoughts to file through, it came as almost an imposition to have Sully speaking.

'Are you all right?'

He traced a finger down her shoulder. Around them the warm timber frame of the room gave out a creak.

Was she all right? She could hardly say. The obvious answer was yes, because there had not been one second when she'd wanted him to stop. There was barely thought, only action, hers as well as his.

She rolled towards him and smiled. 'Yes, I . . . I think maybe I've never been better in my whole blessed life.'

He let out a deep belly laugh and squeezed her. 'Heaven help us, woman.'

She broke into laughter too, and they carried on like that, their bodies shaking against one another. Eventually, they softened and stilled.

'Seriously, is it always that wonderful?'

He thought for a moment. 'No,' he said. 'I think perhaps not.'

They lay like that for quite some time. Every so often, she felt a smile break across her face, then fall away. The word changeling came into her mind and wouldn't leave, although she knew it was hardly apt. It was just that she did feel categorically changed. There was a sense that she could not turn back, that this substitute self was hers for life.

Then there was the sound of men out the window; a group of them, travelling up the path to the men's block. They were laughing and breaking into a crude chant about a girl. Jimmy could have been among them, she thought, but their voices – so uncouth and yet so evidently not of the lowest class – bled into each other and could not be picked apart.

When they'd gone, she said: 'The way those men are with each other. It's so, so . . .'

'Intimate?'

'Yes!' she exclaimed.

'Well, they love each other.'

'Is *that* it?'

'Perhaps not romantic love, but yes, I think it's a kind of love.'

She looked at him quizzically.

'A good number of them fought together,' he went on.

'Yes,' she said.

'They faced the depths of hell – together. I saw it during the war, the way a man can be stripped bare, right down to his manifest humanity. That's how love is formed, is it not?'

She smiled and listened as his words – love, humanity, stripped bare – redoubled in her ears, not really understanding what she was hearing but believing in it all the same.

In time, he shifted away from her and switched a lamp on. Lit a Chesterfield for her, and one for himself. Now the room was aglow, and she could make out details earlier lost: cobwebs in the rafters, a wooden chair in the corner, a shirt draped over its frame. There was barely space for the two of them in his tiny bed, so he hauled himself to sitting and she rested her head on his leg. With his spare hand he stroked her hair and, like a magician pulling hares from a hat, questions came to her that she'd never thought to ask before.

'Sully?'

'Yes, my dear.'

'What're your parents like?'

'Ah, the sixty-four-dollar question. Well, my mother is very . . . mumsy. Not at all glamorous. Very dutiful. Warm, too. Very warm. You'd like her.'

She smiled to herself. 'And your father?'

'My father . . . hmm. What is my father like?' He sucked on his cigarette and exhaled a fine stream of smoke. 'Respectable. And steady. And quiet. Terribly quiet.'

'I see.'

'The enduring memory I have of childhood is walking next to the old man, him striding at quite a pace, me racing with my little legs, trying to keep up. He never slowed for me. Never.'

She laughed a kind of sad, sympathetic laugh.

'Never miss an opportunity to shut your trap, that's what he likes to say.'

She let out another chuckle and rolled her head up to face him. 'That's not really your forte, is it?'

'No, my dear. I have failed him miserably, again and again.'

When their smokes had run dry, Sully flicked the light, shuffled back down into a lying position and they held each other in the dark. There was a moment's pause as the night settled around them.

'Well,' she whispered. '*I'm* rather fond of you, imperfections and all.'

He chuckled a little at that, at the corniness of it perhaps, but then he whispered more seriously, 'Thank you, my dear. I feel the same.'

And in that moment, with the heat of his flat hand upon her head, a strange sort of play on baptism, she believed she could not hope to hear words more beautiful than that.

September rolled by. Joe's letters spoke of Chifley's senseless petrol rations, a terrible plane crash that killed thirteen, Hawthorn's dire showing in the home-and-away season. But life in Australia was far away, easily forgotten. One day Mary realised her homeland had taken Japan's place as the surreal landscape, the unknown territory. Now familiar was the cakey, sweet smell of the Dew Drop, the sight of the ragged hills behind Kure and, from time to time, a kiss from Sully stolen in the dark. It was Noreen's lowing giggle and Ida's haughtiness, Mrs Richards and her ever-evolving benefactions, and the presence of Nancy and the other local women who braided in and out of their lives. She could stay here, she realised, for years – maybe forever if she had to. The rare moments of homesickness were easily managed, because Sully and her freedom eclipsed the loss of home.

Their love affair was as much about anticipation as it was physical togetherness. The days between their meetings were long and repetitive; her work at the Dew Drop had become routine, many of the tasks barely demanding thought. But then suddenly Sully would appear and suggest an outing, and off they'd go, even if it was only a brief journey on the train to a small village halfway to Hiroshima. Through the narrow laneways they would wander, following the trail of the remaining streetlamps, where the pavement hadn't been blasted to smithereens. Sully's updates from the SCAP office or the tribunal or China or Israel were always infinitely more compelling, and yet he listened to her recounting of café diversions with the same enthusiasm he might have committed to the emperor himself. All the while, he would hold her hand as if it were a wounded bird, with such fierce care.

In the dorm, the other women ploughed on with their lives, entirely unaware that Mary had been radically altered. Perhaps they were too consumed by their own love affairs to maintain much interest in Mary's, or perhaps they'd simply grown bored by her insufficient answers. And ever since the launch picnic – the way they'd laughed on the beach, possibly *at* her but maybe not – she'd developed a new feeling about their coalition. Now and then, it occurred to her that if she granted them access to some private fact about Sully – what they were getting up to on those evening walks, how very different it was to the whole Thomas chapter, how very *adult* she felt – she could draw the women back into her orbit, she could be a part of them again.

But she did not want that, for reasons that were only half-clear. She'd been here before, displaced from friendship – nothing overly dramatic or acrimonious, but a quiet separation. There had been Margaret, whom she'd knocked around with in the final years of school and in the first year afterwards, who'd been a 'best friend', in fact. After Margaret had married, there was Flo and her tag-alongs, who in retrospect Mary had simply been one of. And then even Flo had vanished into adulthood, and all the other St Helena girls too, moving with their husbands to suburbs and towns further afield, and then children coming along, and finally the war. There were still the Christmas cards, and an annual morning tea at Margaret's mother's house, but Mary had come to dread that occasion; it was so hard to know what to talk about.

The one woman, oddly enough, that Mary felt genuine affection for in the living quarters was Nancy. It was the equanimity, perhaps; the composed way she held herself, the practical attention to detail, the never asking for anything. Mary had this whimsical, entirely unwarranted feeling that if they had more than a few words in common, they might well agree on some key aspects of life.

Then one day, Mary returned to the room to find a tiny sprig of white flowers arranged in a vase on the dresser. She'd heard other girls speak of this phenomenon; a 'presento', they called it. Mary was flushed with pride at the sight of the little gift, humble as it was, knowing in her heart of hearts that it was intended for her and not her roommates.

In turn, Mary left presentos too – a handful of sugar cubes, a bar of soap, a tin of condensed milk – wrapped neatly in a discarded towel in the corner of the room. She supposed Nancy understood these gifts were for her, because they disappeared along with the soiled laundry, but Nancy didn't ask, and Mary felt it would be crass to spell it out.

There was something extra special perhaps about leaving the whole routine inferred. And yet Mary did not know what it was she felt for Nancy. Perhaps it was a friendship, a funny sort of one. For all she knew, Nancy went home in the evenings and spoke of Mary, but to where and to whom Mary could hardly imagine. A husband? A mother?

After contemplating these mysteries, Mary decided upon a life for Nancy, and even though she knew the little thatched-roof cottage and the little plot of blossom trees were a figment, still Mary could picture so clearly the young woman with the blackest black hair returning to that place as the sky bruised and darkened. She could picture Nancy coming through the door and, in the entryway, freeing the tie on her cotton jacket with the same precise fingers she used to scrub and wipe and rinse. She could picture, too, Nancy coming to the fire pit to warm her cracked palms, and another body, a young man, coming up behind her to rest his hands upon her shoulders. The two of them standing like that for a moment, watching the flames in the pit lick and tumble over one another.

Sometimes Mary let her mind's eye break away from the couple and wander about the room, and she saw then their little dwelling on the inside looked much the same as the house they'd all gone back to after the rugby match on Etajima. Same plain walls and grass floors. And she supposed this was how notions of culture formed, one image endlessly overlaying the next and the next and the next, the imagination stretched to the limits of its ability.

Once, when she revealed a little of these thoughts to Sully, he'd laughed at her and said, 'She's not a character in a storybook, Mare.' After that she understood more deeply that Nancy's cottage *was* a fabrication. Her real home, in fact, might be a great deal more dismal. And so Mary decided that she would be more honest with herself and not entertain those thoughts anymore.

In the first week of October, a solitary case of measles was reported on base. Soon there was another. Before the week was out, there were six, eight, ten cases to manage, and the women's dorm was segregated into the sick and the well. First Ida was sent to quarantine, then Noreen, and for one glorious night Mary found herself unsupervised in the dorm. It was a dangerous thing, of course, for a young person so in love to be left unwatched, left to manage her own poorly understood lust. And Mary followed the script precisely.

It was daringly simple. There was no madcap escape required, no prising flywire or slipping through open windows. She only had to be in the desired location (Sully's lodging) before lights out and as long as the lamps were not on in her own empty room, no further evasions were necessary.

She embarked on this night of lovemaking with terrific enthusiasm. Freshly showered. Clean, pressed frock. Hair pinned back to accentuate her neckline. A little extra work around the eyes. She hoped he would like what he saw, but Sully came to her straight from the shower block and almost immediately took her into his damp arms, mussed up her hair, slipped her dress from her shoulders. Of course she resisted, squealed, felt momentarily annoyed by how fleetingly he had admired her efforts, but finally she surrendered.

'Thank god for transmissible diseases,' he whispered. She laughed and felt the tension in her chest slacken.

Now that she was soft, pliable, he drew her closer to the bed, kissed her neck. A flume of warmth flowed down her body into her arms, fizzing at her fingertips.

When Mary was still very young, not long after her mother's death, there had been a holiday to Queensland. The defining feature of the trip was a man, bare-chested and wet from the ocean, heard shouting at the far end of a beach one day. Her father had instinctively taken hold of her hand while her brothers ran ahead to see what the commotion was all about. Mary and her father had started out too, walking for some time, or at least that's how it felt to Mary, squinting into the rays of sunlight falling over the beach tableau until the stretch of white sand contracted and there were only rocks jutting out into the sea.

When they reached the bare-chested man, they found him holding something within his cupped hands. He was clasping this thing with enormous care, elbows out, shoulders taut, as if it was god himself in there. Finally, the man knelt down before Mary and, in the manner of a performer, revealed an open seashell.

'See? See there?' he whispered with great reverence.

Nestled in the folds of glutinous tissue lay two glistening white balls of light. Two pearls in the one shell.

'A miracle,' the bare-chested man had said, beaming.

This was what she thought about lying in Sully's bed that night, after the work of the body was done, pressed against him in the narrow cot, his breath in her hair. A marvel. A wonder. Astronomically improbable. This image – two perfect gleaming spheres nestled against each other in a darkened room, or a darkened shell. For this moment at least, they were one and the same.

Eventually, she drifted off, then woke. Slept again. Each time she came to, she listened to the pattern of Sully's breathing. How changeable it was. One minute deep and slow, the next light and fluttering. His eyes twitched beneath his eyelids and every so often his hand leapt off her shoulder, flinching like a frightened beast. This went on for what felt like hours. Finally he panted a peculiar sort of noise and his eyes sprung open. She made to soothe him with a hand on his cheek, but that only caused him to startle further.

'Sorry,' she whispered in the very moment he uttered the same word.

'Did I wake you?' he asked.

'No, not exactly.'

He stretched his legs down the bed and moaned a quiet almost-morning sound. Through a gap in the blinds she saw that the night was fading.

'I'm sorry, I must be hard to . . .'

'It's fine,' she said.

He shifted away from her and shimmied up the bed into a seated position.

'Night terrors,' he muttered. 'Bitch of a thing.'

He switched on the lamp. Lit cigarettes for them both. Reposed against the bedframe now, his pale, almost hairless chest was sunken, his shoulders bare nubs. The side of his face was crease-marked from where he'd been lying, and all of this together – the marks, the bareness, the relaxed arc of his body – gave him a tired, world-weary look.

She pulled the sheet up over her breasts and took the cigarette.

'What's on for today then?'

'More of the same,' she replied. 'Always the same. And you?'

'Nothing much. Perhaps I'll visit a girl I know at the Dew Drop.'

He bumped against her gently, and even though she felt spent just thinking about the long day ahead, the promise of such a visit was already alight in her. She turned away, blushing, and it was in this moment that an object on the bedside table caught her eye. She reached for it, gathered it up. A tiny metal thing. Twisted. Charred. Minuscule Japanese characters had been etched into one side.

She rubbed a thumb across the rough incisions. 'What's this?'

'A relic,' he said. 'From the market.'

'Oh, it's from *there*.'

'I have it to remind me.'

'Remind you of what?'

'What we did,' he said matter-of-factly.

They lapsed back into silence. She hardly knew how to say the next words. They sounded spurious even before they'd escaped her mouth. 'Oh, but we had to, didn't we? Think of all our men buried on the islands.'

He murmured a grave, ambivalent kind of agreement.

'It was an impossible decision, but if we hadn't . . . if the Yanks hadn't, how many others would have died? Japanese as well as our men. The war would have just gone on . . . for years. A ground assault. Starvation.'

He took another draw on his cigarette. 'Maybe.'

She returned the object to the table and leaned her head back, sighed.

'I find it hard to picture,' she said, quietly. 'The bomb. Or what happened after, I suppose.'

He was silent.

'They weren't just wiped off the map, were they? There must have been a time afterwards when they suffered.'

'Yes,' he said.

'I've tried to picture it, I truly have, but nothing comes. It's just . . . unreal.'

'You can't picture it because they haven't told you. They don't want you to know.'

'Who? Our side?'

'Yes,' he said. 'It's all censored, the whole damn thing. Drip-fed to us, piece by careful piece.'

'Oh. I didn't realise.'

'No one does.' He slipped his warm hand into hers. 'Do you really care to know what happened that day?'

'Yes.'

'I'll tell you what I know. If you're sure?'

'Yes, I'm sure.'

'Here, close your eyes.' He released her hand and took up the dregs of her cigarette. She did as he directed, shutting her eyes without hesitation.

'First you need to imagine the city before. Can you picture it?'

She shook her head.

'Stand at the station, then. Behind you is the mountains. Can you see the seven green branches of the Ōta river snaking their way down to the ocean? The city is more a patchwork of islands than solid ground.'

She mumbled a yes.

'Directly ahead, you've got the harbour. It's summer, of course, and the horizon is shimmering in the heat. Our blokes say it's a city rebuilt, as if the bomb, the war, was all just a brief interruption. But they don't have the faintest clue what they're on about. Yeah, shacks and shops have been slapped together, but this was a real city, a place of commerce. It has an ancient history and an ancient culture.

'There's a large university. A grand castle. A department store. A museum. A brewery. Crowded shopping precincts with lanterns hanging from street posts. Elegant bridges and fishing boats bobbing on the river. A whole street of temples with long, curved eaves. Schools and sweet shops and thousands of homes. Shiny automobiles and men riding bicycles and children playing in the streets. Can you see it now?'

She nodded. 'Yes.'

Above them, the light *tick-a-tick-a* of a bird could be heard on the iron roof.

'All right. So, the second thing to know is they'd already been through hell, even before the bomb came. Half-starved from the rationing. And the constant threat of an attack, it'd messed with their minds. Every night, every morning, for weeks, air-raid sirens had been wailing. Mothers had dragged their children from bed, over and over, night after night, walking them down to the parade ground or to bomb shelters, only for it to be another false alarm. You can imagine what that does to you.'

'Yes.'

'It's like torture, really, that kind of anticipation. Wears you down. So they hear the plane on the horizon, and the sirens, of course, but no one breaks a sweat because there'd been recons before, never deadly. They could not imagine . . . what was coming.'

She breathed deeper, waiting for his next words.

'They say there was no sound, just a blinding flash of light. But of course there was sound. There had to be. Perhaps it was just so colossal, so unnatural, every sound known to the human ear all at once. Perhaps that's why they couldn't hear it. It was too immense.'

She inhaled sharply.

'You would have seen the terrible wounds. The way it melted their skin.'

'Yes.' She grimaced, thinking of the lady in the market who she could not bear to be near.

'The people at the centre were simply vaporised by the intense heat. In other places, bodies were piled so deep you had to step on them to pass through.'

'Oh lord.'

'There was also a great fire that raged through the city, and many people crushed by collapsed buildings. There were women and children trapped under warped metal. No one to save them. Most of the hospital workers were dead or injured. There was just this grisly, horrifying reality to live through, the smouldering flesh and mutilated bodies, second by second, stretching out before them like some interminable purgatory. There were cadavers still standing, in mid-flight . . . frozen in place by death. Desperate maimed toddlers stumbling alone through the desolate streets calling for their mothers.'

Mary's eyes sprung open. She was crying, trembling. 'Stop. Don't.'

But Sully was already ploughing on; a crazed, mean look had consumed him. 'It's important, Mare. We need to know. Pregnant women birthing dead babies.'

'Please —'

'They found orphans dead with stones in their mouths. They were that hungry.'

'I said *stop*.' She swung her legs out from under the sheet, placed her feet onto the cool floorboards. Wiped the tears from her cheeks.

'I'm sorry,' he said.

She sat up straighter, her back to him. She was holding her bare breasts, for self-protection as much as decency. There was a long, ghastly silence between them, but she could not simply bury her anger. Why would he say such things? In such a dreadful way? At the end of a night like this? Perhaps he really was cruel after all. But then he spoke in a tiny, mineral voice.

'I can't get the pictures out of my head,' he whispered. 'From all the things I've seen, the things I've been told.'

She turned back to him, saw the wretched look in his eyes. He hadn't meant to hurt her. 'What kind of pictures?'

'The adults, I suppose I can manage. But the children, the hungry, sick, wounded children . . .'

She looked back to the floor. Her chest was tight. She could not imagine there were words to ease such pain.

'You see though, don't you?' he continued. 'There's no right or wrong here. No "we had to" or "shouldn't have". No moral victory. This place defies order.'

'Yes,' she said.

'So, what shall we do when confronted with all that suffering?'

She let out a last trapped breath and felt his hand reach out to her, the warmth of it against her shoulder blade.

'I have no idea,' she said.

'I think perhaps, it's this simple: one learns humility.'

They sat like that, his hand on her curved back, thinking. It was rightly morning now. The air was warmer. A bird could be heard calling. Bright streaks of early light cast into the room and fell in shapes across the floorboards. The time to rise was upon them. To go out into the world, to smile and make jokes and put this twilight feeling behind them.

A week later, he found her in the Dew Drop before the lunch service had begun. She was wielding a deep ladle, slopping pea and ham soup from a big pot into serving bowls. There was little time to chat, so he got to the point abruptly.

'Would you come with me to meet Haruki's family?'

She put the ladle down, wiped her palms against her apron, turned to him. 'But wouldn't I be intruding?'

'They've asked.'

'Oh.' She could think of not a word more to say. She looked down to his clasped hands; one pinched the other, biding time. They had entered unfamiliar territory, and she was both thrilled and utterly terrified at the prospect.

'I think perhaps . . .' he said slowly, coming around behind the counter to be closer to her. 'I think they have come to think of me as a son. Or something akin to that anyway.'

'I see.'

'Because of the brother, who . . .'

'Yes, I see.'

She wanted to say, but what about the rules? She was forbidden from fraternising with the enemy. Sully knew this. The whole damn occupation knew it. But to say such a thing would be to paint herself as a child. Even worse, it might come out sounding like a head girl – priggish, humourless. And she was not that person, not anymore. She was someone else entirely.

'Would you come, then?' Sully pressed on.

'Yes, of course.'

'We won't tell anyone.'

'All right. No one will care anyway. I'm practically invisible.'

'Don't say that.' He reached out and pushed a strand of hair from her cheek. Then the door swung open and a woman's voice punctured whatever was holding them there. Mary by instinct turned back to the bench, to the ladle, to the enormous pot of green slop.

'I'll sort out a day,' he whispered.

Haruki's family home was one of those small dwellings of traditional style that speckled the ridgeline between Kure and Hiroshima. Mary had seen its kind many times; seen but never truly examined, she supposed. She had imagined they clung recklessly to the foothills, and it wasn't until Sully parked the vehicle at the base of a rise that she saw the little houses were not in the least precarious, each sitting on their bed of stone. Aged and worn, yes, but also venerable in a sturdy, unyielding sort of way. They had endured what many had not.

Below Haruki's house, the land spread out in a gentle descent, and as they walked, Sully pointed out the various crops he could see in the fading light of a quarter moon in the lilac sky. Barley, oats, buckwheat. There was a large orchard to the side of the house bearing all kinds of fruit – lemon, mandarin. A single slender pine stood at the front door, and for a moment Mary didn't see the old man crouched in the shadows beneath its zigzag arms. He was puffing on a long pipe and did not look up, barely seeming to register their arrival. Sully spoke to him all the same. 'Konbanwa, Yamada-san'. The man simply nodded.

Now Haruki was at the door, saying, 'Welcome, welcome,' with his long-limbed, spectacled, almost British mien so at odds with the grandfather's disposition. He bowed, then indicated where to deposit their shoes and ushered them inside.

Although the house was bare and dim, there was a pastoral elegance about it. A patchwork of grass mats fanned out within the timber frame. Light from a single hanging bulb played in the ceiling rafters and across the paper walls, causing them to glow dramatically against the shadowed recesses of the room. On a timber mantel, someone had placed an arrangement of small wooden boxes, incense and fruit.

Haruki guided them to a low table hemmed by cushions – 'sit, please' – and Mary watched how Sully lowered himself onto his knees. She did her best to emulate the shape of his body, upright at the shoulders, folded and contorted below. She released her hands onto her lap as Sully did, tried not to feel the bones in her toes pressed against the floor beneath her.

She looked across at Sully and he returned a small, reassuring smile. He'd already warned her; she would experience some discomfort sitting like this, perhaps even pain, but she was not to relax. He had also gently, kindly suggested that she speak at a modest volume ('the Japanese are never demonstrative'), that she smile often, that she bow when bowed to. One should not drop one's head to eat, but slurping was permitted, encouraged even.

There were so many things to think of, and despite her wanting desperately to make Sully proud, already she'd been set upon by a terrible panic that she would absolutely mess it all up. Kneeling at this family's table, she was plagued by all these thoughts and, most of all, by a thought never uttered by Sully but easily intuited: whatever you do, do not speak of the past. Do not mention the dead father. Do not talk of the dead son. For this night, she must pretend away the war, the occupation, the very reason for them meeting.

On the other side of the table, Sully was poised, clearly devoid of the fears she was harbouring. Never before had she seen his face arranged quite as it was now. Fallow. Waiting. The line of his mouth curving neither up nor down. The extremes of jovial and serious had been smoothed away, making room for something more attuned to its surrounds, more in keeping with this sombre but not unhappy moment.

Haruki disappeared. From behind a wall there was the familiar rustle and whispering of a family preparing for visitors, and a jolt of homesickness overwhelmed her. Oh, to think of supper in the good room in Beaumaris. The faint whiff of the wallpaper, still new. The best plates, sunshine yellow with a gilded edge. The roast chicken and potatoes, garnished always with a sprig of rosemary from the garden. The first gasp of steam released from the crackling carcass as her father sank the knife in. No rules to think of. Nothing to mess up. Even the sight of the wicked stepmother and the noisy children and Joe with his dark eyes did not deter her. For half a second the memory was so distorted by sentimentality she didn't even think of how it would be *her* cooking the meal, *her* cleaning up afterwards, *her* retiring to bed with that lonely, empty feeling in her gut.

Haruki appeared in the doorway, and the trickery of nostalgia was soon banished.

'Mary-san, this is my mother, Kiku.'

A tiny woman materialised beside him. Not much older than Mary, with a soft complexion, she wore plain trousers and a cotton vest that tied at the breast. Her hair was pulled back into two dark waves, one at each temple. The woman bowed and moved into the room with a tray of teacups. She did not make eye contact with Mary or Sully, but in the bow, in the swift shuffle across the room, there was a sense of deep reverence that made Mary feel horribly uncomfortable.

'And these are my sisters,' Haruki continued. 'Naka and Sachiko.'

Two young girls appeared now. The oldest immediately burst into recitation – 'Konbanwa, Sully-san. Konbanwa, Mary-san' – while the littlest, piggy-tailed and dressed in a bright cotton frock, hid behind the older sister. A small round face emerged, then vanished. Emerged again, was gone. Each time, Mary glimpsed two little eyebrows dancing with excitement high on the girl's forehead.

'My apologies, Mary-san,' Haruki said. 'The little one is not accustomed to visitors.'

'No, please. She's very sweet.' It was now that Mary remembered the lumps of sugar she'd stashed in an envelope in her purse. She reached for them, and the girls' eyes grew large as the mysterious package was revealed. 'Is it all right if I . . .'

'Of course, thank you.' The girls snatched up the gift, whispering high-pitched sounds of wonderment, and Haruki shooed them back into the kitchen.

At one end of the table, the mother poured tea into small

handle-less cups. At the other end, Sully and Haruki fell naturally into conversation about their work. Mary nodded along, trying to keep up with the fast-paced exchange of ideas and names foreign to her. Every so often, one of the men would turn to her and say something like, 'That's the General's main man on the tribunal,' or, 'That's in Okayama Prefecture.' But it was Haruki's mother, Kiku, that drew Mary's attention. There was something impenetrable about the woman, her liquid movements, the lowered angle of her face, the careful precision she applied to the tea pouring and cup arranging and the art of not looking up. When she placed the cup in front of Mary, she gave another little jerk of the head and whispered something Mary didn't understand.

'Sumimasen,' Mary whispered back. Just the fact of having said one word in their language made Mary flush with embarrassment. She'd almost certainly said it incorrectly.

In time, the young girls appeared again. They were hustled by their mother into the far corner of the room and left to play quietly. The older one scratched shapes onto a slate of blackboard while the littlest was crouched over a small pile of clear marbles, making patterns on the mat. The clack of the glass could be heard in the brief silences made by Sully and Haruki, and from time to time one of the girls would look up, gaze at Mary, break into a sheepish grin, and turn to the other to giggle and whisper, presumably about this strange creature who had appeared in their home like a friendly ghoul or an alien from outer space.

The mother arrived again with bowls of rice and other food, arranging them just so in the centre of the table. When the job was complete, she stood between the men and indicated with another half-bow and a flat open palm that the guests should help themselves. Just as Mary wondered if the mother would join them, the grandfather appeared in the room, barefooted and bowed, and took the final place at the table.

'Dōzo meshiagare,' the woman said proudly, and for the first time looked up, right at Mary. Finally, Mary saw there was warmth there in the seams of those tired eyes, in the wide, soft stretch of the woman's smile. She understood now that the averting of her gaze was merely shyness, or respect, not disdain.

The men responded, 'Itadakimasu,' nodded their heads over prayer-clasped hands, and began to talk amongst themselves. Sully's laboured Japanese was understood by the old man, and they spoke on in blunt, covert syllables.

Mary was left to evaluate the meal spread out on the table. Rice she knew, but the small whole fish with tiny bulbous eyes she could not name. There was a pancake sort of thing, and a pile of wilted greens. The smell was pungent, thick – nothing like the meals served in the mess. Kiku had placed in front of her a small empty bowl and a spoon whereas the men, she saw, had been equipped with chopsticks, Sully included. And although this disparity branded her as different, she was grateful for it. What a mess she would've made of the wooden instruments.

The men dished out their meals, and Mary followed. As she ate – bowl tucked under the chin as she'd been instructed – she resisted the urge to wash the food down with tea. She made herself hold each item in her mouth and really taste it – the rubbery, the salty, the bitter, the almost flavourless.

The conversation turned to education, and Haruki began to talk at length, slipping between languages for the sake of the grandfather, about how schools had been transformed after the Americans arrived. Where once children wore a military uniform and performed drills, overnight they were issued plain uniforms and new classes emerged. Suddenly they were learning art and physical education and being taught the finer points of democracy. It was such a rapid change, Haruki explained, at least one teacher in the area had reportedly experienced a total breakdown.

'It was too much you see, Mary-san. Too much for some people to grapple with.'

'Yes, yes, I see.'

And Sully now, piping in: 'Imagine the trouble it would've caused. After so many years of believing one thing, all of a sudden, you're asked to not believe.'

'Or,' Haruki added, 'to believe in something else altogether.'

'Indeed.'

The two men carried on like this, in two languages but earnestly in accord on much of the detail, while the grandfather nodded and quietly ate. After the meal was done, Sully explained he must get Mary back to the base before curfew. The family escorted them to the door, and they exchanged bows and final remarks.

'Itterasshai,' the mother said. Her face had turned serious again. The tired eyes were cradled deep in the skull by her gentle face.

'She says,' Haruki explained, 'please go and come again soon.'

'Sumimasen, sumimasen,' was all Mary could muster.

As they turned and walked away, down the crop-laden rise to the waiting vehicle, Mary realised she'd been smiling so hard for so long, the sides of her face were aching.

The night was still mild as they bounced back down the track and onto the main thoroughfare. At speed, the wind rushed in through the open windows, filling the cab with the damp smell of the night. There was so much for Mary to think about; so many new items to catalogue, to let seep into her bones. There was Haruki's home, now a real place – she could even pick it out if she wished, sitting there on its one and only hillside in its one and only village. There were the little girls, not nearly as bereft as she had naively imagined. And there was the mother, who was so kind, so generous, so utterly duty-bound, who seemed to carry her body from place to place with her heartache sealed inside, like a walking tomb.

There was something else bubbling up too. The ever-so-faint hint of disappointment. A let-down. She couldn't say what she thought a grief-stricken family should be – how they should walk or talk, or eat or act – but whatever she thought they might be, they were not.

Sully took a turn into the outskirts of Kure. Ahead, a cockerel paced across the road, its comb pulsing in the headlights with each thrust of its spindly legs. They slowed to a crawl to let the creature pass.

Mary chose her words carefully.

'What happened to the brother and the father?'

'That day?'

'Yes.'

'Well.' Sully checked the rear-view mirror, brought the car back up to speed. 'The brother came home, very ill. Died soon after, I believe. A rather grisly death.'

'Oh goodness.'

'And the father . . . well, he never returned. I mean, evidently he didn't just disappear, but his body was never discovered. Haruki went into the city the next day and the one after, searched and searched through the corpses. Imagine that. Just picking through all those bodies, burnt and swollen and rotting.' Sully seemed to remember their previous conversation and stopped himself from sharing further graphic detail. 'It was just a hellscape, Mare.'

'That poor boy.'

'He's a brave kid all right.'

On the roadside a man and his horse approached. They were out collecting nightsoil it seemed, loaded to the hilt with tubs, and the whiff of excrement hit Mary like a jab. Sully gave the tired animal and his master a wide berth and they continued on.

'Why were they in the city and not on the farm?'

'Went to help a friend pull down his house. They'd been promised the timber, for firewood.'

'Pull down his house? In the middle of a war?'

'Government decree,' he explained. 'They needed firebreaks between the buildings.'

'So people just had to destroy their own homes?'

'Yes.'

'Were they compensated?'

'Not a penny.'

'My word.'

They drove on. Out Mary's window, the black sky above the buildings was enormous and barren.

'Kiku was in the city too, that day.'

'Oh.'

'And Sachiko. Thank god they weren't near the centre. They hid behind a wall at the station. It saved them, I suppose.'

'Thank goodness,' she said.

They slowed as they approached the base.

'Sully?'

'Yes.'

'Why don't they hate us?'

He sighed. 'I have no idea.'

'They should hate us,' she repeated. 'They should damn well hate us beyond any measure.'

He reached out a hand and laid it on her leg. Gave it a gentle squeeze.

'It makes no sense,' she said, but her voice was small, and the words were blown straight from her mouth into the dark night.

The following afternoon, after she finished at the Dew Drop, Mary returned to the dorm to change out of her uniform. Ida and Noreen were almost never in at this time of the day, and she had this barely thought-out notion that the room would be motionless, deliciously so. That perhaps rather than going to the camphor immediately, she would rest a while. But in fact, the room was not deserted – Nancy was there, by the window, wiping the glass with a cloth.

'Oh, Nancy, I didn't expect you.'

The intrusion seemed to compel Nancy to work harder, and she muttered, 'Good afternoon, Mary-san,' with rapid swipes of the arm. Her long hair, always strikingly untangled, whipped across her back with each motion.

Mary flopped onto her bed and stared at the blank ceiling. After a time, she turned her face to Nancy and watched her work. Despite the urgent strokes, Mary saw that every inch of the windowpane was dealt with, right to the corners. There was force, speed and a satisfying attention to detail, one never detracting from the other, and Mary felt a pleasure wash over her as she lay there watching Nancy excel at this task. There was some vicarious success in observing it unfold; how clear the glass looked afterwards, and the liquid movements of Nancy's slim frame shifting left to right, right to left.

Her mind turned to the previous night. She thought about these Japanese women, Kiku and Nancy, the little girls too, trying to fit them into the picture of the war Sully had painted for her. They'd been through hell, even before the bomb, he'd said. Tortured by the mind games of war. The to-ing and fro-ing from evacuation centres, driven on by the primal urge to protect their children. And then the actual violence. Not nearly as catastrophic in Kure, but still terrible. It was still a city that had burned like a funeral pyre. Still many thousands dead, including – if the rumours were true – Nancy's child.

It was just sort of unfathomable, Mary thought then, that these women were the ones serving her, after everything that had come before.

She sat up on the bed and rested her back against the wall.

'Nancy.'

Nancy stopped her work and turned to face Mary. 'Yes, Mary-san?'

'May I ask you a question?'

'Of course.'

'It's a strange question. I hope you don't mind me asking . . .'

Nancy did not speak, nor did she indicate any objection. Mary cleared her throat and swallowed. 'Do you hate us?' she blurted out.

Nancy's face was transformed. 'No, madam.'

'No, I mean – do you hate the Allies? The Yanks and the Aussies, all of us together. Not me exactly.'

Nancy spun to the window, then back to Mary, unsure what posture to take.

Mary carried on slowly. 'I met a lady last night whose son died, and her husband too, on . . . that day. But she was very kind to me, very kind indeed. Too kind.' She breathed. 'I'm not sure if this makes sense, but it didn't feel right, how kind she was.'

There was a pause while Nancy wrung the cloth in her hand and straightened her back. Mary was just about to go on when Nancy spoke.

'I do not hate you, Mary-san. But sometimes, when I watch your men talk to the children, and give them sweets, then, then sometimes . . .' She beat her chest with a fist. 'I feel hate,' she concluded.

Mary nodded slowly and tried not to feel Nancy's words as a blow to her body. So there was, after all, discontent that ran beneath the surface here. Perhaps she'd always known it was there but had not wanted to face it.

'All right,' she said. 'I think I understand.'

Nancy's face had dropped now, and her hands wrapped themselves around the cloth again. 'If my child take sweets from those men, I would be very unhappy.'

It was the ease of these words that struck Mary; they might've been spoken by a person who believed their child would skip into the room at any moment. For half a second, Mary thought she should ask about the child. If ever there was an opportunity to enquire, it was now. But something almost mechanical inside Mary's throat prevented her from forming the words. She thought of Sully, how readily he would act in this moment. Sully with his knack for gaining people's trust and asking intimate questions.

She was curious, desperately curious to hear Nancy's story, to touch this woman's pain, to turn it over in her hands, to really truly examine it, but she couldn't shake the feeling that it was not her place to ask, not her artefact to touch. She was not entitled to the story; this was the prevailing wisdom that passed over Mary.

Nancy turned back to the window and began a slow stroke across the pane, her body a silhouette against the bright frame of outside. The moment, as slight as it was, had run its course.

November brought a cool wind, and a reminder of all that had come before the warm months: the journey across seas, those thrilling lonely early days, her first sight of Hiroshima, of the maimed, even of Sully, who was once, not so long ago – unbelievably – a stranger. There was a sense that she was coming full circle, that soon the days would be repeated because there were only a finite number of experiences to be had in this place and they were all somehow linked to the seasons.

She could not bear to give up the rhythm of her day, so despite the weather she went on sitting and reading under the camphor. Sometimes that meant pushing the chair right back under the eaves of the branches, snug up against the trunk, while the rain made a dull melody on the path beyond her feet. Other times she resorted to wearing a double pair of stockings and her greatcoat again. Some days her mind even returned to Melbourne, where the wattle would have long dried and fallen, where the billy buttons would be pushing their happy little crowns out of the soil in her father's garden, and where delighted children, Sallyann and Robert among them, would be pedalling pushbikes and tricycles in the streets in anticipation of summer.

Letters from Joe arrived like clockwork, but reciprocation had become more difficult, and she found herself putting off the sitting down and turning her mind to a response. It was not that she didn't miss Joe, but she seemed to have run out of words for him. Letter writing now involved starting and stopping and starting again. Wandering the room, gathering up her rosary beads and thumbing them. Sighing. Gazing out the window. Giving up.

How strange it was to think of her big brother in the hallway of the old house, applying his hat to his head with routine mundanity and heading out into a world she knew so well, while she was here in this far-off place, in a life inconceivable to him. Every so often she gathered up the pen with renewed commitment and thought she would try harder to tell the whole truth, to render Japan real for him, and yet she didn't do this and couldn't say why.

Sully again disappeared to Tokyo, this time to cover the final days of the war-crimes tribunal. He was gone a week, but the days passed quickly, and his farewell – rushed but ardent – had provoked a certain calm in her. She felt sure this time; there would be no other woman, there was nothing to worry about. She must only endure the hours and the days, enjoy the loneliness in a way, with the comforting knowledge that he too was missing her and that he would return. Had his journey been longer, or the mail system more efficient, he'd probably have sent her a postcard of the Imperial Palace.

Their reunion was unremarkable. She was working the lunch hour when she saw him across the café, caught in the eddy of uniforms, and she thought merely, yes, of course, that's him. That's the face of the man who was gone and has now returned. A little piece of the puzzle slotted back into place. He nodded and smiled, and she smiled back, and that was that.

In the afternoon, he dragged a chair onto the gravel path like old times. He was smoking a fat cigar, unusual for him, and, gripping it hard between his teeth, he hauled the chair across the uneven ground. Beyond her shelter of the camphor, the wind was howling; the sky threatened to pour.

'Champion weather,' he muttered.

'Yes,' she agreed.

He seemed to notice her then, and he reached a hand out to hers, squeezed it, smiled.

'How was the big smoke?' she asked.

'It was . . . ah, cripes, I don't know.'

He released her hand and leaned back into the chair, gazing at the rebellious sky. He took another deep puff on the cigar.

'What're you smoking?' she smiled.

'Oh, this? Ridiculous, isn't it? I feel like Al Capone.'

'Why, then?'

'A gift,' he said. 'And it's all I had left.'

A gift from who was the obvious question, but she did not feel she could pry, and he did not offer an explanation.

She opened the cover of her book and found the page. He sucked deeply on the cigar again.

The strangeness of this moment was undeniable. She had not expected a public embrace, absolutely not, but she had hoped for something more perhaps. She dropped her book back onto her lap and looked at him.

'You seem distracted,' she said at last.

'Hmm?' He turned to her, his face blank with private thoughts. 'Sorry, what?'

'I said, you seem distracted.'

'Oh Mare, I'm sorry. I am.'

'Something on your mind?'

'It's the tribunal. There's something most unsatisfactory about it. Now that it's drawing to a close – now that I can see the grand shape of it – it's really beginning to bug me.'

'Oh.'

'Well, the fact the Americans are in charge, for a start.'

'All right.'

'And the fact that Hirohito isn't up there. They've just conveniently bypassed the empire's true power structure. For diplomatic purposes.'

'Yes, I see.'

'Sure, Tojo is an evil bastard, but some of them – some of them were piddly little nobodies just serving their living god.'

'Obeying orders,' she said flatly.

'Precisely. When you're trained from the womb to perform one duty —'

'That hardly absolves a person from moral obligation.'

'But from the *womb*, Mare. An entire lifetime. Believing one thing . . .'

'All right,' she conceded.

'And, and' – his voice rose an octave now – 'the fact we haven't tried the Yanks for dropping the bomb, doesn't it make the whole damn thing a farce?'

'The *Yanks*?' She couldn't help but snort out a little laugh.

'Yes,' he said. 'Why not?'

'I'm not sure how that would wash with the folk back home, Mr Darling.'

'Well, anything else is ludicrous. We condemned the Germans

for trying to bring the Great War to a swift conclusion. Kaiser's battle and all that. Indiscriminate murder. And yet the Allies did the same with impunity.'

'My darling.' She put a hand to his wrist. He was edging towards hysteria, and there were passers-by rather near, wandering up the path, their heads turned by the urgent sound of his voice. 'Be careful,' she said in a low tone. 'The two things – Wilhelm and the Yanks – cannot be uttered in the same breath.'

'I just did,' he said, shaking her hand off and taking another drag on the cigar.

There was a long silence between them. Finally, he released a puff of smoke and sighed. 'I'm sorry. I'm . . . I'm rather worked up, aren't I?'

'It seems so.'

Another long, drawn-out sigh. She waited.

'It's just, I watched General Tojo – I watched him walk into the courtroom each morning, so upright, so . . . serene almost. He'd lay his briefcase on the table. A rather fine briefcase, too. Top-quality leather.'

Sully's brows were furrowed, as if he was trying to grasp the most confounding enigma.

'And I . . . well, I . . . I couldn't imagine what was going through his head. He was a complete and utter mystery. But I'm sure, utterly convinced, that whatever he felt, it was not remorse. Nothing like it. It looked more like' – his voice faded to a whisper – 'certainty.'

'Oh gee.'

'But isn't that what we all feel, Mare? Isn't it?'

She didn't answer, but this question sat between them both until a cool gust whistled through their tree cave and sent a shudder down her spine. Sully blinked and again seemed to notice her anew, seemed to realise that she was in fact there and had been all along.

'Haruki's sister is sick,' he said then in a different tone. 'The little one, Sachiko.'

'Oh dear.'

'Yes, quite.'

'What sort of sick?'

'Fatigue, sore bones, mysterious ailments.'

'Have they been to the clinic?'

'I asked the medic to make a home visit. He was very obliging.'

'And?'

'He's not sure how to help. He suggested broth. Rest.'

'All right,' she nodded. 'So it'll pass?'

'He can't say.'

She was silent, waiting for Sully to say something reassuring.

'Apparently she's not the only one. The medic says there are others.'

'People with the same symptoms?'

'Children. Otherwise healthy children, suddenly quite ill. It's like radiation sickness all over again.'

'Lord, that doesn't sound good.'

'No.'

'But it can't be the atomic plague. That's all passed now.'

The distracted gaze had returned to his face. He paused for a moment, then said with an odd, strangled casualness, 'Did I ever tell you I had a sister?'

She smiled. 'No.' Then she heard his words again, retraced them. Something in her gut dropped. Had?

'She died, at three years.'

'Oh, Sully.'

'Her name was Lillian. She was a sweet kid. Adorable blonde curls. Followed me around like a puppy.'

'May I ask . . . how?'

He paused.

'An accident,' he said finally. 'A terrible accident. My father, in the driveway . . . well, he didn't see her behind the car.'

Mary brought a hand to her mouth involuntarily, then forced herself to drop it back onto her lap. The smell of the cigar had soured in her throat.

'I can't imagine how terrible that would be.'

'No more terrible than all the other children who die every day, I suppose.'

'No, but . . . still . . .'

He looked at his wristwatch. 'I'm sorry, forgive me. I promised Haruki I would visit.'

'Of course.'

He stood abruptly, and she felt she'd said something wrong, that she'd failed an important test. Nonetheless he pressed his lips together and blew her an absent kiss.

She smiled up at him. 'Send them my love.'

'Will do.'

Then he was gone, off down the path, his shoulders an inch higher than normal. She knew him that way now. What an extraordinary and peculiar thing.

Winter arrived as a reprisal. Snow began to fall, unseasonably early; each night it came down in a quiet flurry, blanketing the roofs and the paths with soft white powder. Drifts collected in the streets and local men were sent out to shovel aside the worst of it. In the hills, whole escarpments piled up against farm buildings and houses.

Mary's walk from the dorm to the Dew Drop took on a brisk pace now that the greatcoat failed to achieve its aim. And yet the first sight of the base each morning, disguised as it was in snow, was magical, like something from a Christmas tale. There was a pleasure in being the first person to break the surface of the ice-crust laid out on the paths, to leave a trail of flawless footprints. I was here, they said. Me. Not others. This is my legacy, however impermanent.

But then she'd pass the camphor, hooded with sleet and dripping runnels of snowmelt from its bent arms, and she'd think of those months reading in its shade. What an impossible vision.

The whole of Kure seemed awash in sadness. The sheer weight of the suffering in this place had turned malignant on her.

All that she'd so readily accepted, or turned away from, or diminished with a tourist's distant eye, had become visible. The hungry frozen child on the street, dirty face pressed between the gate posts. The women who moved about the base, so reserved, dressed in black as if perpetually in mourning. How on earth hadn't she seen it before?

And what was the Australian response to all this pain? What good had they done, if any? They were all busy, eight hours a day, but the sum total of that effort seemed mostly in aid of *their* world, the one they had imported here. Indeed, it was Mrs Richards who might have singlehandedly achieved the most noble deeds of all.

If Mary was honest, the sadness came from a personal loss too. There was no prospect now of glancing up from that place under the tree and seeing Sully strolling down the path, hands tucked into his pockets, shirtsleeves rolled up, a grin beginning to spread across his face. Sully travelled, and worked, and when he was not travelling and working he was nearly always at Haruki's house, or making deliveries to Haruki's house, or gathering information about the other sick children. There was talk of a blood disease related to exposure, but the medics mulled over it in hushed tones and wouldn't put their names forward for a story.

It was not so much that Mary didn't see Sully, more that the opportunity for spontaneous discovery was gone. She understood nothing lasted forever, that change was inescapable, and yet there was also a seed of resentment in her. She was familiar with the notion of losing a man to another woman, having heard these stories frequently enough, but the idea she might be losing Sully to a *family* – a foreign family at that – was not part of the playbook.

When they did arrange to meet, she found the words didn't come as they used to, and the touching of skin had become a thing of intention, not instinct. His affections would emerge – a hand placed low on her hip, the press of his body in a momentarily deserted laneway – but they came in all the wrong moments, when she was ill-prepared. They were intended to make amends, she started to see, which only caused her own gestures to become forced.

And so she felt the slow slippage of her mind and body into different realms, like wheat and chaff, milk and cream. She should want him, she knew this, or at the very least she should think of him and his needs. She should, she should, she should. But then, an intrusive thought, an ignoble one – what of him and his duties to her?

It was impossible, this task of loving. She'd begun to suspect that to love a man was to set oneself aside, for him, but also for his hopes and desires, thereby withering away on the vine of his grand plans.

So now, with all that was lost or unresolved, she left work in the afternoons and headed straight back to the dorm, back along the path that over the course of the day had become a tributary of brown sludge, her finely appointed morning footmarks long disappeared.

A nativity scene was erected in the rec room, and paper chains were strung up between the windows. But the evenings were so frigid and the rec room never quite warm enough, so often they stayed in their rooms, under their covers, and wrote letters or read until lights out. Without the welcome interruption of a party or a picnic, the days bled into one another and a grim endurance seemed to take hold. It was as if they'd silently agreed, let's just put our heads down and get through this bit, all right?

Every so often, Noreen would be struck by a moment of brightness, or desperation, or both, and outright demand they go for a walk around Anzac Park. She'd drag Mary out of bed, Ida too if she'd tolerate it, and they'd traipse in marked circles around the sodden athletics track. But these moments were infrequent, and the deficit in their social calendar had revealed a certain conversational vacuum between them. There was no one to gossip about. Nothing much to report. Just the inclination to moan about the weather and their frozen toes and the impending misery of a glacial Christmas. Sometimes Noreen would remark wistfully that the tree would be up at home, or that her father would be due to kill the pig for Christmas supper. Mary would smile sympathetically, and then they would fall silent again, listening to the crunch of their feet on the icy track and the muted cry of far-off birds in the hills.

Just before Christmas, two things happened. The snowfall ended, just like that, and HMAS *Westralia* appeared in the bay. At first it was an almost indiscernible white fleck on the coal-black horizon; it might even have been a mirage, only they knew it was coming.

As the afternoon wore on, the cruiser drew nearer, all eight thousand tons of it. Details emerged like an artist's impression, sketched into existence: masts, smokestack, landing crafts strung up along its pale hull. They had become so acquainted with the local fishing boats and other small vessels that bobbed and weaved through the freezing waters, the spectacle of this enormous ship felt improbably festive, like a finely decorated sponge had been placed before them on a giant silver tray.

Like all grand liners, the ship heralded a beginning as well as an end. Newcomers would come ashore, wide-eyed at the ruins, green as spring buds and misty-eyed in their delusions of what this place meant and how they – barely out of their youth – might make their mark on history. They would be dispersed amongst the various BCOF campuses; some to Bofu, others to Iwakuni, wives and children to Nijimura. A small number would stay in Kure and be instantly recognisable at breakfast by their prompt, eager arrival.

But along with the neophytes came the inevitable departures, and it was this spark that woke them from their winter slump. That evening, the rec room was gripped by an intense buzz of female energy. Two of their kind were pulling out, and there was much chatter and rowdy exclamations, the exchanging of cards and drawings and dried posies, the keening and lamenting as they unsnarled themselves from one another. Whether justifiably or not, the friendships formed here were considered by many of the girls to be categorically lifelong.

For Mary, there was the sense of a troubling conclusion too. It sat in the base of her skull as a niggling reminder always just out of reach; the product of blind intuition and nothing more. She submitted to the farewell celebrations, said the right words, made the right movements with her body and face, but she could not say she was really there in that room or touched by the fizz of the party. She was somewhere else entirely, floating, untethered.

The following morning she woke early, well before the winter sun had peeped over the eastern ridge of the city, well before it had danced like a flame over the labyrinth of tin roofs washed clean by the snow. She could not put words to this uneasy sensation; she knew only that her body felt peculiar. Not ill, nor injured. Nothing as severe as that. But something was askew. Undone, or splintered, or overlooked.

She lay there in the dark, dwelling on this thought for many minutes, warm under the blankets, the cool air at her face a warning of what the day held. Winter. Work. The wilfully merry Mrs Richards popping in with her girls to practise their English. The cooks in the kitchen clanging pots and pans. Tiredness overwhelmed her and yet she could not sleep, shifting and tossing, sighing and thinking.

When finally the sun did crack through the blinds, she reached for her greatcoat and retreated into the corridor. It was now, standing at her full height in stockinged feet, that she felt that troubling blight again, stronger, no longer in her head but in her body. The weight of her breasts seemed to have changed, and when she brought her hands to them, she felt a tenderness the likes of which she'd never known. She tiptoed urgently down the hallway, her mind flipping wildly through pages of an imagined calendar, rounding the corner of the washroom just as the alarm in her head was sounding at full intensity. Hands firm against her breasts, she converged on the basin at break-neck stockinged speed and came face-to-face with a reflection of herself in the tiny, blotched mirror.

Holy mother of Jesus. This was how it felt. To have your whole life unravel, just like that.

She clutched the sides of the basin and breathed. The colour had run entirely from her face. The crags of her cheekbones, the deep pockets of her eyes – this face staring back at her was a remote and distant version of herself.

With. Child.

These were the unlikely words that bubbled up to the surface.

With child.

The next thought came parcelled in a deep and abiding embarrassment. To be *that* girl. To have fallen at the only hurdle girls really ought not to, under any circumstances, stumble at. And she of all girls, the most unlikely. Not particularly pretty, or adored.

Not Ida with her feminine guile. Or Noreen with her serene beauty. The plain, solitary one. Knocked up. With child. It wasn't that she imagined the other girls were so chaste, it was just that one should not mark oneself with the evidence of one's infraction.

You silly, silly thing, she could hear Penelope saying across the oceans, followed by a small snippy jerk of the shoulder, yards of fabric trailing out of the room. To even contemplate telling her father was unimaginable. This shame ran deep, like a seam of opal in ironstone.

In amongst all these jumbled thoughts, there was also a queer notion that emerged, forming itself into an object. A thing. A baby thing. A soft-skinned, cooing baby thing. Not so much *her* baby but an archetype. Rosy-cheeked. Gurgling. Legs and arms flailing with delight. Even if she could rid herself of this problem, would she wish to?

This impossible question was disrupted by the shrill mock-wail of a girl in the corridor, then another. The signal twins, she thought. A moment later, the women came sailing around the corner of the washroom, towels tossed over their shoulders.

'Oh, Mary. You're up early.'

They paused in the doorway, assessing her. It was as if they'd caught her in the act of something illicit. 'You look like you've seen a ghost.'

'No, I mean . . .' Mary turned to face them. 'Just . . . couldn't sleep.'

The women murmured in understanding and, satisfied, continued on into the room, draping their towels over railings, shedding their greatcoats.

'It's getting terribly cold in the mornings, isn't it?'

'Why on god's earth did we complain about the heat?'

'Fools, I tell you.'

'Utter fools.'

Mary withdrew from the bathroom and headed back down the corridor. The arctic touch of the ground at her feet drew her back to reality. So too the thought of Ida and Noreen inside their room, each of whom must be dealt with in their own way. There was a day to get through, she told herself, and then another. There were decisions to be made. A grown-up, adult fortitude to inhabit.

At certain angles and with a little luck in the weather over the bay, the *Westralia* could be seen from base. An enormous thing propped up behind the cityscape, white on top, black down below. Docked now, she was empty; she'd expelled her passengers. She would wait a day, perhaps two, while stocks and fuel were replenished, and the freshly departing came aboard. Then she would set off again, out of the harbour. She would pass back through the Inland Sea, out to the ocean, and back to an Australian dock where order reigned, setting in motion yet another beginning.

That morning, Mary caught a glimpse of the grand ship on her walk to work. And later, patrons at the Dew Drop commented on its immense girth. But it was not just the endless re-filling of serving platters and the collecting of plates that stopped her from thinking too much of the ship. Every so often, those words burbled up – with child – and she slapped them back down, into the abyss of her subconscious, better there. And yet, again, they emerged, a monster of her own making.

With time, the most difficult of all questions stirred and

took shape. Could she tell him? Could she utter the most humiliating words a woman can ever say to a man?

For one deranged moment, she allowed herself to imagine a response. A look of wonder spreading across his face, softening it, smoothing the lines. *A baby?* he might say, a sparkle in the eye. *Our own baby?* Then he might reach out a hand and touch her, wrap his arms around her body, peel away for a moment to break into a hoot of joyful laughter, the discovery of a new thought. *My god, yes!* he might say. They could board that grand ship in the bay tomorrow and be home in time to marry. They could make a life in Melbourne, or maybe with his family in Sydney. Perhaps they might buy a small farmhouse in the country, if his salary allowed for such things. A small little place, nothing fancy, but with birds in the trees and a soft patch of lawn for the baby to crawl on.

'Dear.'

'Sorry?' Mary was brought back into the room by the sight of Mrs Richards in the doorway, bearing a bundle of donated pullovers.

'Where the devil have you been, girl?'

'I'm here,' she said.

'With the fairies, more like it . . .' The woman clucked her disapproval, then dumped the pile of goods onto a table to sort.

The day went on. The hours grew like weeds, one tangled into the next, no sense of order. And her thoughts ran wild too, from one marshland to another. She was tainted now, daubed with a moral stain, and the understanding of this fact was beginning to settle in for the long haul.

At the end of the day, she swung the door open and a winter chill rushed into the vacuum of the warm café. There, standing before her, was Sully. He had both hands tucked into his greatcoat pockets, the scarf around his neck swaddled right to his chin.

His cheeks were scalded pink from the inhospitable weather, and when she stepped over to him he did not take his hands from his pockets, he only leaned forward and pecked her briefly on the cheek.

'Damn chilly, huh?'

'Yes,' she agreed. A wisp of dragon's breath escaped from between her lips, and again more breath when she uttered the words, 'I wasn't expecting you.'

'I had a few minutes spare,' he said plainly.

'All right.'

They shrugged down deep into their coats and headed north by instinct, towards Anzac Park. Another couple, a man and a woman, approached from the opposite direction, their arms knitted into each other, and they smiled and nodded as they passed.

'Bloody outrageous weather!' the man cried out.

Sully laughed. 'A Shackleton dream, I'd say.'

They walked on until the amusement fell from Sully's face and a quiet abstraction washed over him. Today, there were those familiar features: the crumpled brow, the flat stroke of a mouth, the hands cemented in the pockets.

'How's Sachiko?' she asked.

He shook his head. 'Not good. Terribly frail.'

'Oh dear.'

'It's the cold,' he said.

'Yes, yes, of course.'

'That damn house of theirs just doesn't hold the heat.'

'Poor child.'

There was nothing to say, nothing to do but trace the long empty silence to its perimeter, right up to the boundary of her own despair. They passed the men's quarters, then a supply block, and rounded the corner of the last building where the land stretched out to the athletics track.

'Anyway,' he said then, some vague remnant of their earlier conversation. 'There's word coming out of Tokyo. One of the jurists at the tribunal, the Indian judge, he's penned a dissent.'

'All right.'

'But you know how it goes.' He spoke in a bitter tone, as if nothing could surprise him now. 'The bastards are gonna bury it.'

A cool shiver ran through her. It was not so much that Sully was prepared to say these things, it was the volume at which he uttered them. As if he cared not a penny who might hear.

'There's the trial, though,' she said. 'That's something, isn't it?'

'Oh yeah, they talk a big game. International law. Fair trial. All the rest of it.'

'And history is written by the victors, isn't that what they say?'

'Yeah.' He snorted out a thread of pale air, choosing his next words carefully. 'It's not the individuals I object to, Mare. It's the machine.'

'But every nation has a machine.'

'Yes.' He nodded gravely. 'That's true.'

They walked on into the dimly lit afternoon. In the distance, the grey sky seemed to be gathering momentum, preparing for an evening of rain, not snow. It occurred to her then that the most significant scrap of intelligence she'd ever been privy to remained inside her. It seemed to have moved into her mouth, a lead weight she wanted to spit out, to eject with force. It took enormous restraint to hold it there.

Instead, she asked, 'What will the dissent say?'

'Not sure exactly, only that it'll be critical of the tribunal, and our lot.'

'Even if it were released, would it make any difference?'

'Perhaps,' he said, tipping his head one way, then the other. 'Perhaps not.'

For a moment Mary had the heartening idea that her news, *their* news, might be the happy surprise Sully needed today. That it might shake him out of this dangerous mood. But then he reached into his shirt pocket and pulled out a folded-up sheet of newspaper, unpeeled it and handed it to her. She saw it had been torn from the body of a broadsheet.

'That,' he said, pointing, 'that's the story they're getting back home. Doesn't matter what I file. Or even what gets past the censors. They're still just running the same old muck.'

The headline read, 'Japs remain insolent, disease rife'. A quick glance made it clear that the story was an editorialised summary of the occupation, covering the full gamut of disobedient locals, venereal disease and the need for Japanese medical officers to be retrained.

'Oh, I know what I'm supposed to think,' Sully continued. 'They're all disease-ridden villains, right?' She handed the sheet back to him and he folded it as he went on. 'You know, up north the Yanks have managed to find some Christian goodness in their hearts. Sure, they're indulging themselves to the hilt, but at least they're the forgiving types. Down here, we act as if we're still at war.'

'Yes,' she agreed.

'It's shameful. I mean, all the vengeance in the world won't bring back one dead soldier, will it?'

He fell silent and it was almost as if he'd been defeated. But then his body positively bristled with a fresh thought and he was speaking again. The tone was deep and careful; she could hear the apology before the words had come out.

'There's a bloke I need to track down,' he began. He was going again – that's what she heard. To Tokyo, or god knows where else. He may already have packed his bags. 'Reckons the Yanks are secretly studying the sick kids.'

'Like Sachiko?'

'Yes, but there's hundreds of them, Mare. More every day.'

So this was really what they'd been talking about for the past ten minutes. Hidden under the anger at occupation lies and deceit, this was the heart of the matter. Sully had given more to Haruki and his family than Mary could ever have imagined for herself. She thought of Sachiko – of the pigtails and the huge, spirited grin – and the sad mother. There was a spark of jealousy inside her. An outrageous one, she knew. How could she be jealous of a small, sick child? It was a repulsive thought, beyond rationality.

'You think the Yanks know something? About the illness?'

'I can promise you they do.'

It took a great deal of courage for her to ask the next question, because truthfully, she did not want to know the answer. 'When will you be back?'

'It could be a while.'

She swallowed. 'And Christmas?'

Now, finally, he looked at Mary, saw the expression on her face, and was forced to think also of her needs. She was not simply a fleeting acquaintance but the woman who he had touched intimately, who was secretly or perhaps glaringly in love with him.

'I'm sorry,' he said.

She grimaced an acceptance, which made him break into a smile. 'Oh, don't be like that.' He stepped in front of her, and she was made to stop. He took her by the shoulders and shook her gently. Laughed. 'Won't be forever.'

She smiled back. The weight in her mouth grew heavier. Could she just say it? Just spit out the words with one exhalation – *there will be a child.*

But Sully was speaking again, thoroughly unaware that a private universe was collapsing alongside him, unabated.

He said, 'This is really important to me, Mare.'

And she said, 'I know.'

'I'm afraid it's what I'm here, on this earth, to do.' He spoke with a resolute firmness, spreading a flat hand across his chest. 'I see that now. It's become not so much a profession as a calling, I suppose.'

These words evoked in her pure rage. The urge to scream overwhelmed her. She wanted to grab *him* by the shoulders, to cry out curse words, to mock this calling of his. The terrible luckiness of it. The way he uttered his wishes with such breezy self-possession. Ah, to follow one's calling. What profound, appalling liberty it was that allowed a man to say such things.

But when she sucked in another breath, forced it out in one long thread of visible air, the anger passed. He was a good man who wanted to do good things. And if she were a good man who wanted to do good things, she would hope others might support her.

Now, now that the bitterness had gone, she wanted to ask, Where am I in all this? But the great conviction he carried in his shoulders and wore on his face made the question superfluous. So instead they turned back to the path, and she asked a different question.

'Sully?'

'Yes, my darling?'

'You don't plan to go home, do you?'

'Well, someday . . .'

'But not soon.'

He considered that notion for a moment. 'No,' he said finally. 'Well, what's there for me? Just the banal – a job, my folks' place. God, that lovely home of theirs is so frightfully quiet.' He released a hand from his pocket, attended to an itch behind his ear, then replaced it. 'There's this harbinger-of-doom feeling that greets you at the door.'

'Because of Lillian and the —?'

'Perhaps,' he said, cutting her short by instinct or accident, she couldn't be certain. 'It's hard to say.'

And she thought, yes, it is hard to say. And then it came to her that this little girl Lillian – blonde curls around the head, cherubic beyond plausibility – was the unexamined stone that sat at the centre of Sully's life; he had built his world around it, but he would not turn that stone, not if he could possibly help it.

'But it's mostly about the work,' he said then. 'And Japan. I'm not ready yet.'

'Yes,' she said, seeing with utter lucidity everything that needed to be seen.

He had spun and was walking backwards beside her now, invigorated by this conversation. 'There's something about . . . being untethered from your old life,' he went on, 'away from everything you know, that really helps clarify things, don't you think?'

'Yes.' She nodded. 'Yes, I suppose that's right.'

He seemed satisfied with himself, lighter for having expressed such private matters of the heart. He thrust his hands deeper into his pockets, spun back, and stepped into line beside her.

She left Sully outside the women's quarters. He kissed her, an ordinary kiss on the side of the face – a distracted kiss, but a kiss nonetheless. There was a final moment where they held one another, bundled body against bundled body and currents of cold air passing around them. She felt that little flare of love she had for him; there was just enough time to look inside herself, to rummage about for that spark of hope, and extinguish it.

She went inside, pressed her body against the back of the door, breathed and counted slowly to twenty. When she cracked the door open again, tentatively, he'd gone from view.

The rain would set in any moment, so she raced down to the office block, the very one she had stormed into on her first day in Kure. Between two buildings, she caught sight of the *Westralia*, a dull slab waiting under the sunless sky.

The Major was alone in his office, head bent over a large book. The towers of files spread across his desk seemed to have halved since she'd last been here, and she thought this must have something to do with the thinning of the force, more members pulling out than coming in. The tide of them was slowly ebbing away.

Soon, perhaps, there would be just Sully and a sprinkling of others left to dismantle their existence here, to remove the King's flags and the photos of the generals on the walls.

'Sir.'

He looked up. 'What is it?' There was something softer about the man's face than she remembered. Perhaps Japan had changed him too.

'I've had a letter from home.'

'And?'

'My father is very ill.'

'You need a discharge, Private?

'Yes, sir.'

He began to search through a pile of papers close at hand.

'Surname?'

'Egan.'

'Lucky timing then, darlin', what with your ride in the harbour.'

'Yes,' she said.

'They set off at the crack of tomorrow. I'd get your backside down there tonight.'

'Yes, sir.'

He continued to search through files, flipping one then the next.

'Ask Millicent down the way to prepare your papers and to find a sub.'

'All right.'

He looked up then, meeting her eye. 'Thank you for your service, Private.'

She saluted him with a stiff hand at the temple, the kind of proud salute she had once rallied on a regular basis, before it had all really begun.

The room was soundless when she arrived back there, discharge papers in hand. She realised she'd been walking rather swiftly; her chest rose and fell with each breath. When she brought a hand up to the light, she saw that it was shaking. Her other hand sprung up and clutched the first, and somehow together they made a more resilient pair.

Now, she said to herself, now we focus on the task. A task like many others. Like serving the soup or buttering the chicken or ironing Father's shirts. This was merely packing. This was merely dragging her case from under the bed and placing an item – a cardigan, a book, a photo – into it one after the other until the vessel was full. So, she did this. All the while, she was thinking that Ida and Noreen were bound to come scampering through the door at any moment, a whirl of hair and breasts and fine scents, and she would have to find the words, some impossible words, or perhaps a lie. But in the end, they didn't appear. The room remained quiet.

When the packing was done, she stood with her case and her kit at her feet, surveying the room. The bare walls, the well-made beds, the streaks of dim light seeping through the cracks in the blinds. Goodbyes were easy, she thought. Goodbyes were simply putting one foot in front of the other. Mechanics of the body. Procedural. One need not *feel* anything.

She bent down and eased the kitbag onto her shoulder just as the doorknob clicked and Nancy pressed into the room. She, too, was laden with objects, the weight of a bucket and other cleaning supplies dragging one side of her body down. When she saw Mary she froze, assessing the spectacle before her. There was a strange mirroring that occurred now. If they were an artwork, it would have been titled *Women, poised with cargo, rooted to the spot.*

'Mary-san.'

'Nancy.'

'You go?'

'Yes.'

'Where?'

'Home,' Mary said. 'Home to Australia.'

There was a surreal silence.

'Will you tell the girls for me? Ida and Noreen.'

'Yes,' Nancy nodded.

'Thank you.'

She bent to pick up her case and edged towards the door. Nancy shifted aside to let her pass, watching all the while, holding every small motion in her gaze.

'Mary-san?'

'Yes, Nancy?'

'Will you be all right?'

'No,' she blurted out, a mad smile spreading across her face. 'No, I dare say I won't be all right. Not at all.'

Nancy wrinkled her brow, made a sombre look. That in itself proved something about friendship, proved that this had been a kind of friendship after all. Fraught and limited, but real.

'Itterasshai,' Nancy said. 'See you again soon.'

She was bowing, deep and slow. When she straightened, she looked at Mary directly, those dark eyes sharp and alert, harbouring layer upon layer of understanding. Mary was compelled by instinct to do perhaps the strangest thing she'd done since she'd arrived on Japanese shores. She dipped her head, let her gaze fall to the floorboards, and gave the deepest, most gracious attempt at a bow she could manage. When she righted herself, Nancy was smiling at her, a broad smile that reshaped her face into something almost entirely new.

'Arigato, Nancy-san. I will miss you.'

It was in the midst of saying these words that Mary felt her eyes prick with heat. A flood of unwanted feeling surged through her. Before she allowed one tear to fall, she tightened her grip on the case and bustled out the door.

At the threshold of the base, under the skeletal arms of the bare, wintered blossom trees, she gathered her strength. Pushed down the rising mania. This was being an adult. This was taking control. This was making the best of the worst situation.

A vehicle pulled into the designated spot and a young driver nodded to her through the open window. His uniform was half hidden by a brown woollen scarf that enveloped his neck and chin.

'Docks?'

'Yes, please.'

'Righto.' He unspooled his long frame from the car and came around to her side, grinning with thoughtless amusement. 'Going home, huh?'

'Yes.'

'Exciting times.'

'Yes.'

He bent and gathered up her bags. His forearms were tawny lengths of muscle. 'Who's the lucky bloke, then?'

'Sorry?'

'Well, I mean . . .' He looked up at her and caught himself. 'Sorry, er, sorry.'

She looked at him, confused.

'Most of the sheilas heading home seem to have a ring on their finger, that's all.'

'Oh, I see.'

'Didn't mean nothing by it.'

'It's fine,' she said, shaking her head into a posture of superiority.

He grimaced slightly, then seemed to remember the task at hand. 'You right getting in?'

'Absolutely,' she said.

They drove in silence down the main street, past the shops and the lovely plain buildings, past the local men pushing carts and a peppering of BCOF members out for a stroll, all of it bearing a sheen of familiarity. It was nearly twilight, and the streetlights had come on.

Eventually the driver – unable to bear the memory of his own ineptitude any longer – cleared his throat and gestured to the vast toy floating in the bay. 'Quite something, isn't she?'

Mary nodded, smiled. 'Quite.'

'They reckon she's a lucky one. Had a close call with the Japs in '42.'

'Is that so?'

'Yeah, well, that's what they say.'

She smiled in detached understanding, turned her face away. How very different the act of saying was to knowing. People said all kinds of things about Japan, but after all this time what did she really know? Perhaps surprisingly little. She knew that, come spring, the swifts would nest in their grass cups under the eaves of old homes, crouching for cover when the big winds blew.

And she knew that, on occasion, a river of air could emerge like a ghost from the Inland Sea, that the gale would scatter in all directions around the warehouses at the docks, forming channels that rushed into the city streets, rattling signs and tossing laundry.

But there was much she didn't know. Why did the women pound rice with a mallet and mortar? How did people keep themselves warm in this cold? Did Nancy even have a child to lose? It occurred to her now that all those imaginings – those flights of fancy, the conjuring of made-up lives – was nothing more than a terrible conceit. She might never learn the answers to these questions, even if she were to stay another year or two or five. She was a traveller, and there remained always many mysteries hidden from the eye of a traveller, no matter how deep their desire to know.

They were nearly there now; the broad side of the ship was gaining on them out the front window and, beyond that, the unceasing grey domain of the sea. The young driver hauled the vehicle into a sudden U-turn and pulled up at the marked spot.

'I'll just —'

'Please no,' she said with a hand up. 'I can manage just fine.'

She was suddenly desperate to be free of him, to be free of all the people that inhabited these shores. She cracked the door open into the cold evening, wrestled the bags from the back, and slammed the door with a heavy finality.

It was now that the rain started. At first a light patter, quickly becoming a thrumming beat. Fat drops bounced off the metal cleats laid out along the dock and collected in rivulets in the dips and crevices of the concrete walkway. She hurried to the gangplank, clutching her case and kitbag as rain streamed down her face.

She maintained a resolute numbness all the way up the bridge, through the corridors of the ship, to her assigned cabin, which she found mercifully empty. Her vacant aspect continued, a remarkable feat in itself, through supper in the dining room (sweet buttered fish, root vegetables – no greens), through her preparations for bed, hanging her wet clothes to dry, pulling back the blankets on her berth, lying down, closing her eyes, drawing a final waking breath, wilfully ignoring all the many questions that squalled within her.

In the morning, she woke to a vague swaying sensation. A tender lurching from side to side, as if the ship were a small child and the sea its mother. She opened her eyes and let the events of the previous afternoon seep back into her consciousness. Thought for a moment more. Yes, that was movement all right. Indisputably.

She reached for the tiny blind on the porthole and flipped it up. The sight that greeted her was an endless stretch of white-tipped charcoal. Not the dock, not Japan, but an unruly sea. Panic struck her in the chest and she leapt from bed, bundled on her coat and scarf, snatched up her shoes.

In the first morning light, she emerged onto the deck a force of primal energy, hair free and wild. The ship's horn let out a fierce blast. She swung her head to the north and took in a great gulp of wintry air. Oh, she had not missed it after all! That last sight of Kure – the ravaged docks, the city, the fractious hills – all of it receding inch by inch into the bleak horizon. To have this moment felt necessary, like the viewing of a body before burial. And in her sleep-dazed state she could even imagine it was the city that was moving off, not her, not the grand ship. A whole city stealing away. Oh yes, she liked that idea. The place as fugitive. And she its blameless jailer.

Yet even in the act of thinking these thoughts, she knew they were lies. It was she, Mary Egan, who had hit the eject button. She who was abandoning Sully and Ida and Noreen with absolutely no explanation. She who was leaving Nancy, and Haruki's poor wretched mother, and the little girl Sachiko who, she saw now, was more than likely to die. And Mr Ogawa, Nakajima-san, and all the maimed creatures who wandered the streets of Kure. All of them unable to escape their terrible grief. And yet here was Mary, walking away, transporting herself back to another life; indeed, her actual life.

She thought of Joe at home. Thought of rapping the old cast-iron door knocker at Pearson Street, pushing open the slab of paint-rough timber, stepping from the summer heat into the cool old house, the look on her brother's face. She could almost hear the call of home on the wind. No matter what Penelope and her father said of her predicament, Joe would protect her.

She would feel no guilt. Indeed, if she was truthful, right now all she felt was unfettered relief. Soon Japan would be distant, immaterial. Merely a place she visited once. It would return to being an image on a newsreel, or a willow pattern daubed on a porcelain plate. Just as war was fleeting and random, so too had been this journey, and now it was gone; already it felt as if it had never happened.

Mary stood on the deck, hands thrust into her coat pockets for warmth, and watched the sea rushing back to shore in sheets of plated grey. It was perhaps six am. Today, in Tokyo, seven men would be hanged by the neck for the unspeakable crimes they had committed in war. Among them would be Hideki Tojo, whose body would be burned and scattered at sea and made invisible, and his lovely polished briefcase that held the impossible dream of an entire regime would be tossed or given away or burned along with him. Closer still, along the hills between Kure and Hiroshima, a mother and her sick child would wake to another icy morning. Noreen and Ida would moan. And Sully would rouse from sleep utterly unaware. Perhaps he would scribble a note to her, push it under the door of the Dew Drop, make his way to the train station. Or perhaps, having had a night to think on things, he would defer his trip to the capital to another day, until after Christmas. Perhaps he would wait outside the café that afternoon. Wait and wait and wait. But how he learned of her departure was, she supposed, none of her concern now. It was the product of another time, another life.

The boat pushed on, out to sea, out, out, away, never to return, free of that place.

1949

On Collins Street, caught in the discord of those terrific gusts of hot wind that whipped at the ladies' dresses, Mary took three deep breaths and thought, perhaps I'll walk a little way after all. Distance was what she needed – inch by inch, foot by foot. The space between her and Tess must be hollowed out until a valley had formed, one the size of half a city.

The semi-controlled chaos of the afternoon offered a strange appeal. The plane trees had surrendered the first of their autumn leaves, and the papery brown fragments scuttered along the pavement like small creatures. She wandered past a chic-looking shoe store, a jeweller, turned into Swanston Street and headed towards the clocks. The familiarity of this scene – the English signs and ornate facades, and the people, of course the people – was still faintly novel. It was too early for the businessmen in their nice suits, and the footpath was mostly occupied by women and manual workers, none of them wearing monpe or clogs, none hauling carts.

Ahead, the gothic spires at St Paul's were lit up like a triptych of flames against the bright sky.

In time, Mary began to feel she could think clearly again, and she let herself revisit the appointment in the hotel parlour. There was nothing particularly shocking about the meeting. It had played out almost exactly as she'd imagined it might. From the moment she'd put down the phone three days prior, she had known. And yet, it was shocking to have actually said the words. *She's yours. Have her*. What kind of woman said that? And to then be confronted with that little dawn breaking over Tess's face. Despite her obligatory show of regret, Mary had seen the joy there in her eyes. A terrible, cruel, mean joy. What kind of woman indeed.

She passed the cabs lined up at Flinders Street Station, ignoring the heavy feeling in her belly and legs, and continued on to Princes Bridge. After she'd returned from Japan, from time to time she'd had reason to travel into the city and, each time, perhaps three or four in total, she had stood here above the Yarra and thought how peaceful Melbourne was, with its seagulls gliding easily down to the water; how untouched it was by war or violence. The whole scene exuded a mediocrity that she only now understood to be safety.

The sharp horn of a riverboat sounded in the distance and for the briefest time she was at the docks in Kure again, racing up the gangway, back against the world, utterly determined to press on, do not hesitate, don't let the doubt creep in.

She shook the memory free.

Onwards. Upwards.

At Sandringham station, the walkway was a parade of long-afternoon shadows. Mary followed their inverted forms – distorted fence-lines, steel poles, feathery branches – through the gates, out onto the blazing bitumen path and around the corner to her father's parked Chevrolet. Seeing her through the half-lowered window, Joe raised a finger of recognition. Not so long ago, the car's distinctive harbour blue, the high grille and glossy arcs, would have screamed protection.

She climbed into a cabin thick with tobacco smoke and Joe there busily lighting up another. His brown felt hat hung from the hook of one knee. In the footwell, his brogues were powdered with pale earth. All of this together meant he'd been at the track; his wallet was no doubt empty.

'Howdy.'

She nodded and grimaced a smile. 'Partner.'

'How was it?'

'Fine, I suppose.'

He looked at her and raked his fingers through the stubble on his chin. Made that scratching noise like an animal scouring in the undergrowth.

'Was it as we thought?'

She gazed out beyond the car park, past the beach road, out to the bay that shimmered like a jewelled wasteland behind a row of she-oak. No sailboats bobbing. No fishermen. Just a vast stretch of useless water.

'Yes,' she said.

'All right.' And then, after a second, 'Well, it's done then, yeah?'

'Yes.'

'Easier this way.'

She spun back to him and examined his grey eyes, the bruised hollows beneath. 'Yes,' she said again.

Joe brought the engine rumbling to life, and it was no good talking then. There was nothing more to say in any case.

They snaked their way out of the car park and onto the smooth road, travelling south-east with the line of the bay advancing then abating to their right. At one point the whole sandy foreshore was laid bare, revealing white-robed mothers crouched over toddlers in the shallows, small figures racing with spades and buckets. A moment later, the entire happy scene was erased by a screen of tea-tree and coastal banksia.

After several minutes, Joe took a left into the backstreets of Beaumaris, past the shops in the tiny village centre, past the church and primary school, past the rows of neat hedging and paling fences and the odd stretch of meadow. The sun was low by now, and it winked every so often behind a large gum or the tip of a roofline.

He swung the car into the driveway. The engine wheezed and drew a final gasp.

'Home,' Joe said in a flat voice that was designed to comfort.

Home, she reminded herself.

She was still acclimatising, she supposed. Funny how returning was so much harder than departing. No one told you that. And even stranger, how simple words could be cleansed of all meaning. What was 'home' if not an assemblage of red bricks, varnished by the green tincture of moss, pummelled for half a century by sea air?

Before Japan, not once in her life had she been ashamed of this house, how lovely it was and how lovely all the things inside it were. What a ludicrous thing to feel shy of. And yet, since returning, she'd found an odd feeling creeping in that certainly resembled shame, and which made no sense at all. Rationally, she knew the lovely things weren't what made her, and yet somehow she suspected now that they did.

This is my home, she told herself firmly. She ought to get her head in order.

She climbed out of the car and followed Joe into the cool, dark corridor where the Indian summer was immediately forgotten. The door to their father's study was shut, so they moved by instinct towards the parlour, where the afternoon light was streaming in through the leadlight windows and throwing coloured patterns across the carpet. In the corner of the room, Penelope was spread recumbent on the chaise longue with an arm flung over her eyes, reams of silk falling like water. She waited a beat, perfectly aware of their arrival it should be noted, before peeling her arm from her face gingerly and executing a finely tuned sigh of ill-health. 'Poorly again, I'm afraid.'

Joe moved towards the kitchen. 'Damn kids, hey.' When he was out of Penelope's line of sight, he turned to Mary and flashed her a wink. He disappeared and she heard the rattle of the fridge door, the clink of a glass bottle being extracted.

'Where are the little sweethearts?' Mary asked.

'In the nursery,' Penelope muttered.

Mary was already halfway out the door when Penelope spoke again in a lower, more deliberate tone.

'Mary, dear.'

Mary turned and examined her stepmother, this dazzling woman, wearer of turbans and large gilded brooches, possessor of an exquisite head of rich auburn hair, who was a whole two years Mary's junior and yet for all intents and purposes her superior.

'How was Tess?'

'Fine,' she said.

'Hmm?'

'It's all sorted now.'

'Oh thank heavens.' She threw a pale arm back over her eyes and said, 'Your father may even sleep again.'

Sallyann had set Robert up in a children's chair with a pile of books and pencils on his wee little lap. His tiny stubby feet didn't reach the ground, and he was balanced there precariously like a bobble toy. She was standing at the blackboard, all three feet of her, left hand positioned on her hip with defiant bossiness. Her lovely russet hair, yet another inheritance, had been pulled back into a tight ponytail, and she was saying, 'Robert, dear, two plus two is not one. Try again.'

Mary stepped into the room. 'Sorry I'm late, Miss.'

The children's little faces burst open with recognition and the pile of books promptly fell to the ground in Robert's rush to extract himself from his sister's dull lark. That only set off Sallyann two-fold, shrieking that the game must continue, and that silly little Robert never played right. Mary dropped down onto her knees and hushed at them both gently, opening her arms out to envelop their hot little bodies.

She'd missed them while she was away, or at least from time to time she had. But they were not hers; she had always been firm about that. Even though she had been there when their plum bruised faces had emerged from Penelope's body. Even though she'd seen them transform from round and fleshy to thin impressions of their future selves. Even though she did care for them, in her own restrained way, they were not hers – they were Penelope's. And for that she could never quite exonerate them.

They climbed and wriggled over her for a moment longer, Sallyann still howling that Robert ruined all the fun. Finally Mary's hushing confirmed that really they were awfully tired, and even Sallyann surrendered, settling onto the floor and falling quiet as Mary ran a finger along her spine. They sat like that, the three of them on the nursery floor, while the sun sank fast behind the jacaranda.

Finally, Mary whispered, 'Bath time.'

They allowed her to lead them into the next room to be bathed, then to the kitchen where they watched her make boiled eggs with soldiers. All the while, their mother was sprawled out on the couch, as still and stiff as a cadaver. At seven, the grandfather clock in the hall pealed and abruptly Penelope was on her feet, miraculously revived from the hereafter just in time to sweep into the nursery and smother the squealing children with kisses.

'Oh, my darlings,' she cried between a hammering of pecks. 'My superb, brilliant little darlings.'

Mary watched this performance from the doorway. Saw how the children ceded to their mother's body, yielded to her scheduled adoration. There was almost a sense that through the patiently waiting and never asking, they had earned it. She was conferring on them what they were due.

On Sunday, they paraded down to St Joseph's on foot, all six of them, under a row of plane trees crisp with browning leaves. Robert was carried in their father's arms because he categorically refused to sit in the baby carriage. He was a round little node of muscle and pent-up energy in his tiny suit jacket and trousers, and her father held him in a gentle lock. Beside them, Penelope had a glum Sallyann by the hand. She didn't attempt to coax, merely strode on, hissing 'c'mon now,' and yanking at the girl's arm each time she fell behind.

Bringing up the rear, far enough to observe the familial spectacle in its entirety, were Joe and Mary. This was what Joe liked to call 'playing happy families', and indeed except for the jerking and the hissing, they did make a rather fine-looking party. Penelope in her loveliest silk. Their father sporting his new forest-green Homburg. Only now and then could Mary glimpse the ageing face below, softening at the jowls, resting in repressed irritation.

'Oh, Mare.' Joe gazed out to the clear sky and the birds that twittered mockingly. 'What a splendid day for some family malfunction.'

She laughed, and he gathered up her arm and placed it into the crook of his. The lumpy rhythm of his gait – courtesy of a school football injury and made worse by the war – pulled at her, making them an awkward syncopation.

'How does this end, do you think?'

She looked at him, quizzical. 'How do you mean?'

'Well, does she die an early tragic death like the first wife? Or do they live into old age, miserable and cantankerous old bastards endlessly quarrelling about one thing or another?'

'Maybe they're happy.'

'Doubtful.'

'I know it seems impossible, but people . . . people can be happy.'

They passed through the gloom of one tree's shade and into the bright gap before the next.

'People are never really happy,' he said. 'Not really.'

She had an unpleasant taste come into her mouth, which brought with it a flash of Sully. The hands tucked into the trouser pockets. The face brindled with shadow after a bitter smile had come and passed. Perhaps it was simply the male body beside her. Or the unchecked cynicism. In any case, it sent a shiver of loathing through her. She yanked her arm free of Joe and walked on.

'What? What did I say?'

'Nothing.' She resisted the urge to look at him. 'I just think . . . some people . . . sometimes . . . are happy.'

'Really?'

'Yes.'

'Are we talking about Jap-land now? Is that where you were happy? Because I sure as hell never saw it before.'

'Don't be absurd.'

'Well, not since childhood.'

Mary could feel her face steel into something tight and private.

'Mare?'

'What?'

'So you were happy there. Is that it?'

'That's not what I said.'

'But that's what you meant.'

'No.'

He grabbed at her arm, tried to slow her pace. 'Say it, Mare. You might as well say it.'

She stopped and looked at Joe. Sighed deeply. Then gazed beyond him to her father and Penelope and the little ones, who were a good few feet ahead now.

'I was happy,' she whispered.

Joe snorted out a breath. Wrinkled his top lip. 'Course you were.'

The children squirmed and squawked their way through Mass, Penelope keeping a firm hold of their little bodies and relentlessly hushing them. Their father was a silent disapproving figure on the periphery, and beside him sat Mary and further along Joe. At the chancel, Father Flaherty was turned towards the altar, the back of his vestments a still life of green and gold thread. He droned on in a long stream of melodic Latin, honed and repeated over years so as to be barely borne from thought. It seemed to Mary, who was listening with renewed attention after months of release, that Father Flaherty did not breathe as the sound poured out of him. It was just a long purr, intoned through the nasal passage, not unlike the church organ, thrumming with some divine resonance.

He was a young man – perhaps Mary's age or thereabouts – and a handsome man too. The kind of dark-haired, tender-eyed fellow that Mary might have had some interest in had he not been the second son of an Irish family and obliged by tradition to enter the Church.

He had resisted the cloth at first, the idea of a calling, of familial duty. And then had come the war. He'd gone off to the front with the best of them, not as a padre but as an average man. He had seen the death. The suffering. Gazed into the deep dark hole of questions a man could get eaten up by. The way he'd told the story to his congregation, the seed of priesthood had been planted in him long ago, and the war had nourished that seed. It had taken root and budded. And it had proved to be a lifeline, he said; something to come back to when the terrible black void threatened to devour him.

Next to Mary, Joe stirred in his seat, moving weight from his bad knee to his good. He brought his hands together on his lap and discreetly cracked a knuckle, the sound muffled by the fist he'd made around it. Despite the blooming heat outside, the nave was cool under its dark timber hood. When she raised her eyeline, the roof seemed to sit like an inverted ship's belly above them.

The deep richness of Father Flaherty's voice carried on, emptied of meaning, a husk with no pith. Despite her closeness to Joe, and Michael and Bernard having served too, Mary had learned more about the war, the *true* impact of the war, from Father Flaherty's homilies than from anyone else. But today, the sermon centred on petrol rations and themes of patience and trust in the Lord. It did not interest her, and her mind swiftly floated away from St Joseph's, from this world into the past.

She had stopped trying to imagine what Sully was doing day to day. Stopped trying to chart the course of an imagined life. He could be anywhere: Tokyo, Sydney, Korea. There were only memories to go over. Ghouls and phantoms to disinter. Magic puppet corpses, reanimating a not entirely untrue version of her personal history. Today, it was the little boat on the river in the mountains. The fishermen and their cormorant birds tied at the neck. The vaulted pit of the vessel was mirrored by the church canopy above her, but there was also Sully here, painfully handsome, perhaps fraudulently so. The remembering mind indulges in all kinds of illusions.

Other tricks came to her. A scrolling effect that allowed her to swiftly think through the events of that night, to stop and start as she pleased. To rerun the charmingly irreverent things he'd said, or at least the charmingly irreverent things she believed he'd said. 'Lousy, two-bit occupying force,' his phantom voice taunted. His smile. Her smile. The kiss. The sensory engulfment; the smell of fish and fire and a damp night. Most disturbing of all, her utter capitulation in the face of a singular male regard. If only she'd recognised it for what it was. He might as well have tied a string around her neck.

A sudden eruption of movement in the church shook her out of the past. Joe and her father, all of them, were on their feet, setting off a chain of echoes that bounced between the roof struts and came back at them like thunder. Mary launched herself from the seat. A bell chimed. An old woman in the next pew turned and shot Mary a stern gaze from under her mantilla. The bell sounded again.

Mary was not a good Catholic – this she knew. Despite the hundreds of hours she'd spent standing and kneeling and praying and chest striking, she had always found it immensely difficult to focus on the task at hand. The mysteries of god were almost entirely obscured to her. This whole business of churchgoing had come to feel like a strange game they all played, once a week, like clockwork, not because they wanted to but because they ought to. Because they must.

She clutched her hands to the back of the next pew and closed her eyes. The odour of her father in a wool suit on a warm day, and from the other side her brother too, came at her infused with the hung scent of church incense and women's perfume. She felt the room spin. A deep meaty force of nausea rose up into her throat. She breathed in through her mouth and swallowed down the feeling. If only she'd been more god-fearing, or god-listening, perhaps, she wouldn't have found herself here in this church with a tiny creature coiling loops inside her.

In the afternoon, their father announced it was a beach day. 'Like old times,' he said. This was of course nonsensical, because in the old times Mary was a child, and even with a dead mother to suffuse her life with a certain adult solemnity, her days had been straight-forward, effortless things. No thought required, just action, and response. A laugh at Joe's antics. A moan for hunger. A short sharp cry for hurt. There was also the small matter of Penelope, who would barely have been out of nappies back in those days. And Sallyann and Robert, who were rightfully unthought of.

Nonetheless, their father insisted: 'The last warm days of autumn should never be squandered.'

He was not wrong. The beach – their beach – was perfectly sublime. A glassy film sat over the water, static under a breathless sky.

The sandstone outcrop to the south lay exposed and wet, glistening like jewels. Families were stippled over the rockpools, and across the sandy waterfront mothers were propped up next to small foraging toddlers. Older children crashed squealing through the shallows. Others again walked a tightrope of jagged reef, arms flapping, on their search for sea urchins and tiny nipping crabs.

Mary was left to guard the picnic basket as her family peeled off into the water; her father and Penelope and the children at the tideline, Joe deeper, charging out to paddle angry, stiff-handed strokes. Ordinarily, she would be out there with him. Following his feet as they churned through the eddying water, the reefy bottom a blurred dark mass beneath, the thrill of the cold unknown sending ripples of delicious fear through her. Ordinarily, she would not be seen dead perched on a towel like another item in the family's brightly coloured beach detritus.

As if to awaken her from a dream, the baby rolled and shifted within her, summoning some long-forgotten memory of riding the rollercoaster at Luna Park. She had this instinct to touch her belly, to form a cup with her hand, a first tentative step towards one day holding the child, but to do so would have been revealing. Would have been downright wrong, in fact.

No, she would not think of the life form within her. She would think about something else. Anything else. Sully emerged – or at least an idea of Sully – like a raging geyser. She could hold him back, the idea of him, for long periods of time. But then, without warning, he was there just as he was now, all eager skin, feverish to the touch, aglow in the night, in the dark, in the infinite reaches of her seditious memory.

She shrugged the thought off and staggered to her feet. In the shoal of a sandbar, Penelope was huddled over Sallyann, who was digging for pipis. Nearby, her father was swinging Robert through the shallows, little legs flinging wildly, metronome style, a gleeful howl catching in the open air. They *were* happy, she thought. In their own way.

Joe appeared then, hobbling out of the water drenched and icy-pale, coming up to where Mary stood. He turned back to the horizon and rubbed a hand vigorously over his wet hair, releasing a spray of saltwater. He was larger than her, much larger, with a stocky, thick-limbed physique that was once athletic, then emaciated, now simply out of shape.

'Howdy.'

'Partner.'

'No swimming for the pudding club, hey?'

She smiled a small bitter smile, and they stood there a moment, their last conversation still alive between them. Finally, Joe said, 'Aw, c'mon now. Let's not quarrel.'

'Fine.'

'And I'm sorry about . . . before.'

'All right.'

'It's just . . .' She could feel him searching for the words. Time hung still and innocent between them, as if there was nothing there at all to sift through. Then, at last, he landed on the words. 'You never talk about what it was like.'

That thought again of Sully naked, a glowing pelt in the unlit night. What could she say about Japan? Which words could she actually turn out that in any way resembled the truth?

'Yes I do.'

'No, you don't.' He dug a toe into the sand, unearthed a wet clod of dark matter. 'Every time it comes up, you . . . you . . . change the subject, or talk about the dances and the picnics and the damned weather. Oh, it was so cold, Joe, or so blazing hot. Or you wouldn't believe how sticky it was. Who bloody cares about the humidity, Mare?'

His eyes flashed with an indeterminate heat. A look so fierce she could only turn away from it.

'I can't talk to you about this,' she said in a small voice. 'You won't understand.'

He let out a pointed laugh. 'Oh really?'

'Yes.'

'I – of all people – won't understand?'

'I should think not, no.' Another thought came to her then, charged by an irrational sense of injustice. 'Besides, you don't talk about it either. The war and the camps and all that.'

Joe laughed, a mad burst of mirth that spewed out of him. 'You've got to be shitting me.'

'Well, you don't.'

'It's different, Mare.'

'How? How is it different?'

He remained silent, the side of his face motionless save for the slow blink blink of an eyelid.

'How am I supposed to know it's different when you never utter a word?'

'It just bloody well is,' he said with an acid totality.

Of course she knew it was different. She'd read enough in the papers. Had seen the feeble size of him when he came off the ship. She knew of the disease and the mud and the back-breaking work. The dead friends and the cruel guards and the endless days of facing into the great yawning chasm of one's own imminent death. The fact that she'd suggested otherwise, hinted at the idea of her trip being anything at all like his trip was utterly ludicrous, hateful even.

And yet at the same time, for some reason she could not and might never comprehend, she felt justified in saying the words.

She stole a glance back at him and saw that all the fight had gone from his face and body. He was just a sad quiet man on a beach, deep depressions beneath his sea-reddened eyes, the booze beginning to show in a veined web across his cheeks. A man with no work, no family of his own, a father who only barely tolerated his laggard son. Just the horses and his friends at the track to keep him sane.

His desolation somehow made the words come easier. 'All right, I'll tell you,' she said. 'I was so happy there I could have stayed forever.'

He nodded slowly. 'Because of this Sully fella?'

'Yes.'

'And the people, the Japs?'

'They were kind, all right? I liked them.'

'Jesus, Mare.' He snapped his head away and lengthened his spine like he was taking the force of an invisible punch. 'You went over there to give 'em hell and you came back some crazy convert. It's enough to make a bloke crook in the guts.'

'I'm sorry,' she said. 'I didn't mean for it to be this way.'

Had she gone there to give them hell? She could hardly recall a reason now; that time was a strange, otherworldly blur.

Joe made a grunting noise. He seemed to have noticed something on the horizon, but when she followed his gaze there was nothing to take in but the far plane of the water, deep blue against pale sky.

'I said I'm sorry.'

For a moment she thought he would remain mute, so sealed off did he appear, but then his mouth was opening and words, quiet words, were coming from him.

'You ever eaten a rat just to survive, Mare?'

She felt her chest force out a breath.

'Have you?' he said, turning on her. And louder now. 'Have you?'

'No.'

'You know what gangrene smells like, do you?'

'No,' she whispered.

'You know what a corpse looks like when it's been beaten so bad you couldn't say which poor bastard it belongs to?' He turned his dark mean eyes back to the horizon. His jaw was as tight as a steel trap. 'Right. Didn't think so.'

He broke away from her and moved towards their dune of towels. Snatched one up and began to scrub himself savagely.

'So don't come at me with that "they were kind" baloney, Mare. Don't you bloody dare.'

Days and weeks went by. A warm late autumn yielded to a cool early winter. In Japan, the enormous camellia and azalea bushes, the daffodils and jonquils, would only just be commencing their cycle of wonder, while in Melbourne the trees had been reduced to rangy, vulnerable things.

The coastal gales arrived with a satisfying force and through the bay window Mary watched them fuse with silver sheets of tinsel rain. They battered the old home's windowpanes and snapped away the last fronds of the crepe myrtle. Low-lying streets in the area were flooded but Pearson Street, being higher and wider, was spared.

Joe found ever more urgent reasons to stay away – the de Groot brothers were in from Tassie, the old farrier Bob McNaughton was looking for an apprentice, there was a promising mudlark paying long odds. All of it was muttered with the grim bravado of the helpless punter, trapped in that seam between hope and despair. Mary did not try to convince Joe of a better life, nor did they speak of Japan again. She simply nodded and smiled and watched him pull on his raincoat, his warmest hat, wrap a tartan scarf around his neck and disappear out into the bleak wet streets.

One evening in late May, after supper, Penelope appeared at the verge of Mary's room, silken and radiant in a cream nightdress. She cleared her throat at Mary, who was seated on the bed with a book in hand.

'Yes?'

The stepmother pursed her lips and leaned an elegant hand against the door jamb. One hipbone could be seen through her nightdress, jutting at a sharp angle.

'Your father,' she announced with importance. 'Well, he says you'll stay home now.'

Mary could not think what to say in return.

'Did you hear me? No more outings.'

'I heard you.'

Penelope sniffed out a small thinking sound. 'You've been lucky, I suppose. Being able to conceal your condition until now. It's the fullness of your hips. And your . . . breast plate being rather . . .' She waved a hand up and down by way of description. 'Elongated.'

Her tone was not altogether unkind. It was true that Penelope rarely understood how her own words were received by others. Even at school, she'd stood out as slightly odd; too proud, and mostly disinterested in her peers. Had she not been so beautiful, she might indeed have been friendless.

'Perhaps you're right,' Mary said in an attempt to move the conversation along.

'But now . . . well, look at you.'

Mary gazed down at her middle, shocked anew to find the shape of her belly round and protruding, almost saggy in appearance under her greying flannel, like a smelly old animal pouch.

'What would people think?' Penelope asked in summary, her face brightening in the most unusual way. It could honestly have been that she and Mary were confidantes in the same conspiracy, the baby their happy secret.

In truth, this dynamic wasn't entirely Penelope's fault. Had Mary not planned to marry Thomas in '41, her father might never have had the urge to remarry. The timing was quite remarkable. Weeks into her courtship with Thomas, her father was suddenly talking about that 'lovely young Penelope' from the women's group at church. That being the same Penelope whose mother had been friendly with Mary's mother when they were young women.

Her father had said these were all signs of a healthy relationship. In a way, they were already knitted together. The union would be seamless. And it would be another person to look out for him in his old age, so that Mary could focus on making a home for Thomas and their future children. He had it all planned out, founded on sound logic. But of course, life rarely followed logic and almost never ran to plan.

The following morning, with the children on the floor rifling through a pile of costume jewellery, Penelope pulled two button-down smock dresses from the back of her wardrobe. They were oversized cotton numbers, daubed with garish fruit patterns.

She held one up to Mary's chest. 'See. That'll do, won't it?'

Mary gazed in the long mirror at the sack shape, adorned with huge green apples and topped by her own tiny, pale face. It so closely resembled a clown ensemble Mary felt she might break down and weep.

Oblivious, Penelope turned back to the bed and began to remove the second frock from its hanger. 'I suppose it's too late to worry, but I could have given you some tips had you asked. Mummy always says, add some drama to the neck to avoid blabbing the news.'

'Drama to the neck?' Mary repeated with only the smallest hint of derision.

Penelope ignored her tone. 'Yes. A large necklace or a shawl or some fur, depending on the weather of course.'

'Right.'

'Certainly you'd never wear something like this until you must. A smock fairly screams B-A-B-Y, don't you think?'

Mary turned back to the mirror and murmured in agreement. The absurd outfit and the swollen belly beneath it made her feel even more severed from reality, and she decided she would have to think of herself as an actress performing a role. This at least meant there was an end in sight, that it was just a minor interruption in the grand scheme of a life, and it was true, she had marked the date the doctor gave her on a calendar in her room with a thick, red-inked star. All entertainers must work to a schedule.

The thought was disrupted by a short sharp squeal. Sallyann had unearthed the prettiest of the costume pearls and now dashed out of the room, little Robert crying and waddling urgently behind.

After a moment, a door slammed and the house fell silent.

'Penelope?'

'Yes, dear.'

'Were you frightened?'

Penelope spun towards Mary. She thought a moment, then a moment longer. 'Yes,' she said finally. 'Very much, both times.'

Mary swallowed and turned back to the mirror.

'No one tells you how utterly terrifying it is, so . . . so I hope you don't mind me giving you the harsh truth.'

'No, thank you. I don't mind.'

Mary had been present at both births, and while it had been clear Penelope was in a great deal of pain, the idea that she was also terrified was hard to reconcile. On the first occasion, the Mummy – a former midwife and a wickedly formidable woman – had taken charge, ordering Mary in and out of the room to gather fresh towels and bowls of warm water.

The following day they would learn that, as Penelope laboured, as perhaps hundreds of women across the country laboured in hospital wards and at home, a series of Japanese midget submarines had entered Sydney Harbour under the cover of night. Those had been precarious times, undoubtedly – indeed, it had been the beginning of a period in which they thought war might truly come to them, beyond the abstract, a period in which Mary sometimes looked up at the night sky and imagined the stars as Japanese warplanes come to annihilate them.

But inside the rose-scented master bedroom of 12 Pearson Street, the Mummy had a tyrannous grip on every detail of the proceedings. It was only months later when the girl down the street died in childbirth that it occurred to Mary that, in fact, the whole birthing business was a powerful exercise in denial.

The situation had been far worse the second time, when Robert in his infantile wisdom had announced himself early and with great haste, and the Mummy was caught out, visiting a grieving cousin in the country. Far from seeming terrified, Penelope had taken command, locking herself in the master ensuite and barking orders through the keyhole, only flinging open the door at the last moment to allow Mary the job of catching the purple slimy creature as it slid from the grunting, panting animal thing that had possessed Penelope's body.

'You didn't seem frightened.'

Penelope screwed up her mouth in such a way as to indicate humility. Then, quickly, surely, the veil of nobility descended, and she gave a little toss of her head. 'Well, there's no good in showing it, is there?'

A strange tenderness moved through Mary then. For Penelope and her social ineptitude, but also for this difficult bond they shared. And she was remembering how Penelope every so often had said, in her own queer way, something in Mary's defence. It had been Penelope, after all, who'd convinced her father on the dental training: *She needs a project, Gerry. We all need a project.* Why hadn't Mary remembered this side of Penelope until now? Why hadn't that thought stuck?

After that, Mary spent most of her time watching the children while Penelope ran errands, and the rest of her waking hours reading or watching the outside world through the window in her room. Joe coming and going from the property. Her father off to meet clients. Penelope and the children all spick and span in their finest. There was so much watching on, so much voyeurism, that some days she could barely feel the edges of herself.

June came and went. July also. The miserable weather intensified, with the odd wild thunderstorm blowing in from the bay. As each approached, the old woman over the road could be seen scampering about her front yard in the drizzle, pulling down wooden shutters and securing loose items. According to Mary's father, the poor dear had raised all her children in British New Guinea and had never been quite able to extract the memory of the tropics from her mind.

In her seclusion, memory was also the lens by which Mary had begun to encounter the world. There was so little 'now' – no outings, no visitors, nothing much to dwell on except the future and the past, and the future was unthinkable, unimaginable, a shut-off quadrant of her mind.

She pored over the paper for any hint of Japan or of Sully, but the reports were small, unsatisfying. The public's interest in the occupation had waned so substantially, now there were just brief accounts of members returning home and the curious phenomenon of Australian men marrying Japanese girls, against government prohibition. One young private had even been imprisoned.

August showed up in spite of everything, and so too a letter that Penelope pushed under Mary's door. It was encased in a fairy-floss pink envelope, the words scrawled in familiar lively loops. A quick scan of the myriad stamps plastered over its surface revealed the item had been lost in the postal system for some time due to an incomplete address. Before Mary had even ripped the thing open, she had the cold sinking thought: Noreen.

The letter began with the usual pleasantries and worries. *I do hope your dear father has pulled through. We were all quite besides ourselves when we learned of your hasty departure. It must have taken you by tremendous surprise, you left in such a hurry.* She went on to describe their Christmas – *inedible turkey roll, roast spuds, beans* – and an inventory of occupation gossip including *a terrible turn for poor Ida.* Jimmy had been *caught by the provost doing unspeakable things with a Jap girl in one of those nasty shipping containers down by the docks – can you imagine?* – and in a matter of days would be shipped home in disgrace. Ida had been *terribly stoic in the face of such indignity* and was *already rather taken by a new RAAF fella stationed over at Iwakuni.*

The letter carried on and on, three more pages of cheerful shapes, before Noreen finally came to the true point of the exercise. Macalister had proposed. He had waited for the full moon in the first month of the year – an auspicious time, or so Noreen believed. He had taken her by car up into the foothills to stand in a snowy field at night with the enormous moon hanging over their heads. He'd got down on one knee. *In the mucky old slush no less!* An owl had apparently hooted its approval. Afterwards, they'd celebrated with a swig of scotch and a quarter-pound block of Cadbury's chocolate that Macalister had secured through a new arrival. Not once that evening had he complained about *his rather soggy trouser leg. Oh, I still can't quite believe my luck, Mare. The most handsome man on the most handsome of nights, proposing to me!*

To define her own reaction as envy would have been to flatten pain into something too simple. No, it was not envy. Not precisely. It was mostly just sadness, a terrible aching lonely hopeless sadness. The kind of sadness that made you want to put away the letter and never allow yourself to think of it again. Most unhelpfully of all, it was the kind of sadness that brought Sully to mind, that made her wonder if a letter etched in his hand was likewise lost in the post-war chaos of the postal system, doing laps around the country in search of her. And then she thought, with abhorrent clarity, that there was no letter of that kind and there never would be, because of what she had done, just up and leaving like that, without even the most basic of notes left for him. It had been a deeply hurtful thing to do but also, incontrovertibly, proper and right.

The following week, as the weather improved, Mary's long days lengthened further. Penelope took the children for more ambitious outings, to the zoo and the city and for high teas with other ladies, and Mary was left for desperate, interminable hours to examine the choices she had made and, indeed, the choices she had not.

There was now, in her consciousness, a before time. A cloudy nebulous place filled with paper-walled homes and the smell of seaweed and men in uniforms and Sully. A whole cosmos that existed right before she betrayed herself. She was too naive back then to recognise the deceit she'd exacted on herself. But now, with the advantage of time and calamity, she understood that she'd allowed herself only the smallest taste of freedom. All those advances towards self-determination – getting herself out of her father's house, not an easy task, and then halfway around the world! – and she'd thrown it away before it had even really begun. She had taken possession of herself, seized the vessel of her own body and filled it up so there could be no other story.

And although she knew she should, absolutely should, turn the shame inward, towards the baby as well as herself, and that she should hate this growing body beyond any measure, instead as the weeks passed the loneliness began to spawn queer ideas of love and anarchy and, dare she even think it, motherhood.

Some nights, when it was dark and soundless in the house, when everyone was asleep but her and the baby that kicked and kicked, sometimes then she was consumed with memories so lost to the crannies of her mind they felt, now that they were exhumed, like new experiences. There were images of her mother, only she appeared as a spook. The family album proved that in life Carol had been tall, handsome, dark-haired, with high cheekbones and a stern line for a mouth. In contrast, the dream mother was wispy at the edges, vaporous, and smiling, a pale gleaming face flashing with laughter. The dream mother seemed to be embracing a small girl, Mary perhaps, bringing the girl into her body, swaddling her, then letting her go, letting her pass from her fingers. And she was clapping then, and throwing her laughing face back. 'Brava, darling! Brava!' There was nothing more than this, just a vague sense of a mother delighted by a child. And the swelling feeling of connection; a scion grafted onto rootstock.

One evening, after Robert was asleep, Sallyann was sent as an errand girl up to the top floor of the old house. Mary had been summoned, Sallyann said, to their father's study. She was wanted. Now.

This was a rare event. It had happened like this perhaps a handful of times in Mary's life, always in exceptional circumstances: marriage, death, etc. And so Mary knew to brace herself. She hurried to pull a dressing gown around the shameful, unconcealable roundness of her belly and shuffled downstairs.

He sensed her presence outside the study even before she had knocked.

'Mary?'

The hinge made a yawn as she pushed the door open. The study was lit only by two desk lamps, one on either side of her father's seated body, and the recesses of the room, the oak escritoire and the ancient spinning globe from her childhood, stood practically in darkness. The silver back of her father's head was bowed over a large accounts book, a pen held aloft in thoughtful enterprise. He did not turn to her.

'I've been a busy beaver, Mary.' He spoke in a clipped, proud voice, and for a moment there was a hint of the man he used to be. The one who would sweep her hair from her eyes and pretend with a playful strike to steal her nose.

'Yes, father.'

'Roger and I have been discussing the arrangements.'

'All right.'

'For when the time comes.'

He raised his head. In profile, she could see he was not so playful after all, more absorbed in the process of putting things right. He looked towards the darkened window. Smudges of inky leaves swayed in the night.

'Roger has an aunt, a widow, with a house in the Ranges. It sits empty for half the year or more. We can pay her a small fee, make use of the place for a few days.'

'I'm not sure I understand . . .' She took a seat in the leather armchair adjacent to her father's desk.

'Must I spell it out? For when you're discharged from the hospital, Mary.'

'Oh, I see. I thought I'd perhaps stay . . . here.'

He did not respond to this thought. His patience with her, with this situation, was rapidly diminishing.

'Joe will drive you up,' he continued. 'Tess can join you when you're ready.'

'Join me? Why?'

He huffed out an exasperated sigh. He was clearly thinking how to say what needed to be said tastefully. 'The difficult thing is, Mary . . . Tess hasn't the faintest idea what to do with a baby. She'll need tuition.'

Mary felt her face buckle into a smile. Why this comment was so amusing was hard to say. Only that it was. 'Tuition, father?'

He gathered up his pen and sighed again. 'You know damn well what I mean. Her mother isn't here. And you've had all that experience with the little ones. You'll need to . . . show her the ropes.'

Mary nodded and looked away. 'I see. The ropes.'

'Discretion, Mary. That's the guiding principle here.'

'Yes, father.'

'We must think of the children, and Penny.'

'Yes, of course.'

There was a moment of silence while Mary's father began to scrawl again in a column of the book. She made to speak, hesitated. Waited a moment longer.

'It's just,' she offered in a low, small voice. 'I've been thinking too.'

He murmured a non-reply.

'Maybe there's a way, father?'

'What kind of way?'

'I shan't be a bother, father. I shan't. But perhaps, if you were able to . . . give me a little money, just a little to get started, it could be a loan, I would pay you back, and I could go somewhere.'

He spun towards her with an alarmed jerk of the neck. He was utterly perplexed by her, that much was evident. But deeper still, in the eyes and the downward pull of the face, there was also the shame.

'I could keep it,' she whispered.

'Keep it,' he repeated, as if she'd just uttered words in a foreign language.

'Yes.' She was trying very hard to manage her voice, to sustain some semblance of professional efficiency. If she didn't alert him to the fact that this was a matter of the heart, perhaps he would simply understand it as a business proposal. 'Yes, keep it,' she said again.

'Don't be absurd, Mary.' He released a deep mournful grunt this time, returned to the book on the desk. 'Keep it,' he muttered to himself. 'What kind of nonsense.'

It was nonsense, of course. But once she had said it aloud, it was impossible to ignore. The next day she spent Robert's nap time sitting in the living room by the open fire, drawing up a budget.

In two neat columns, she listed all the things she might need and their associated costs. She knew from the country girls she went through nurses training with that there were rooms in the city going for less than seven pounds a month. She already had a good twenty saved up from her work at the Dew Drop, and she could look for shifts at the hospital, perhaps leave the child with Penelope two or three days of the week.

Even as she was transcribing this plan, though, she knew it was the most preposterous trick she'd ever played on herself. When she was finished, she held the sheet of paper up to the light and took a long hard look at the shapes on the page. Another future, spelled out in black and white. Then she sighed, folded the paper up into a neat rectangle, folded it again into an even smaller square, and fed it directly into the eager flames of the fire.

Birth came like this – not as a body thing, but a mind thing. A creeping sensation. An unravelling. The husk of the world being peeled back. At first, astonishingly, there was no pain, only knowledge borne from some deep and abiding place.

She was sitting in the low embroidered armchair in the corner of her room when it happened. Slowly, she placed her book on the little round table. Rested a hand on the great round bluff of her belly. Downstairs, there was the purr of family, muted by a barricade of ceiling plaster and timber joists. It was afternoon and a waxy light was pouring in through the curtains, falling in a bright pool on the rug. It was not so much panic that she felt, more a vigilance. Her hearing had become sharper, the skin across her palms more sensitive.

She sat like that, listening to her body, locked into the moment. She tried to imagine what the next few hours held, but that was hardly straightforward; the details had been released under censorship and all she had was an entirely outlandish idea that a baby would come, one way or another, for right or wrong.

Soon enough, the pain began. She thought she should call out for help but stopped herself. Perhaps she would just sit there a little longer. The fear had finally curdled into something real, something comprehensible. There was a sense that to penetrate the threshold of this moment, to turn stillness into action, would be to invite terror into her life. If she just went on sitting, not moving, with the afternoon light flooding in, then she could avert disaster, she could throw destiny off its tracks.

At some point, when the pool of light on the rug had faded and the room had abandoned its colour, she heard the creak of the stairs, then footfalls in the corridor. The door swung open and, framed against darkness and with terrifying proficiency, Penelope grasped the situation.

'Oh dear.' She snort-laughed. 'Were you not going to tell us?'

'No, I . . .'

'Thought you could just have it here and sneak it out the window, did you?'

Mary didn't respond because she couldn't. The air rushing in and out of her lungs – the peeling back of the husk – was so intense, so pronounced, even shame didn't register.

She heard Penelope, already out the door, dashing down the stairs, crying, 'Bun! Oven! Now!'

Looking back, she would know that action had taken place, undeniable action bringing her ever closer to the horrors of that day. There was her father and Joe coming into the room, helping her down the stairs. There was Joe in the car, silent, the ridge of his brow set like bronze. There were streetlights lit up for evening, shivering as they passed, and there were other drivers in other cars, oblivious, heading home for tea. There was Joe at the hospital desk giving a false name, saying he was the father. But she couldn't make sense of any of it. The pain had pushed everything out. She did not so much feel her body as become it.

As time passed, feeling and thought receded from twilight into a vast black maw of nothingness. There were nurses handing her pills and wrapping her head in a towel. There were walls tilting and collapsing. Light sparking, wheeling. Sound reflecting in on itself like an infinity mirror at the fairground. The sharp snap of leather that meant her legs and wrists were immobile. The walls of the cot a cage. There was the becoming of an animal, the terrible, long howls that eructed from the depths of it. A terrible crushing thirst. A thrashing about. The smell of shit and piss and vomit. There were long periods of solitude when her soul rose like a leviathan, seeking vengeance for all the world's crimes, the maimed women and dead children with their bloated faces and burnt skin hanging loose in sheets, piles of bodies, the stench of death, the world shredded and torn. And it was seeking order too, seeking a mother, any which one would do. And it was seeking grace, god's grace, the grace of touch and love and oblivion and the hot skin of a man against her and inside her, pressing his lips to her like it mattered.

Time went on and on and on like this. Interminable hours of nothing splintered through by the unabridged history of human anguish.

Finally, the madness retreated. Sound and vision welded themselves back to real time. And then a baby, *the* baby, was placed in her arms. 'A girl,' a voice said. Of course. A girl who was bundled tight in a white cotton blanket and who, in that instant, opened her eyes. Who looked at Mary with such ferocious love, looked at her like she'd never look away.

Mary woke the next morning in a bright room, feeling small and shaky, rootless, the fringes of herself frayed and woolly. The memories from the night before were almost unreachable, more dreamscape than life, but there were raw welts across her wrists and that's how she knew it wasn't a dream at all.

The baby ward was a long room, with a dozen or more metal-framed beds set at intervals under the windows and along a blank wall. A nurse was shifting between the cots, pulling open curtains, letting in the new day. Mary instinctively shut out the light and rolled away, but somewhere behind her eyelids she'd captured the image of other women sprawled in beds.

The closing of the eyes did the trick, and she drifted back into a dreamless state. She was woken again, some hours later, by the chatter of women, the growl of metal bearings, the small squawk of a baby.

A voice spoke. 'Mary, *Mary*. Time to eat.'

And so she sat up, sipped the soup and chewed the bread she was given. Across the aisle, a young woman with rollers in her hair was bent around a baby, cooing. Another, a few feet away, was blathering on about her new kitchen design; all the knotty pine cast off and a sleek, linoleum look installed. 'French blue,' the girl said. 'Voted colour of the season in three separate magazines.'

The nurses came and went, insisting that Mary eat, drink, sleep, eat, drink, sleep, and she did as she was asked, submissively, like a child. She hadn't the energy to fight them. From time to time, they brought the baby in, but the visits were fleeting and there seemed to be an unspoken agreement that she would need to get stronger before she could handle the child on her own.

The day passed. Then another. She gathered the other women in the room were also following this strict nurse-appointed routine, but she could not bring herself to look at them, and they naturally turned to each other instead.

Finally, on the third day, Mary was feeling better, so an older nurse showed her things she already knew; how to prepare the bottle and hold it at the right angle, how to secure the nappy pins to avoid spiking the baby. Mary went through the motions, never making a fuss, pretending with all her might.

Under the turned-back brim of her starched cap and severe hairline, the nurse had the lithic, unsparing features of someone who had seen it all and then some. Mary knew the mystery of the missing husband could not have escaped her attention. Still, the matter was not discussed, and they worked alongside one another easily, like two old hands on a factory floor, speaking only rarely. All the while, Mary was soaking in the sight of the child, the peachy melt of her skin, the folded dark eyes, the pelt-like brows as soft as velvet; and she was thinking how to behave like a normal mother, the kind that has all the time in the world.

Near the end of the day, as the nurse gathered the child back into her arms, she said, 'Is there a name yet, Mary? For the chart.'

And Mary said the first plausible thing she could grasp at. 'We haven't decided yet.'

Lowering the swaddled babe into the trolley crib, the nurse gazed up at Mary for a moment, dropped her lower lip a tiny degree. She was thinking whether to challenge the lie; there were any number of ways she could put Mary in her place. But then she seemed to stop herself, grimaced a kind of acceptance, and moved with the baby out of the room.

On the fourth day, Mary was woken in the early morning by an agonising pain in her chest. She began to weep and could not stop, no matter how she tried. A pit had formed in the gully between her engorged breasts, but the pain had refracted like light through a cut diamond, striking out through her body, to the tips of her fingers, to the very limits of her person, almost righteous in its intensity. Somehow, she understood the sensation was linked to her own mother; she was grieving not only for the girl, but also for another relationship that ended before it had begun. A whole lineage of rupture, right back to god knows when.

She rolled away from the other women and cried and cried and cried. The rock-faced nurse came and went, offering mild remedies like, 'It'll pass.' But Mary knew it couldn't and it wouldn't, and the nurse's words only brought on another keening lament.

On the morning of day five, a nurse informed Mary she had visitors in the day room. 'Best jolly yourself up, dear.'

Mary nodded, smiled. 'Yes,' she said.

As she donned her dressing gown, pulled back her hair, dabbed a little red on her cheeks and lips, she was almost able to imagine a husband waiting for her in the next room. Maybe it was Sully. Maybe it was some other man. In any case, it was not until she followed the nurse and the baby crib into the day room that she allowed the story to fall away. Sitting at a table in the far corner of the room, outlined by a vivid stage of purple iris out the window, were Joe and Father Flaherty. Their large bodies and dark clothing brought reality back with a shuddering heft.

Father Flaherty stood and moved towards her, arms swept outward. 'You look well, Mary. Oh, and look at this little one.'

Behind him, Joe was still seated. He rapped a knuckle on the table with a dull clip, didn't even glance at the child. Mary came to join them at the table, and they all settled into the chairs. The girl in the crib was within arm's reach, but she was silent, sleeping, and the scene seemed to go on without her.

Father Flaherty was gazing around the room. His face was bright, his high cheekbones flush with colour. His hair was swept back into a rather stylish wave.

'This is a bit flash, isn't it?'

'Yes,' she said, forcing a smile that hurt.

'Not a sterile kind of place at all.'

'No,' she agreed.

Father Flaherty seemed afraid to make eye contact with her, and he went on looking around. Finally he mustered his strength, cleared his throat. The tone that emerged was flat and contrived; the voice of a much older man, someone who Father Flaherty had learned from, perhaps, or fashioned himself after. 'So, Mary,' he said. 'We just thought we'd have a little chat. See how things are going.'

'All right.'

Joe was still eyes to the table, knuckle rapping – clip, clip. A lock of hair had fallen over his brow.

'Your father tells me you were having some trouble, in the weeks leading up to the . . . huh.'

She felt her mouth fall open. No words emerged.

'Well, Mary, he seemed to think you were harbouring some ideas of . . . fiction. Of how things might be.'

Although they were the only people in the room, he was speaking at a discreet volume, just a few degrees bolder than a whisper.

'You can talk to me, Mary. This is just between you, me and god.'

'And Joe,' she pointed out.

'Well, yes, and Joe.'

She smiled, let the silence linger.

Father Flaherty went on. 'It could very well be worse than this, Mary. You know that, I imagine.'

'Yes, yes, I do.'

'Boy, some of the girls I see . . .' His voice trailed off in a long breath, almost a whistle. 'You're lucky to have a good family willing to help.'

'Yes, Father.'

'They're protecting you,' he said. 'You know that also?'

She didn't respond. She understood this task. She only had to smile, nod, and smooth the way. And yet a strange contrariness had come over her. The kind of feeling that makes you want to touch a hot element, just to see if it will burn. She could feel the heat of her stare directed right at him, vulgar in its intensity, downright juvenile in fact.

'Is there anything you'd like to say?'

'No, Father.'

'You won't do anything foolish will you, Mary?'

'No, Father.'

The moment between them tarried. Father Flaherty took stock of her and this placid rebellion. His handsome face was hard to read.

'I'll tell you what.' He shifted back in his seat, crossed one leg over the other in a simple conciliatory action. 'What we could do is . . . if you prefer . . .' He was speaking very slowly, like this way she might truly, finally understand. 'There's a home I know of not far from here, for girls like you. Would that make things easier?'

The strength of his words made even Joe look up. She felt all the power in her gaze vanish, just like that. She had been neutralised.

'No, Father, that won't be necessary.'

He stood then, and Joe followed. As they moved past the crib, Father Flaherty gave another passing glance to the girl and muttered, 'Sweet little thing.' And then to Mary, 'Enjoy your time with her, Mary. This is how we grow in god's image.'

Joe turned back, just the once, and frowned a goodbye.

She was left in the day room, dazed, one hand upon the side of the crib, with the spring sunshine bleeding in bright shards through the windowpane and blooms of purple iris buds jeering at her.

A few days later, Joe came to collect her and the child. The rock-faced nurse, who had by now made an accurate calculation on the state of Mary's life, said with a deep ironic slant to her voice, 'Your *husband's* here to take you home, dear. Best not leave him idle.'

Mary was bundled into the Chev without a second to mull over the significance of this inflection point. Joe, flat-featured but not unkind, had secured her bags in the boot and placed the baby in her bassinet on the floor behind the driver's seat. The move from the warm hospital into the cooler air had disturbed her and she was awake, grizzling and threshing about in her blankets like a trapped animal. Mary managed to squeeze an arm between the seats and pat the child into submission as they exited the car park and headed east, passing under a succession of Dutch elms whose shadows flickered across the windscreen.

They were a good few streets away when it came upon Mary, the sense of escape, a brilliant aching deliverance. Of course, it was madness. And yet she felt it, the girl and her, away now, spared the nurses' routine, the other women's eyes, that undercurrent of scrutiny and performance. Now it was just them and the world, and as it stood in this instant, she did not really care for the world. If she pushed right back into the seat and swivelled her neck just so, she could see the girl's face in the bassinet. For a moment they locked eyes, and Mary smiled at her. Freedom.

They drove with only the wind whistling through the air vents to keep them company. Eventually, Joe began to speak in a plain, unassuming tone. He talked for a time about the house in the hills they were driving to, the layout of the rooms, the garden and so forth. Then he moved onto the way things would work. Tess up tomorrow. Two nights more. Home Sunday. Penelope had made Mary a pie. It was in the boot in a box. Also, she'd turned up more teats and bottles at the back of the cupboard, forgotten but not in bad nick.

There was no mention of the meeting with Father Flaherty, and Mary was too pleased to dwell on the betrayals of the past. She wanted only to soak up this brief period of time; the girl in the bassinet, the motion of the car as they passed by unknown house after unknown house, street upon street, suburb upon suburb – somehow it all together made for an irrational sort of happiness.

They arrived at the house before midday. It was a small cottage nestled between two hills, beset by an unruly mass of trees and shrubs of both the native and mother-country kind. A small assortment of daffodil blooms had reared their crowns under the windowsills, and rising up behind the house like an enormous, furrowed wall were the foothills of the Ranges, sheathed almost entirely in vivid green ferns.

Joe said only, 'C'mon then,' before climbing out of the car and busying himself with the luggage. He left Mary to manage the bassinet, and again, at the door and in the house, there was this sense that he would not look upon the girl, that it was better this way, not to think too long on the matter of his niece. Mary followed him into the first bedroom, a musty space decorated simply with an embroidered bedspread and lace curtains. He turned to her.

'Hell, there are worse joints.'

'Yes,' she agreed.

He seemed on the verge of saying more but stopped himself, and in the end the only sound he emitted was a thoughtful little huff that could have meant anything at all.

He vacated the premises just as quickly as one could, leaving Mary with the baby and the long afternoon to stare down. She was not altogether unhappy with the solitude, she told herself. In fact, she decided, she should be rather pleased to have this little house in the hills, this lull in proceedings, to gather the stray parts of herself into some kind of bundle resembling her.

After the sound of the car had gone, she came to stand over the bassinet that'd been deposited in the hallway. She stood there for a long time, watching the breath go in and out of the girl's body. After some hesitation, thinking what she knew of babies – daylight in the day, to help them sleep at night – she moved the bassinet into the sitting room.

Mary occupied herself unpacking her belongings, hanging out the dress and cardigan she'd stowed days ago, back before the girl was wholly a reality, and she sorted through the bag Joe had left in the front bedroom – the girl's things, the bottles and teats.

At some stage of the afternoon, the child woke and Mary tended to her, feeding and changing her, feeling a great deal of satisfaction at the sight of her soft features flagging as she fell back into a deep slumber. Mary returned her to the bassinet and then wandered from room to room. In the kitchen, she stood at the timber bench under the window, looking out upon a small square yard. It was terribly quiet, and with the onset of dusk the forest's bracken and duff had turned into a flat plane of vegetation that seemed to conceal a malevolent force.

Any moment, the girl would cry again, and Mary thought she must nourish herself, sterilise the used bottle, prepare the milk. But suddenly she was more tired than she'd ever imagined possible. Whatever joy she'd felt earlier had evaporated, replaced by a grim clock. She could hear it now, the tolling of time, the seconds, the minutes, the hours, an aphotic creature drumming a claw against the great rostrum of life. She felt herself untether; let herself acknowledge the profound loneliness of this house and this moment. She had but three days to live a whole life.

Around noon of the following day, she heard the Chevrolet on the path outside; a series of violent groans as Joe revved the engine, revved a little more, creeping over the gravel. The sound filled up the house and then it was gone, and the garden was returned to itself, eerie under the surveillance of hidden birds.

Mary tiptoed to the window and through a crack in the blinds caught a glimpse of harbour blue. When she nudged further, there he was, brother Joe, fixed for a moment, one hand still saddled across the steering wheel, frozen by some thought or other. She edged towards the front door, teased it open and stood behind the screen, watching him through the wire. He was reaching for his hat on the passenger seat and climbing out of the car. His movements were timid, almost fearful, she thought, as if he'd been sent to conduct a welfare check at the insane asylum and was not quite sure what he would find.

Traipsing up the path, he couldn't see her – a trick of light on the screen, perhaps – and it was not until the seam on his shirt collar was visible, also the stubble on his chin, the shadows beneath his eyes, that she thought to speak.

'I'm still here,' she said.

He gasped a little flume of air. 'Christ almighty, I didn't see you.'

She swung the screen door open and gazed at him. For some reason she did not move from her place in the doorway, did not invite him in. Perhaps this was her only power.

'No ritual suicide to speak of,' she announced.

'Jesus, Mare.'

'No blood-spattered walls, no pool of guts to clean up.'

His face contorted. 'God, you're dark.'

'What do you expect? Leave a girl out here in the sticks, nothing to do but think and think.'

'Been a long night, has it?'

'You might say that.'

He looked at her now, really looked at her; evaluated the uncoiffed hair, the rumpled nightie, well into the day. And then another thought.

'Where's the baby?' he asked, and before she could muster a word he was pushing past her into the hallway. 'Where is the baby, Mary?' he said again, firmer now.

So, this was a welfare check. She smiled to herself. Even after all she'd been through, she still had a knack for reading people.

Joe shunted between the sitting room, the bedroom, the bathroom, moving swiftly, urgently. She shuffled behind him, powerless to articulate the precise location of the precious cargo. Finally he saw the girl in her bassinet beneath the kitchen window, asleep, bundled in light cotton, almost purring with each in and out breath.

He expelled a long current of air, barely able to conceal his relief. 'All right then.' He brought a hand flat to his chest, then rested the other on the slumbering mound as if to convince himself of the girl's safety.

When he turned to Mary, she could feel the lead weight of her arms against her side. 'What do you take me for?'

'Nothing, Mare.'

'You thought —'

'No, no, I didn't. These are just . . . difficult times. We're all a little on edge.'

'Oh, we are, are we?' A loud, sour chuckle escaped from her mouth. The force of it shook her head from its axis, flushed her cheeks pink. And once it started, it wouldn't be stopped. The laugh went on for several moments. Poured out of her like a tidal wave, one surge after the other, she a mere shell of a thing at its mercy. Joe was staring at her, alarmed. She must have looked insane, she knew. Perhaps she was insane.

Eventually the tide went out and what was left was merely seafoam that welled in her eyes.

Joe reached out a hand. 'Sit down, Mare.' He guided her back into the sitting room, to the couch, and found a blanket to rest over her knees. 'Tess'll be here in a few hours. We need to spruce you up a bit.'

'Yes.'

He laughed lightly. 'Can't very well invite her in looking like this, can you now?'

'No.'

He went into the kitchen to fill the kettle. 'Just need a little spit and polish, that's all,' he called back into the sitting room.

It was no good responding; her voice would only be lost in the stream of water gushing from the tap.

When the tea was ready, Joe carried a single mug back into the room, placed it in front of her and eased his way into one of the armchairs. He'd clearly been thinking how to say the words that needed to be said.

'This is hard, of course.'

She did not respond. What on earth was there to say?

'You're going to feel like this is the worst thing that ever happened to a person, but it's not. It's not even close.'

Despite everything, she knew he was right about that. You could not count the ways in which she had been lucky in this life, or the ways in which other people had suffered more. It was unfathomable mathematics.

He shuffled now in his chair and said, 'You've been through worse, anyhow.'

She looked up at him. She could not imagine what he meant. 'When?'

'You know, when Mother died.'

'Well . . . it was hardly the same.'

He let out a strange sound. 'You didn't utter a word for months, Mare.'

'No,' she said aghast, although she could not think why she would resist this notion. Even though it was unlikely to be a lie, the words that came out next were, 'That's not true.'

'It is. You don't remember?'

She was silent, thinking.

'Everyone was terribly worried about you. It went on for months and months. So long, the doctors thought . . .' His voice trailed off, which she took to be kindness.

'How did I not know?' she whispered.

He leaned back into the chair, stretched his arms down the armrests until his big thick fingers came to cup the ends like stoppers. 'I guess we're not much good at raking over old territory, are we?'

'No,' she said.

'Before, beforehand . . . you were a right little show pony. Always making us laugh with some dance or jingle.'

'Really?'

'Yup, little performer you were.'

She was utterly mystified by this information, because it felt so far from her or anything that was true, but also she was remembering the visions she'd had of her mother, laughing, clapping, saying, 'Brava, darling.'

'Anyway,' Joe went on. 'It was hard. You were little. But you got through it. The point is, you got through it.'

He examined her face for a moment longer.

'Aw, c'mon, Mare. It's time to be brave now.'

She nodded, felt the tears welling up again and blinked them away.

'So this is what you do, all right? You stand up, and you go and put on a frock, and you do your hair real nice, and you come back out here, ready to smile and make this okay for the both of you.'

'Yes, all right.'

'Piece of piss.'

She huffed out a laugh of sorts.

'Just like that. Dress, hair, smile.'

She took in a deep breath and pulled her battered bones to standing.

At four, Mary was seated in a wicker chair on the back porch, watching small brownish birds dart and flicker in a shadowy corner of the garden. She was decked out in a peach square-necked dress, her hair curled and set like a silly doll. Her hands lay motionless in her lap, fingers slightly open, the creases on her palms visible. There was a cup of tea beside her, a fresh one, again made by Joe. It rested within arm's reach on a sun-bleached stump, and yet it sat untouched, untasted, seeming to exude bitterness.

In the time taken to bathe and dress and paint her face, a strange aura had settled upon her. Even though she knew and could see that her body existed there below the neck, she could not make the necessary connection from brainstem to muscle, and so what was easier was to just sit in this deathly inertness and not even try to break through the veil that had fallen over her.

Tess's car announced itself on the gravel outside precisely on schedule. Wheels crunching, engine trembling to silence. Mary listened to the arrival of this firing squad – albeit a femininely attired, nicely scented, politely spoken one – with a rush of adrenaline. She heard through the open door Joe and Tess greet one another in muted tones. There was a good long minute of faint discussion, then shuffling that Mary ascribed to them moving through the house towards the sleeping child, followed by a pause in which they were presumably standing over the babe in pious devotion.

Finally, there was a sudden burst of more talking, and Mary caught the trace of Joe's words – 'a little flat, I'm afraid'. And, a moment later, 'rotten luck'.

In the backyard, a whipbird burst into view, landing on the branch of an orange tree and making a long falling crack of a sound. The sombre alarm of the call filled the garden and Mary's head.

Footsteps. Joe's low thudding and a higher clip-a-clip. The screen door squealed. Tess's frame appeared in the doorway.

Mary found the strength now to engage her muscular system and face her cousin's apple-cheeked, barely contained radiance. The words that came next she could not claim as her own, but were instead issued from some deep, mean, other place. 'So you've come for her, have you?'

A pall came over them. Tess was speechless. She turned to Joe, who angled his head as if to say, *See, I did warn you.* He dealt with Mary's resistance simply by ushering Tess deeper into the garden.

Tess took in a little rasp to equip herself with the necessary courage and stepped onto the porch. 'Hello, Mary dear.' She edged closer.

Mary sighed and finally stood. The women embraced in a kind of ill-fitting mutual arm-grasp that required no intimacy. They were almost but not quite a reflection of their former selves, just months earlier, greeting at the hotel under the bright arched window, minutes away from settling an important accord.

'Isn't it a lovely day,' Tess said. Her travelling case had been deposited in the second bedroom, Mary realised. And then with an added satisfying miserliness she thought: already making herself at home.

'Yes,' Mary agreed. 'Terribly lovely.'

They angled their faces away from each other to gaze upon the garden.

'Warm for September.'

'Indeed.'

A long moment passed.

It was Joe who spoke next. Joe who was unable to bear them a minute longer. 'All right then. You ladies make yourselves at home. The shopping's in the kitchen, hey. And remember, the aunt says no fires this time of year, but there's blankets in the dresser, and . . . and . . . the girl, she'll need a little extra. No cloud cover tonight.'

Tess followed him back into the house, and a few seconds later Mary did the same. In the kitchen, Tess had swept up an apron from somewhere mysterious and was crouched over the shopping bags, gathering potatoes and onions into the bowl of its fabric.

'Is there anything you don't eat, Mary?'

But Mary didn't, couldn't respond. She was already trailing, without volition, up the hall, away from them. She heard Joe answer for her, and give another whispered apology. Of course she should've helped Tess prepare the evening meal, but there was that nasty voice in Mary's head saying, make her work for it.

In the bedroom, the child snuffled with the intrusion and rolled her head away from the glare of the window. Mary stood over the bassinet. Took in her perfection. The glassy half-moon eyelids, ever so lightly trembling. The lips as rosy and silken as the inside of a conch. The round fleshy cheeks. There was no world in which this child, this flawless, untainted, trusting creature, did not belong to Mary. And yet Mary heard that tick of time again, like a bomb in her head. There was tomorrow. And a part of the next day. And then no more.

The thing to do, she thought, was to not let the baby out of her sight. Keep her close. So even though she knew she must not spoil the girl with cuddles, she lifted the sleeping babe into her arms, and they lay together on the bed, listening to Tess's hand thrum the knife against the chopping block in the other room. Mary fell asleep this way, one body bowed around the other, as if still one.

At supper time, the girl was fussy after her feed, so Mary pulled the bassinet up next to the kitchen table and patted a rhythm against her tiny back as they ate.

Tess was chattering on inanely about Roger's plans for their house extension. 'The carpenter advises we wait a few months, and that's quite right, I think.'

'Of course.'

'Everyone seems to have forgotten what a Melbourne spring entails.'

Tess took another bite and chewed. Her fork clinked lightly on the plate once, twice, three times as she gathered up a collection of stray peas.

'Oh!' she cried suddenly. 'You'll never guess what I read in the gazette today.'

'What's that?' Mary could hear how flat and uninterested her voice was, and yet she could not contain the malice.

'A young woman went head over heels into Sydney Harbour yesterday. Fully clothed. Can you imagine?'

'Gee,' Mary muttered.

'The report said she was leaning over the railing of the Manly ferry and just fell right in. She was safe, of course. A boater came by, picked her up, and all was well. But still, fancy that. All those eyes on the ferry, watching you as they chug off into the distance.'

Mary forced a smile.

'It was a funny old write-up, actually. Said she was treated for "shock and immersion". Fancy that. I wonder what the treatment is for immersion.'

'Dry clothes, perhaps.'

Tess let out a loud crack of laughter. 'Oh, Mare, you were always a hoot, weren't you?'

Mary smiled again, and perhaps this time it was almost genuine. Nonetheless, Mary had committed herself to confinement, so as soon as the meal was finished she bundled the child up into her arms and began to move towards the front bedroom, dragging the bassinet behind her.

Tess was on her feet immediately. 'Won't you let me help?'

'No need,' Mary said as she disappeared into the hallway.

Tess of course followed, and when Mary reached the bedroom and spun around she found Tess in the doorway behind her, too polite to cross the threshold. The girl had begun to cry out in big, gasping fits so Mary placed her on the bed and reached for a fresh nappy.

'Will you feed her again?' Tess asked, still trapped in the doorway out of sheer decorum.

'Yes, I suppose so.'

'Could I be of assistance, perhaps?'

'You can warm the bottle.'

'All right.' Tess was out the door and back again within a few minutes, brandishing the glass vessel with an eagerness Mary could barely bring herself to register.

'Thank you, I'll be fine from here.'

Mary bustled Tess through the exit, and before Tess had a moment to argue, the door had been sealed and Mary had returned to the bellowing child. Tess's defeat was almost audible, a thing that seeped through the walls of the small house, but Mary wouldn't allow herself to dwell on that fact, nor the function of the exercise they were engaged in; two women and a baby in a house together. There was a point to all this, and isolating the mother-to-be was hardly it. And yet, Mary was steadfast. She would not think deeply, not for a moment. She lay down on the bed, letting the girl burrow into the crook of her arm and snuffle fervently on the teat. Not for the first or last time did Mary feel a futile little tingle in her breasts.

The morning meal was already spread out on the table and Tess was in full doing mode when Mary and the girl emerged. It was after eight at least; perhaps it was nine. Sunshine was streaming through the kitchen windows in dazzling fragments and illuminating the small round table tucked into the corner of the room, its linen tablecloth, the workaday china plates, the little ceramic salt and pepper shakers made into the image of two women in long dresses and bonnets lugging market goods.

Tess's face stirred at the sight of them. 'Oh, how did you both sleep? Here, please, sit. Shall I take her?'

'No need.' Mary felt her arms tighten around the child.

She let Tess draw the chair for her, though, and furthermore, she let her race around pouring tea and buttering the toast. There was some vague memory of all this inverted, of Mary fussing over Penelope in the days after Sallyann's birth, albeit with less graciousness.

'I think I heard a little peep at four. Is that right?'

'Perhaps,' said Mary, yawning. 'There's really no sense in obsessing over the time. They wake when they wake.'

'Oh, I see. But I thought, well, I was under the impression that keeping baby on schedule was of the utmost importance.'

'A furphy, I'm afraid.' Mary bit into her toast and tried to ignore the superiority that had crept back into her voice.

'Oh.'

'Well, they find their own schedule.'

'I see.'

'And you'll only send yourself mad.'

'All right, I see.'

Mary could feel Tess gazing upon the sleeping girl. But when Mary looked up, right at her, Tess's gaze snapped away.

Finally, after a time, Tess inhaled and said brightly, 'What shall we do today?'

Mary screwed up her face and laughed.

'Oh dear, what did I say?'

'It's only, well . . . one doesn't really *do* anything when one has a small child. She's barely out of the womb.'

'Oh, of course, yes. I know —'

'This is it, I'm afraid.'

'I only thought, well, perhaps a walk.'

'If you think it's too boring, being at home with a child, perhaps this isn't really for you.'

'Oh no, it is. It definitely is for me.'

Mary felt a mean smile spread across her face. She felt her body rise from the seat and her hand gather up the last triangle of toast before she had made the decision to do so. 'I'm still feeling rather tired. I think I'll rest a little more.'

Tess's chair made a loud scrape as she followed suit. 'Could I . . .'

'You could sterilise the bottles.'

'Of course.'

'Use the big pot.'

'Yes.'

'Do you know how? It's rather important it's done right.'

'No, yes, I'm well qualified. I've read all the books. Five minutes at the boil. Use tongs, no touching, clean towel.'

Mary took a moment to really see Tess. Standing there in her lovely pink dressing gown, soft curls falling around high cheekbones, fingers caught in an anxious web at her front. For a moment, Mary almost felt sorry for her. It was a rather unpleasant game, this one. The other adoptive mothers simply popped off to the hospital with their husbands by their side and got handed a baby – a clean slate – never having to think of what came before. To be forced, as Tess was, to confront the damage wrought, to have that on her conscience forever after, and being a kind person as she was, well, Mary could already see how this would haunt her.

She tried hard to soften her tone. 'Make it six minutes, just to be sure.'

Tess nodded. 'All right.'

The day carried on in much the same vein. Mary stayed in the front bedroom, leaving Tess to rattle around the house, diligently retrieving things at her request, cleaning up, preparing meals and cups of tea, sterilising the bottles and scrubbing the soiled nappies. Mary justified all this as some kind of apprenticeship. Had she not done the same for Penelope? Over months, not days, it should be noted. And, truthfully, she did learn a lot in the process. It was a training by osmosis. To be near, to be witnessing it all. It was still valuable, even without the touching and the holding. It meant that when the time came there was an ease there, a comfort with the protocols that made space for the loving and the cherishing.

In the early evening, the baby became fussy and unable to be put down. Again, Tess offered to hold her, to give Mary a moment's peace. Again, Mary declined.

For her part, Tess was beginning to swell with some new emotion. Her movements had become sharper. When she enquired before supper about Mary's meal preferences, her questions were taut, muscular things. She was unusually quiet and careful over dinner, as if her words might expose some dark nadir, and afterwards she crashed the pots and pans around in the sink in a thoroughly un-Tess way.

Far from disturbing Mary, this new rendering of Tess added another gratifying layer to the whole affair. She understood her own cruelty, she truly did. And yet the ticking in her head and the constant piercing cries of the girl, the pacing back and forth across the room, the endless jigging and shushing and patting – it was all so consuming, there was little room left for compassion.

Finally, after Mary had succeeded in calming the tiny tempest inside the girl, Tess appeared at the doorway again.

'Well done,' she said. Her face was rigid, as if she had made a promise to herself that she would not go back on.

Mary let out a long exhale. 'Finally.'

'Mary?'

'Hmm.'

'I have a question, if you'll indulge me.'

'All right.'

'I don't want to intrude, it's only your brother will be here in the morning and . . .'

'What's the question, Tess?'

'Did you have a name in mind?'

Mary felt her face crack into a strange form. 'Oh.'

'I'm sorry, it's none of my business.'

'No, no, it's all right.' Mary felt the tight knot in her chest ease a fraction.

She thought on this for a moment. 'Lillian,' she said finally.

'Oh, that's a lovely name. Do you know a Lillian?'

'No,' she said. 'But a friend of mine did.'

Mary turned her back to Tess and walked to the other side of the room, gently holding a warm hand against the girl's back. When she reached the far wall, she turned and paced back.

'Did you?'

'What?'

'Did you have a name in mind?'

Tess gave a sad smile. 'Oh, no,' she said. 'I haven't . . . wanted to let myself even imagine. In case . . .'

'In case I changed my mind?'

'Yes.' She dropped her gaze and busied herself with a torn nail. 'I suppose it all feels a bit . . . surreal. Trying to imagine her, in my house, with Rodge and I, and you not being there.'

'It's absurd, that's why.'

This made Tess look up and laugh, a real ironic chuckle. 'It's utterly bizarre, isn't it?'

'The strangest thing in the world!'

The force of their laughter, controlled as it was, startled the girl, and both women, in unison and by instinct, brought a finger to their mouths and shushed themselves.

They looked at one another. A moment in time to consider the impossible. And then the girl relaxed back into Mary's chest, and they were left depleted.

Tess cleared her throat. 'I dared not tell you . . . but I had a dream last year, when you were still in Japan. That I would have a daughter that came from a far-off land. She would be given to me, as a gift, swaddled and perfect.' She stymied the cry just as it broke from the surface of her mouth. 'I'm sorry,' she said, turning away and shifting down the hallway. Her faltering voice disappeared into the depths of the dark house. 'I'm sorry. I shouldn't . . .'

Mary stood eerily still. The weightlessness that came over her then was so profound, so complete, she felt she might faint. Never had she felt this light, this obliterated. The dark carcass of the house pitched in towards her, and without cause or logic she was off, pursuing Tess through the house with the girl still in her arms. She had thought that Tess's pain could not in a million years penetrate the crust of her. But here she was, misshapen by a storm of rage and sorrow and wicked loathing.

She found Tess perched on her bed in the second bedroom, drying her face with a hanky.

'I'm sorry,' Tess said again. 'I don't know what I was thinking.' She ran the hanky under one eye, then the other. 'I suppose I thought it might help us both to talk . . . frankly for a moment.'

'Frankly?'

'Yes, woman to woman.'

'Woman to woman.'

'Yes.'

'And what exactly were you hoping for? For me to weep like that, to pour out all my feelings? Just lay myself bare in front of you?'

'No, no, not at all.'

Tess was upright now, spine like a brace, eyes unblinking, as if she was preparing for the admonishment before it had even really begun.

'You get the baby, Tess. You can't also have *me*.' There was a tight kink in Mary's throat, and the warm body of the girl against her breast was a heavy burden, but she continued, lips firm and thin in order to extract the next words. 'If you want honesty. If that's what you truly want, how's this —'

Tess's gaze dropped.

'There is just the smallest scrap of solace in all this for me. And that is . . . that is knowing . . . that I knew how to love her first.'

The pain came out of Tess as some animalistic groan, but Mary would not look back. She was out, stomping back down the hallway and slamming the door of her bedroom with such force that the house shook, and the baby woke with a start, and Mary was required to begin the process of cooing and shushing and patting all over again.

In a senseless twist of fate, she was back on the dock at Kure Harbour. Small vessels bobbed in a golden light. A low sun sat over the horizon, firing beams of heat at metal; a polished cleat here, a flagpole there. An abandoned anchor – alarmingly new – lay glinting like a blade on the quay. Protrusions of land jutted and sagged beyond the water, at the furthest reaches of sight, and in her chest her wild heart bucked. Somehow she understood the baby had been snatched away, out to that archipelago, and she, Mary, the mother, the real and only one, must reach her and save her.

She leapt from the dock fully clothed. Formed a graceful Olympian arch of the body as she fell. She hit the black sea fingertips-first, but the shock of sensation unravelled something and now the water was an enormous swathe of dark silk, giving way beneath her. The more she beat her arms, the more the fabric pooled around her, cocooning her, a siren song of cloth. And still she tried; thrashed and writhed and beat and jerked, cried out a silent howl – but no matter how she struggled, there was no going forward, she would never get there, never save the girl, there was only down. Down to a watery silken death.

She woke with a rush.

The window was haloed by the soft glow of early morning. The house was noiseless. The girl in the bassinet slept.

With a cold pulsing in her extremities, there was just this lofty, utterly deranged thought: take her. Take her now while you can.

She stole from bed, dressed in her warmest clothes, stuffed the girl's belongings into a small woven bag, all with clean-fingered precision. The adrenaline was coursing through every vein and artery of her body, yet somehow she managed all this in silence. The final task was the most difficult, but she managed this too, scooping the babe into her arms.

They were out into the cold blue light before she'd had a chance to conceive of even the most elementary plan. The wind buffeted a chevron of pale-leafed birch trees. The sweet, cool smell of spring was buoyant in the air. She followed the path by instinct, then the road, downhill, towards the hum of morning traffic. Already the baby was growing heavy in her arms, and she stopped once, twice, carefully adjusting the bag that had been thrown hastily over one shoulder. Ahead, the tip of a church spire reflected the first rays of dawn.

As her feet beat a dull rhythm on the path, slowly her mind began to clear, and the clenched horror of the dream began to pass. Soon. Now. She saw that of course she must be mad. She had no money, no prospects, no resources, no help. Not even a baby's bottle. The delusion of a moment earlier slipped into outright despair.

By the time she'd reached the crossroad and committed herself into the shadowy domain of the bluestone church, ruin was upon her. She was weeping, keening, gasping great sobs. Now that the tears had begun again, she feared they might never stop. The baby was awake, eyes wide, watching with alarm as they pushed through the great heavy doors of the church. Any moment, the girl was sure to let out a fitful wail.

Mary stalled at the back of the nave. Row upon row of vacant seating stretched out before them. She felt a presence to her right, turned, saw daylight beating through a towering stained-glass image of the Virgin Mother, clasped hands framed by reams of blue cloth. A lifetime of religious ambivalence seemed to vanish in that instant. How truly curious it was – to have sat through hours and days and weeks and years of Mass and for it to all add up to naught. And yet, remarkably, whatever had been obscured for all that time now came into the light. There was a flash of her mother, throwing her head back and saying 'Brava, darling. Brava!' Ah, Mary thought with a teary smile, this place had nothing to do with the living. It was a place to commune with the dead.

Whether this next moment was divinely appointed or an invention of the mind was honestly beside the point. Because it *felt* real, utterly real, in this eddy of pain and madness. Time unspooling like a fallen ball of yarn, the months and years passing out, reaching some crescendo and now reversing, spooling back in, the baby a woman now, swaddled in fathoms of silk, a high-boned, soft-lipped woman's face etched into vast coloured shards of glass.

'How much do you love me?' the baby's womanly form murmured from on high.

'So much,' Mary cried. 'Too much. So much. I —'

'All right.' The woman gestured kindly for her to stop. She cocked her head, and a brief look of pity passed over her immaculate features. She was a woman of her time, but also a woman who was not afraid of the truth; she could see what needed to be done. 'All right, you love me,' she said. 'So prove it.'

Tess was perched on the front step when Mary and the baby emerged onto the sunlit gravel path. She stood. Dropped her hands to her side, fluttering her fingers as if she was preparing to run a long race, then brought them together into a knot at her front. She remained in her nightdress, hair pulled back in a net. Without the gloss of cosmetics, her scrubbed face seemed both more and less real, like another person was living inside her skin.

Mary covered the last stretch of the path in silence, until they were standing face to face, not two feet apart. She was aware that some rare mix of emotions had settled over her; something that spoke to shame and agony, and hatred and love.

'How long have you been up?'

'A little while,' Tess said.

'Did you call him?' (Joe, she meant. Or father. Or Roger. Any one of them would do.)

'No.'

'Why? Why not? I stole her.'

'Because . . . because . . .' Tess looked down to her feet, exhaled a heavy rasp, then brought her gaze back to Mary. 'Because I might have done the same.'

Mary felt herself again begin to unravel. She fought back the tears that threatened to spill. Swallowed the creature in her throat. The fact was, Tess understood. It was indisputably clear that this kind-hearted, soft-faced woman did in fact understand. She was not a villain, no more than Mary was. She might even have been a victim too.

Mary saw then how this would go. In an hour or two, the men would arrive en masse. A battalion of family men who were doing the right thing – the only thing, under the circumstances. There would be no big scene. Mary would not have the child ripped from her bare hands. She would not weep or howl. There would be no thief, no perpetrator. Mary would, in the end, hand the child over willingly. She would rip out the heart from her own chest, amess with blood and gore, and serve it up on a platter for them all to see. Turn herself inside out. And no one would utter a word of solace because this was, after all, an everyday kind of suffering.

'Here,' Mary said. She reached out with the child. 'You take her for a bit.'

Surprise passed over Tess's face, but she did not hesitate. She gathered up the mewling parcel with careful arms. Mary could see in her features, in the gentled puckered lips, the downcast eyes, the beginnings of an understanding that this was more than a dream, and that yes, there were such things as miracles; she would be a mother after all.

1954

Mary brought a flat hand to her brow, holding back the sharp Bondi sun. The wide sweep of the beach revealed itself. Thousands of bare-skinned people agitating in the clinquant light. Mothers and children. Bands of teenagers. Men. There was no reason to examine their faces, they were strangers, and cast through this frame the waterfront was reduced to a theatre of gloss and shadow.

She had hastily pulled linen shorts and a loose blouse over her bathing suit in the back room of the nurse's station. Her long hair was cinched into a high ponytail, more an expression of function than form. Over one shoulder, she had draped a soft-worn towel. She contemplated the scalloped edge of the bay, the jag of white-washed apartment blocks that jutted ostentatiously from the coastline. Between the hilltop properties, bitumen ran like chines. She wondered at those mysterious sealed-up lives of others, gifts waiting to be opened.

She followed the arc of the promenade to the south, past the surf club and on past an improvised game of cricket where a young boy was stumbling backwards, arms overhead, squinting at the ball as it descended like a planet falling out of orbit. The concrete was warm under the thin soles of her sandshoes, and the sun hot against the side of her face. It'd been a long shift, extended by a troublesome extraction, and her feet were tired, her head woolly with exhaustion. The chill and bite of the ocean called.

She recognised his feet first. Lord knows why she knew those pale feet belonged to him and no one else. And yet she did. Knew it with an instant thrilling tremor. Also, too, that as she raised her eyeline she would find those calves, that body, that face. The fact of him being there felt so blindingly inevitable, the only shock was that none of it was shocking at all. Even the ice-cream cone which he held aloft, the soft vanilla twirl, seemed to fit.

Of course they'd come upon each other here; it could scarcely have happened anywhere else. He was practically a visitor to this city now, such was the length of his absence, and she a bona fide tourist through and through. A little room in a boarding house and a few knick-knacks to call her own hardly changed that. Perhaps she had tricked herself again, in the most elaborate fashion; the move up north *was* in aid of finding him, even if she'd never let herself believe it.

He was leaned over the ice-cream half a degree, shading it with his body, preparing for the drips to land beside those lovely feet. He was still handsome, she supposed, and yet the shape of him bent over an ice-cream cone of all things struck her as indescribably artless. He was wearing a rather prosaic shirt, too, and rolled-up trousers. His hair had been cut short. Without being able to pinpoint the precise issue, it was perfectly clear that the lustre of youth had gone.

He had not seen her, and she felt the mechanisms of her body slow in order to buy some time. Every moment of her life had been distilled into this moment. Every choice crystallised into this choice. All reason had taken form in the need, now, to be rational. A decision must be made, a clear-headed decision and the right one too, one she wouldn't regret in the years to come. But she was working against the current of sightseers on the promenade, and almost immediately a man rushed past and knocked her heavily sideways. That was enough to draw attention, and without her making any decision at all Sully was glancing up, seeing her. A mystifying, unclassifiable look crept over his face.

She took a step towards him, and he seemed to understand that they would talk. The ice-cream cone in his hand had become the most unwanted, awkward prop imaginable, and he held it out at some distance, as if to negate its existence.

'Hello,' she said.

'Hello.'

'What a pleasant surprise.'

'Yes.' He smiled, but his face still hadn't recovered from the shock of seeing her. She thought it could almost not be him, such was the strangeness of it.

There was a pause as a group of young women strode between them.

'My father was ill,' she offered finally.

'I heard.'

'Oh, you did?'

'Yes,' he nodded.

'It was a hurried decision . . . a difficult one . . . with the boat in the harbour . . .'

She fell silent with the terrible realisation that no excuse was adequate. No explanation could atone for the pain she'd inflicted.

'How did he fare?'

'Sorry?'

'Your father.'

'Oh! Yes, he's fine. The illness was . . . rather less dangerous than I'd been led to believe.'

'Right.' He looked out to sea, then back to her. A cloudy film sat over his eyes. 'Perhaps, then, your family wanted you home?'

'Yes. Perhaps that was it.'

He appeared to be keeping himself from saying anything further, and she wondered if they would part ways now. They were eye to eye. People flowed past them like the months and the years had done before.

Something broke Sully from this reverie, and he seemed to remember the vanilla twirl in his hand, wilting at a brisk rate. Fat drops of cream had begun to slip down the cone and were falling onto the concrete below. He made to swap hands, then decided against it.

'Hold on a moment, will you?'

'All right.'

He turned and moved ten paces or more towards a wastebasket. The fact of him depositing the barely touched treat seemed to mean something, but what, precisely, she could not say.

As he came back to her, he conjured a hanky from somewhere and wiped his fingers. Now unburdened, he could achieve a more familiar posture, hands tucked into his trouser pockets, chest wide, head high, and it was no surprise at all that he did this. The effect on his personal power was rather astonishing.

'So how have you been?' he asked.

'Fine. Just fine.'

He smiled back, nodded.

'Are you home for good?' she said.

'No, no, just a quick voyage to see the folks.'

'I've been reading your stories from Korea.' She offered these words like an olive branch, immediately regretted the fawning tone, then continued all the same. 'The one last year about the children, in that village, in the demilitarised zone. It was very moving.'

'Thank you.'

He held her gaze for a moment, but she could not bear it. She turned her face to the sea. The next words were pouring out of her before she really had a chance to think them.

'I'm glad,' she said. 'I'm very glad you were there to bear witness for us all, to be the one to tell us. It's rather an important job, isn't it, your journalism. I see that now. How important it is, the bearing witness . . .'

She brought her attention to the pavement in an effort to interrupt this flow of hopeless thought. The shadows at their feet were contained little ellipses, distinct from one another, and it was this observation that reminded her five years had elapsed and she should not imagine for a moment that one random encounter changed that. Five whole years and, contained within that guardhouse of time, thousands upon thousands of little moments. Love affairs might have occurred. Marriages. Babies!

The idea of this, of small humans being brought into the world, prompted a crushing wave of blackness to wash over her. She thought momentarily of the girl's small face in the silver frame that Tess had sent her in the post. Sitting there on the dresser beside her bed. Only now and then did she feel the need to flip the image down, to wait for that devastated feeling to pass.

Then something else came to her, a more selfless notion perhaps, a distraction at the very least.

'I've wondered all these years . . .' she started. 'About the little girl – Sachiko.'

'Ah,' he sighed.

'Did she . . .?'

'Yes, I'm afraid so. It was winter that did it.'

'How terrible,' she said. 'For that family, of all families, to lose another.'

'Indeed.'

They looked directly at one another now. The wave of his hair was settled across his brow in rather a stately way. He had grown into himself.

'One learns humility,' she offered.

He gazed at her quizzically.

'One learns humility – you said that once. I couldn't imagine what you meant back then. Not really. But now, yes, now it makes rather a lot of sense.'

He smiled a small, tired smile, and she thought she'd become quite a bore, not being able to think of anything cheerful to speak of, nothing at all. She took in a breath and rearranged the towel on her shoulder in the way one might adjust a handbag, ready to be off.

'All right then,' she chimed. 'I should let you go. I've babbled on long enough.'

'Sure.' He squinted a little at her. He was at risk of speaking again, of holding her there against her will.

'It was truly lovely to see you again,' she said summarily.

'You too, Mary. You too.'

They hesitated for a moment, the distance between them an unbridgeable gap. But then he brought a hand to his brow and made a sort of ironic casual salute, and this, at the eleventh hour, allowed both Mary and Sully to loosen their grip on themselves and laugh. Shriek in fact, almost insanely. They stepped away from each other, wild laughing like that, and it took several seconds for the smile to fade from her face.

She continued south to the next set of stairs, took them down onto the sand, and headed towards the ocean. All the way, her mind was flashing with unsettled visions like birds wheeling far above a clifftop.

She found a place between two families where the sand was dry and stripped down to her bathing suit. Here she was, then. One woman in a throng of humanity. There'd been pictures of this beach in the newspaper during the war. Barren of life. Barricaded with iron stakes and coils of barbed wire. All street signs removed to keep the enemy witless. But now, squeezed between a mass of lively, epicurean day-trippers, it felt extraordinary that both scenes could be true. That one might not belie the other, but in a way offer proof of its possibility.

The first and only thought that came to her as she hit the water was this. Japan. What on earth was that place to her? That place of hills and sea. That place she both longed for and despised. Perhaps, after all, it had not been a small blip in a life, a momentary pause, a fleeting disruption. It was compressed into tiny filaments and woven like gold thread into the fibres of her being. It was, she thought, like prising open a small shell and finding the whole universe.

She waded out past the children and mothers. There were days when she didn't think of him, or of Japan, but today – it was plain to see – would not be one of them. Her head was reeling with memories. Bombed-out cities. Maimed women. Dancing. The flash of his grin in the dark. Nancy's graceful arm sweeping back and forth against a windowpane. The forest. The cormorants. The balm scent of a timber and paper home. And then, the mind, that treacherous thing, always taking the path most dreaded. The very reason she did not and would not think of him. The girl. Lillian. Both inextricably linked to and utterly abstracted from every memory she held of Japan.

She was waist deep now. The white lip of a wave was nearly upon her. She duck-dived under and rose, the slug of cold water against her chest and in her throat. She planted a solid hand, one after the other, through the darkening water. Felt the pull and release of the waves. Once she was out past the breakers, the beach a distant hum against the totalising roar of the ocean, she turned onto her back and let the tide roll and sweep her this way and that. Above, a cloud had been detonated into fragments of wispy hair.

This much, she knew – there was hope in surrender. She felt it now. The great strength of the ocean under her, around her, and she just a jot at its mercy.

She was once a person who cried at lovely things. At *trivial* things, trees and paintings. Now she was a person who could not summon even one tear for the greatest loss of her whole life. Perhaps this was what it was to survive. It would never not be sad. The pain was enormous. So vast it reshaped the world. She would fumble on in the dark, clutching at shadows, looking for something that wasn't her, something else to fill the days, to fill the void, and yet there would never be anything else. There would only be the girl in her ivory-skinned snuffling perfection. And yet, miraculously, Mary could hold all that pain inside her and keep moving. She was strong enough to bear it.

Always, there would be the outline of the Kure hills branded in her mind, and the harbour and the islands. But there was also a lifetime ahead of her. Onwards, always, forever.

NOTES ON THE HISTORICAL RECORD

The Occupation was inspired and animated by true events, particularly my maternal grandmother's experience working for the British Commonwealth Occupation Force (BCOF) in Japan. But while it's situated within a landscape of true events, and extensive research was conducted to bring this work to the page, much of the story is invented. Ultimately this is a work of fiction and should be read as such.

That said, it was important to me to be truthful *in essence*, particularly with regards to the cross-cultural elements of this story, and to render this period in Australian and Japanese history with the respect and solemnity it deserves. The following notes outline the factual basis for elements of the novel.

In the building and portrayal of my Japanese characters, I leaned heavily on a number of deeply moving works of fiction and nonfiction, including but not limited to: *Michi's Memories: The story of a Japanese war bride* by Keiko Tamura, *Japanese Reflections on World War II and the American Occupation* by Edgar A Porter and Ran Yin Porter, *Widows of Hiroshima: The life stories of nineteen peasant wives* edited by Mikio Kanda, and the unforgettable 2016 animated film *In This Corner of the World*. In choosing not to inhabit the perspectives of Japanese characters, I offer a work that is inherently limited in its view of another culture and should be read with this in mind.

The discriminatory racial and cultural views expressed by Ida, Jimmy and others throughout the book are indicative of views frequently encountered in my research, including in letters, diaries and contemporaneous novels held in library collections around Australia.

The scene in which Lieutenant General Sir Horace Robertson administers a scathing rebuke of the Japanese people at the third anniversary peace festival is based on recorded events. The words uttered by Robertson are taken from newspaper accounts.

News reports from Australian and British journalists who visited Hiroshima in the aftermath of the atom bomb provide an insight into the dominant cultural views held by Australians at the time. While views varied, a common theme emerged – that is, the inclination to diminish or erase the suffering of the Japanese. Perhaps a more generous interpretation is to say cultural and language differences made it hard for Western reporters, often in-country only briefly, to grasp the extent of the suffering. Or, indeed, the desire for people who had suffered to move on with their lives. Australian writer Frank McClune, visiting in 1949, described the atom bomb as 'merely an intense flash of heat in the air'. Also that year, British reporter G Ward Price described the stricken city thus: 'Hiroshima once more has a quarter of a million people, with daphne and peach blossoms decorating their gardens as before.' British–Australian reporter Sefton Delmer went further: 'I expected to see something of that ordeal written in their faces. I expected to find men and women suffering physically and mentally . . . I have inquired and questioned. But I have found none of it. Instead, I have found the people of Hiroshima to be a cheerful, entirely normal, hardworking folk.'

There were, of course, sympathetic approaches within the ranks of the media. In dispatches to the *Australian Women's Weekly*, Dorothy Drain delivered more humanising accounts of local people and their struggles. Australian journalist Wilfred Burchett was the first Westerner to report on the destruction at Hiroshima in September 1945 in London's *Daily Express*. And Allan S Clifton wrote the notoriously revealing *Time of Fallen Blossoms* (1950) about his experience working in the occupation, which included unsubstantiated claims of sexual violence by Australian army men. The character of Sully is loosely based on Clifton.

The no-fraternising rule was real, and many occupation members seemed to have limited interactions with local people. Cultural differences were often misunderstood, with Japanese social norms, etiquette and rituals considered by some to be childlike or inscrutable. There was a cohort of Australians who made a genuine effort to learn the language and interact on a more meaningful level and, in general, these people expressed far more sympathetic and well-rounded views of the Japanese – views that often proved unpopular at home, where the war against the Japanese remained fresh in the collective psyche.

Around 650 Japanese war brides migrated to Australia after the Australian government lifted the ban in 1952, paving the way for a shift in cultural views and, ultimately, the first tentative steps towards ending the White Australia policy. Many more Japanese women dated Australian men during the occupation period, between 1946 and 1952.

The scene in which Sully describes meeting Haruki – 'lo and behold, in flawless King's English . . .' – is heavily inspired by an event described by TAG Hungerford in his semi-autobiographical novel *Sowers of the Wind*. Other views held by Sully, particularly in relation to the role of the occupation, were influenced by commentary from academic Robin Gerster.

Aspects of Mary's travels to the hot pools at Etajima, the launch picnic at Horseshoe Bay, and the markets in Kure and Hiroshima, were briefly described in letters from my grandmother to an aunt in Australia.

Scenes in which Sully and Mary explore the hinterland of Honshu Island, stay at a village inn, learn about the guardian deity Jizo and observe cormorant fishing are inspired by brief mentions from BCOF members Allan S Clifton and Clement Govett (who was also vice-president of the BCOF Tourist Club).

Mrs Richards is an amalgam of several women's voices gathered from personal accounts and is informed by the work of historian Dr Christine De Matos, who has examined gender, race and class roles within BCOF.

Some artistic licence has been taken with the locations of various BCOF army facilities in and around Kure in order to smooth out the narrative.

'Atomic remnants' were real items sold to BCOF members. Also true was the haggling that occurred in markets where Allied forces sold supplied items (like soap and condensed milk) to local people at dramatically inflated prices. 'Presentos' gifted between BCOF members and housegirls were described in a number of personal accounts. Soldiers' wives and children were sent to Japan as agents of 'civilisation', the Y's Dew Drop Inn was a real place, and Japanese school children were taught English by Australian women.

All mentions of the Tokyo war crimes trial and the Japanese

Constitution are based in fact. The 'Know Japan' guidebook was indeed distributed amongst BCOF members.

In the late 1940s, the Americans began studying the human effects of the atom bomb through the Atomic Bomb Casualty Commission (this included investigations into leukaemia and other cancers). 'Study' is the operative word, as the patients were not treated, and the ABCC's work remained censored for a number of years.

Last but by no means least, that fated meeting in Melbourne's prestigious Hotel Australia did take place, although the precise details of the conversation are not known. My biological grandmother (also a Mary) was pressured by her male family members to relinquish her baby. After the birth of my mother, both Mary and my adoptive grandmother Sheila were forced to endure an agonising few days shacked up together. Despite the difficulties, the two women remained in contact throughout their lives.

This book is dedicated to my mother, Gillian, who has loved us fiercely.